Praise for Anne Louise Bannon
and Fascinating Rhythm

Fascinating Rhythm is reminiscent of Agatha Christie or Dorothy Sayers' novels of the time period. A very nice story to cozy up to a fire with and imbibe. Legally, of course.

Literary R&R

Those who love a great (who-done-it) mystery will enjoy Fascinating Rhythm.

Sheri Wilkinson

JuniperGrove.net

Praise for Tyger, Tyger

I like Bannon's main character, Brenda, enough to follow her anywhere. Her boyfriend (no! wait! they're "just friends") trains animals for the movies, and between Brenda, the BF and his tiger, "Sweetness," they are a fun, crime-solving trio. I enjoyed this book.

Petrea Burchard

Author of Camelot and Vine

Bring Into Bondage

Anne Louise Bannon

Healcroft House, Publishers

Healcroft House, Publishers, a subsidiary of Robin Goodfellow Enterprises, Altadena, California, United States of America

Cover art by Helen Kim

ISBN 978-0-9909923-6-3

Library of Congress Control Number: 2016910441

Expression of Gratitude

There are always tons of people to thank when one undertakes the writing of a novel, especially one that is set in a different era than the author's own. There's the nameless reference librarian that ferreted out information on wedding rings. My late friend Joyce Madison, who was always available as a resource in the days before Google, especially at two a.m.

Then there were all the nice folks who, thanks to the Internet, answered emails and strange questions for me as I updated my research. Betty Macdonald, the archivist at the Ellis County Historical Society Museum, went to great lengths to help me find maps of Hays, Kansas, in the 1920s and is solely responsible for my new addiction to Sanborn maps. Dan Condor, of the Model T Ford Club of America, helped with ways to sabotage a Model T, even though he was perplexed that I'd want to.

And there is the usual crew of wonderful people who provide support and encouragement: Lori Webster, Jane Rollins, Carol Wuenschell. My husband Michael Holland, my daughter Corrie Klarner.

Special thanks also go to Nancy Raven Smith for her exceptional notes on the manuscript, my brave and diligent copy editor Petrea Burchard, and to Helen Kim, graphic artist extraordinaire, who went above and beyond to take my cover concept and turned it into the beautiful cover you now see.

Dedication

To Shirley Holland - how great it is when your mother-in-law is also one of your True Fans

*Yet now our flesh is
as the flesh of our brethren, our
children as their children:
and, lo, we bring into bondage
our sons and our daughters
to be servants, and some of
our daughters are brought unto
bondage already: neither is it
in our power to redeem them;
for other men have our
lands and vineyards.*

Nehemiah 5:5

Chapter One

"Marriage of true minds..." Freddie grumbled as he gazed at the row of red, calf-bound volumes. "Marriage of..."

He pulled a book off of the shelf and whipped through the pages, heedless of the fine paper and the ash that floated off the cigarette whose holder was firmly clamped between his teeth.

"No. No. Ah. 'Let me not to the marriage of true minds admit impediments...'" He read the rest of the sonnet and smiled.

Kathy would like that one. Freddie closed his eyes and tried to recite the words.

"Sir," said Roberts, the valet, from behind him. "Your car is ready."

"Thank you, Roberts." Freddie looked at the book and sighed. Perhaps between the light of the stars and the city, there would be enough to read by. He slipped the volume into the inside pocket of his light gray summer wool suit jacket, checked his vest pocket again, and left the apartment.

In the cream-colored Cadillac, he left his cigarette case and lighter on the dark brown leather seat beside him. The top was down, and the last lingering traces of another sweltering day in New York City wrapped around him as he pushed the starter. He checked his vest pocket again for the ring that he knew was still there, then pulled into traffic.

Dodging flivvers and buses, he yanked the butt of his cigarette out of the holder and tossed it onto the street. A new cigarette was fitted and lit in seconds. The action was barely soothing. He was smoking too fast, and he knew it. Then again, he felt he had the right to. He again touched the ring that waited in his vest pocket.

He'd planned the evening carefully. They would dine casually at a small Italian restaurant in the Village where the food was excellent and the proprietor served wine as if there were no such thing as Prohibition. Then a pleasant drive along the East River to a spot north of town where one could look back and enjoy the beauty of the city lights, but still be quite alone. And there, on July ten, nineteen hundred and twenty-five, Freddie Little would try his damnedest to convince Kathy Briscow to become his wife.

Kathy had every reason to refuse him. For her, marriage meant a loss of self so profound it only started with the loss of her name. Unfortunately for Freddie, it was that same independence that made her so attractive to him.

They'd been going out together for over six months, supposedly as friends. But even Kathy had been calling him her beau for at least four months. Of late, there was a decided tendency to get rather overheated when alone together. The previous Saturday had been the worst.

They were celebrating the Fourth of July at a private picnic in the country. An accident with a strawberry pie had led to some intense necking and even petting before Freddie abruptly called a halt.

"Freddie, it's time we were lovers," said Kathy, blunt as always.

"I think not, Kathy."

She smiled softly. "I'm not talking about easy

pleasure, to be taken lightly. Freddie, I love you."

"And I love you." Freddie took her hand and lightly caressed it, marveling at how easily the words had come. "Which is precisely why I will not take you as my lover."

"I don't understand."

"Kathy, dearest, you have a dream of coming together as equals. With no promises or contracts, if something goes wrong, as it could all too easily, you will have no recourse to the courts or social conscience. You will be defenseless, and that is not equal."

Kathy hadn't argued back, not that she'd agreed. She merely knew the futility of trying to change his mind on that issue. It had put a significant damper on the afternoon, although they still stayed out quite late that night.

Something had to be done. Freddie had always known marriage was the best answer, a marriage in which they defined the terms of their relationship, in which they were equal partners, and at long last, he felt ready to do it.

He lit another cigarette and touched the ring. At least, he was fairly certain he was ready. By the time he stopped the car in front of the brownstone on East 9th, he was not at all certain. He checked his watch. Three minutes after seven. Kathy was probably in the parlor of the boarding house, wondering why he was late. He forced himself out of the car and up the stoop.

Mrs. Lynne, the landlady, was surprised to see him.

"Mr. Little!" she gasped. "That's right, it's Friday. Kathy!"

She pounded up the stairs, fluttering and dithering, as fast as her chubby little legs could carry her. Puzzled, Freddie put his panama on the hat rack. Kathy had never forgotten a date before. Curses, in Kathy's voice, floated down from the fourth floor. Mrs. Johnson, another tenant in the boarding house, came out of the parlor shaking her graying head.

"Good evening, Mr. Little," she said, then looked upstairs. "Poor thing. Not that I approve of such language, but she's been in such a state since the telegram arrived."

"Telegram?" asked Freddie, fearing that he knew. "From whom?"

"Her mother," said the widow. "It must be serious."

Freddie nodded. It had to be. Kathy's parents were dirt poor farmers living someplace in Kansas. Mrs. Lynne came dithering back down.

"I'm sorry, Mr. Little. The poor girl's not thinking straight," she said. "She's so busy packing."

"Packing?" Freddie started up the stairs.

"Mr. Little! I can't have you up there," shrieked Mrs. Lynne. "I told her that."

Freddie ignored her and took the stairs two and three at a time. Kathy was indeed packing her clothes in a trunk when Freddie got to the doorway. She was wearing a dark blue cotton dress, with blue gingham cuffs on the sleeves and the collar. Technically a day dress, Freddie knew it was Kathy's best one and her favorite for less casual evening excursions.

"What's the matter?" he gasped. "You got a telegram from your mother?"

Kathy nodded and wiped a tear from her cheek. "It's Pa."

She swiped the yellow paper off the bureau and handed it to him.

"Pa ill, stop," it read. "Please come quickly."

"It doesn't say it's serious," said Freddie.

"For heaven's sakes, Freddie," Kathy snapped. "There's two words there she didn't need!" She started sobbing. "Oh, hell, you wouldn't know. Ma wouldn't wire me in the first place if it weren't serious. And she wouldn't use please or quickly. She'd know I'd know it was that urgent. She's got to be awful upset, and that can only mean one thing. Pa's dying."

Overcome, she sank onto the bed. Freddie slid next to her and put his arms around her.

"There, there," he said soothingly, and kissed her hair. "You don't know that he is."

"He's fifty-nine years old. That's not young, Freddie. And Ma's last letter, she was worried. I got it yesterday. Things haven't been going well on the farm. She won't say what, exactly, but Pa took a ducking in the creek last week and took cold from it, and if his heart goes bad..."

"You don't know that it is."

Kathy got up abruptly. "I've got to keep packing. The train leaves at ten."

"The train, eh?" Freddie did some thinking.

"Oh, damn. I forgot about tonight." Kathy wrapped up a summer shift and shoved it in the trunk. "I'm sorry, Freddie."

He smiled. "No apology needed. It's perfectly understandable."

She looked at his light wool suit. "At least you didn't make any reservations. You don't have tickets anywhere, do you?"

"None. And I would have gladly put them aside if I had. Please, don't waste any time worrying about my evening."

"Somehow, I knew you'd say that." Kathy's smile was weak but grateful.

"When do you plan to arrive in Kansas?"

"I'll get to Topeka Sunday morning. Then I have to catch a local into Hays. With luck, I can get the morning train and be there by two thirty."

"Hays is how far from New York?"

Kathy frowned as she looked at him. "About fifteen hundred miles. What are you getting at?"

"What if I could have you at your parents' farm by..." Freddie did some calculating, "...Saturday evening?"

"How on earth could you...?" Kathy suddenly shook her head. "Oh, no. You're not getting me into that plane of yours."

"That's a whole day sooner you'll be at your father's

side."

Kathy wavered. "There isn't room for my trunk. I'll need that."

"There is room for a valise or two." Freddie smiled. "Just pack what you'll need for a couple days, and we'll send your trunk by train. It will also be a lot cheaper."

"And what good will it do me or my parents if I end up mangled in bits and pieces in a haystack in Ohio?" Kathy tossed a pile of step-ins and camisoles into the trunk.

"My plane is perfectly reliable, and I am more than an able pilot." Freddie put his hand on her shoulder. "Your mother did use two words she didn't need to."

Kathy trembled. "You bastard," she whispered.

"Have you bought your tickets yet?" he asked softly.

"Not yet."

"I'll make a phone call or two first. I'm certain my sister can arrange to loan you some flying gear. Why don't you finish packing?"

"Freddie, are you sure it's safe?" she asked in a small voice.

"Very sure, or I wouldn't have offered." He kissed her cheek and left.

Downstairs in the hall, Freddie sent Mrs. Lynne to help Kathy. The other tenants were elsewhere, for once. Freddie called his apartment first and had Roberts pack a trunk and valise for him. Then he called a shopkeeper who was quite happy to fetch things at odd hours for a price. Not that price mattered to Freddie. Being fabulously wealthy did have its advantages.

But it had made things awkward for Kathy on more than one occasion. She was a working girl, a junior editor at a publishing house, and quite proud of having achieved that much. She and Freddie had an understanding that he would assume the cost of whatever they did together, but even that had its limits. Freddie's sister, Honoria, had at least solved the clothing problem by "loaning" Kathy dresses for those occasions when Freddie wanted to take her places that required evening dress. As Honoria was tall and slender like her brother, and Kathy wasn't, there was no hiding the fact that Honoria actually bought the dresses for Kathy. But it was politely ignored.

Freddie took charge of Kathy's trunk after it was filled, and put it in the back seat of the car. He put her valise there also, then seated her in the front with him, and they left.

"Freddie, why aren't we going straight up to Grand Central?" Kathy asked, as he turned onto 23rd.

"Because we shall have to detour to my place," Freddie explained. "I have a trunk to pick up, not that I'm presuming upon your parents' hospitality. There must be a hotel or something in your little town. In any case, it wouldn't be very kind to drop you there and not remain to bring you back."

"Don't you have appointments or something?"

Unlike Kathy, Freddie did not have to work, and didn't, except as a writer.

"Nothing I can't cancel, and be happy to at that," said Freddie. "And I'll be bringing my book with me, so you needn't harass me about letting it go."

Kathy snorted. She had edited Freddie's first novel, which was to be printed soon, and had all but nagged him into writing a second.

"But that does remind me of a curious aspect of this adventure," he continued. "What about your job? I can't imagine you just flying off and leaving it, no matter how dire the circumstances."

"I contacted Mr. Healcroft, and he agreed to let me take a vacation."

"He did?" Freddie's eyebrows lifted in amusement.

Kathy shrugged. "He seems to feel obligated to be kind to me. For the moment, I'm glad."

Freddie nodded. The trunk and valise were waiting in the apartment lobby. The doorman loaded them, and soon the luggage was duly dispatched to the train station.

"Well," said Freddie as they left the ticket counter. "Shall we find ourselves a bite to eat?"

"Aren't we going out to the airfield?" asked Kathy.

"We don't have to immediately. The inn won't give our rooms away."

"What inn?"

"The inn at the airfield. It's a lovely little place, but the food is terrible."

"Aren't we leaving tonight?" Kathy's voice became strained.

"Of course not. I can't fly in the dark."

Kathy panicked. "You tricked me! I thought you said we'd get there tomorrow."

Freddie grabbed her shoulders. "Now, now. Calm down. We will. I figured the time leaving tomorrow morning. We'll be taking off at dawn. We should get there in time for dinner."

"Oh." Kathy sniffed.

"Here." Freddie handed her a handkerchief. "It's clean."

"Thank you." Kathy dabbed her eyes and wiped her nose. "I'm sorry, Freddie. I should have trusted you."

"My dear, you are overwrought, and deservedly so. Let's get some food into you, and then we'll head out to the inn. We'll both need a good night's rest."

Kathy nodded. But at the inn, she couldn't sleep. Putting on her red artificial silk dressing gown, she slipped down the hall to Freddie's room. Dim light shone under the door. She knocked.

"Yes?" he called quietly.

"It's me," she hissed. "I can't sleep."

Freddie opened the door. "What's the matter?"

"I'm frightened." Kathy slid in.

He was wearing his shirt and pants. In spite of her fears, Kathy couldn't help admiring the tall, lean figure that was all arms and legs, the soft, strawberry blond hair that was usually slicked down, but had gotten rumpled since he'd left her in her room.

"Kathy, I promise, I won't let us crash," he said soothingly.

"You would have to mention that." Groaning, she sat on the edge of the bed.

Freddie gazed at her fondly. Even worried, Kathy had that spark of liveliness that made a face and figure that should have been plain quite beautiful. Her brown hair was cut to her chin, after the current fashion. But her figure had a little healthy padding, and she had real bosoms. Quite squeezable bosoms, as Freddie had found out to his everlasting regret and joy. His fingers itched, but he chased such thoughts from his mind. Now was not the time.

He sat down next to her. "If not tomorrow, what are you worried about?"

"Pa." The tears trickled down her cheeks. "Freddie, I haven't seen him in six years. I couldn't afford it, even if I could have gotten the time off from work. What if I never see him again?"

"Then you'll just have to rely on your memories of him." Slowly, Freddie put his arms around her. "It will hurt a great deal, but time does heal."

"I suppose you're right." She shook her head, then nestled in. "It was so hard when Grandma Briscow died. She lived just long enough to see the Eighteenth Amendment passed. I was in New York by that point. Ma said not to come back for the funeral, which made sense. She died so suddenly, what could I do for her? I hope I make it in time for Pa."

"You'll get there as fast as I can get you."

"Freddie, why are you doing this for me?"

He kissed her hair. "You know why."

She looked up into his soft green eyes. "You really do, don't you?"

"Amazingly enough, yes."

Her eyes filled. "I'm really glad you're here. I don't feel quite so helpless anymore. This afternoon, I was wishing you would come with me, but I couldn't ask because I didn't have the right to. Damn you, Freddie."

Freddie winced inwardly. Kathy only cursed when the two of them were alone together, and usually only when she was emotionally overwrought. He often heard worse from his male friends and chose not to make an issue of it.

"And I want so badly to be your lover," Kathy continued. "But you're right. As long as I don't have rights, we can't be equals. Lord. What would Pa think of me, if he heard me like this?"

"He'd probably come after me with a shotgun," chuckled Freddie.

Kathy laughed sadly. "He just might. He's an Old Testament man and one stubborn old mule. Won't take a mortgage on the farm, and he's got more acres than he can work. But he won't take a mortgage to buy anything. All the new machines, he paid cash for."

"Given how badly crop prices are doing, I'd say he's pretty smart."

"He's that, all right. Self-taught, but he's quite a student. He taught us to read before we were five. He always told me the good Lord had given me good brains; it would be a sin and a shame if I didn't use them. I don't know if he meant for me to be an old maid. But he was pretty proud when I told him I was going to New York to work after college instead of coming back to Hays and waiting around to get married."

"It's a good thing he was. It would have been interesting to see him try to keep you at home. You come by your stubbornness honestly."

"Pa can out-stubborn me any day of the week."

Freddie laughed. "This I will have to see."

"Freddie, you don't like it when I'm stubborn, do you?" Kathy sniffed.

"If you're disagreeing with me, of course I don't. You don't like it when I get stubborn. But I do respect it, and I admire your tenacity."

"That's only a nice way of saying I'm cussed."

"I wouldn't have you any other way."

"You won't take me, either." Kathy got up. "It's

just as well, I guess. It'll save me a lot of explaining to Pa, assuming I get there in time. Thank you, Freddie."

"You're welcome, Kathy." He stood.

There was an awkward pause. Slowly, he pulled her to him and softly pressed his lips against hers. The warmth grew with quiet sighs.

"If you're going to kiss me like that, the least you could do is take me to your bed," Kathy whispered.

"Then you had better start kissing me like a brother because I cannot help what you start."

Chapter Two

The jump from the peaceful shadows of a new
morning to the bright flood lights of the hangar
made Kathy's eyes recoil. She blinked several times
to adjust. Freddie, whose hand had triggered the
switch, merely stood and gazed. Here, at last, were his
two greatest passions: Kathy, and a customized dual
cockpit Curtiss biplane with wing surface radiators
and a D12 engine. He'd told Kathy at length of the
hours he had spent with the designers at the Curtiss
factory, developing the plane. There was no other like
it that he knew of.

Kathy shivered, unaware that she remained the
greater object of Freddie's passions. She watched as
Freddie made a point of checking everything twice on
the biplane. He was clad in tan serge pants and boots,
although in deference to the heat he'd laid aside his
worn, leather flying jacket. Kathy was only marginally
convinced they'd arrive in Kansas in one piece. Freddie
even explained the principles of air flowing over wings
and lifting them, demonstrating with a piece of paper.
Kathy said that was all right for paper, but not for
some big heavy monster.

She shut her eyes the moment the propeller caught

and grabbed tightly onto the sides, and didn't open her eyes until Freddie assured her over the roar of the engine that they were safely airborne. She looked over the side of the plane and almost lost her breakfast.

Then the plane bumped. Kathy screamed.

"It's just an air pocket," Freddie yelled. "Perfectly normal."

"Like hell," Kathy grumbled, hoping Freddie hadn't heard her curse. She readjusted the blanket that Freddie had tucked over her lap. She wore a leather jacket and helmet with goggles but had on her other best dress underneath, a flowered cotton lawn with white dotted trim on the collar and sleeves.

Freddie was behind her, in the second cockpit. Kathy watched the stick in front of her move as if by magic. But it was Freddie's hand that moved it, from his controls.

Two hours later, they landed to refuel at a small roadside gas station. The garageman seemed rather bemused to be selling gasoline to a plane instead of a car. Freddie chatted with him amiably while Kathy used the garageman's toilet.

Flying was cold, windy, noisy, and bumpy, and she didn't like it at all. She tried to console herself with the thought that she would arrive that much sooner at her father's side. It was small consolation.

They made their third landing at one o'clock in the afternoon for lunch, in a field somewhere in Indiana. Kathy wasn't sure where, and cared even less. She was stiff and sore from hanging on so tightly and tired of being cold.

"You seem less than happy with the experience," observed Freddie.

"I don't want to sound like an ingrate, but it's awful."

"If it will make you feel any better, we've already passed your train."

"I almost wish I were on it." Kathy shivered and tried to blink back her tears.

Freddie handed her a hip flask. "This ought to warm you up."

"Oh, wonderful. You're drinking, too." Kathy still took the flask and drank.

"Not me, for once. I prefer to stay clear-headed when I'm flying." He smiled at her sorrowfully. "You know it might help if you relaxed a little. It can't be very comfortable staying clenched up all that time."

"Somebody's got to hold that plane together." Kathy took another hit from the flask.

Freddie laughed. "It's doing perfectly well on its own, Kathy. But do as you like."

Kathy did manage to relax a little, even looked over the side once without getting nauseated. A thunderstorm grounded them for an hour south of Springfield, Illinois. Kathy turned peevish until Freddie reassured her they would still be in Hays before dinner. After they refueled in Topeka, Freddie dipped the plane more and more often to check his location. The sun started down towards the horizon.

"I thought you'd said we'd be there by dinner," she yelled at Freddie.

"What time is it?"

"Close to seven."

"We just passed Lincoln, Kansas. How far is that?"

"I think a hundred miles."

"We'll make it."

Kathy groaned. "Freddie! We eat at six out here."

"Oh. I meant dinner in New York."

"Obviously." Kathy cringed.

Freddie was used to being pampered with servants and valets. Anything he wanted was his, and if it wasn't at his fingertips, all he had to do was pick up a telephone. Kathy's parents did not even have a telephone at their house. Or electricity. And they had only recently gotten indoor plumbing. They were as likely to go to town with a wagon and a team of horses as they were in the Model T truck Pa had broken down and bought, used, a couple years after Kathy had graduated from college. Freddie was in for some shock if he ended up staying at the house, and crisis or not, Ma would want him where she could keep an eye on him.

Freddie swooped down one last time.

"We're over Hays," he announced over the rush of the wind.

"Right. There's the old fort."

"How do we get to your parents' place?"

"Follow the road to the dirt fork, and hang to the right. They're about six miles out."

"That look like it?"

Kathy looked down at the white, two-story clapboard house, with the battered red barn and nearby tool shed. An empty, green pasture surrounded the back part of the barn, and beyond that, fields spread out, filled with wheat turning from green to gold. The outhouses were gone, but Kathy could see where they'd been. A young boy came running from the side porch, looking up and waving at the plane.

"That's my parents' place!" called Kathy. "That's got to be Gammers."

"Who?"

"My brother, Gamaliel. He was five when I last saw him."

Freddie circled around over the farm. "I'm going to land on the road. See any cars coming?"

"No."

Freddie took the plane down. Kathy cringed at the final bump. But they were down, and Freddie shut off the motor as they drifted up to the front gate. Kathy bolted out of the plane before Freddie could help her.

A blast of buckshot sent her scurrying back. Freddie scrambled behind the plane. Kathy ripped off her flying cap and goggles.

"What in tarnation is going on here?" she screamed.

"It's a lady!" an adolescent voice cried from behind the corner of the house.

"Who's that?" Kathy called, approaching carefully.

"Isaac? Gideon?"

"Damn it, Kathy," yelped Freddie. "Get back before they blast you!"

"Kathy?" A young man in his mid-twenties came out from behind the house, a slight limp rocking him back and forth. He wore dusty, dark trousers with suspenders over his open shirt, with the sleeves rolled up. "Kathy! What are you doing in that get-up?"

"Joshua!" Kathy ran towards him. "At last. Aren't you supposed to be in California? And how's Pa?"

Three other boys came out, the smallest holding a double barrel shotgun. They all had Kathy's face and brown hair, but the smallest, a boy of eleven, had a preponderance of freckles. All of the boys wore overalls in varying states of dirtiness and repair. Kathy realized that the only brother missing was Abraham, who was presumably still on the train from Boston.

"I'll be. It is Kathy," said the oldest of the three, a stocky youth just shy of manhood. His overalls looked the newest but had a long streak of grease down the front. His dark shoes were scuffed, but almost new.

"Uh-uh," insisted the youngest, setting his bare feet in a stubborn stance. His shirt was gray and worn, and his overalls faded and threadbare, with the bottom hems fraying badly. "Kathy's got long hair."

Kathy finished embracing Joshua and grabbed the youth.

"Gideon!" she crowed. "My god, you've grown. And Isaac, good lord, you were eight when I last saw you. So how's Pa?" Kathy hugged the middle boy, a fourteen-year-old, as well.

The youngest boy still looked at her suspiciously. Joshua laughed and rumpled his hair.

"Gammers, this is your sister, Kathy. We promise you."

"Gam, I cut my hair in New York," Kathy explained as she hugged him. "Everyone's doing it there. How's Pa?"

Gam pointed the gun at Freddie, who was kicking

wooden blocks under the plane's wheels.

"Who's he?" the boy demanded.

Kathy waved Freddie over. "This is my friend from New York, Mr. Freddie Little."

"You're Mr. Little?" Isaac gushed happily. "Boy, won't Pa be happy to meet you!"

Freddie flushed a little.

"I'm sorry." Kathy turned to him, blushing furiously herself. "My uncles must have been exaggerating again."

Freddie nodded. "So I gathered."

"These are my brothers." Kathy pointed them out. "This is Joshua, Gideon, Isaac, and Gamaliel. We're missing Abraham. He's probably on the train still."

"It's a pleasure to meet you, gentlemen." Freddie started to offer his hand.

The younger boys looked at him as if he were doing some weird ritual. Joshua laughed and shook Freddie's hand vigorously.

"It's a pleasure to meet you, Mr. Little," he said, grinning. "These young'uns just don't know about fine city manners."

"Boys?" called a woman's voice. "What's going on out there?"

"Ma," said Kathy softly, then louder. "Ma? It's me, Kathy. I got here a little earlier than I thought."

Kathy's mother came from a huge clan of New York Irishmen, which she had left to marry Kathy's father in Kansas. Freddie had met several of Kathy's aunts and uncles in New York. The Callaghans tended to be stout, especially when they were living well. Mrs. Katie-Marie Briscow had the family padding, but years of hard work had left her somewhat leaner than her siblings in the city.

Her face was worried, and her dusty brown hair was pulled back into a bun. Her cotton dress was simple, waistless and faded to a light brown with a hem that reached her ankles and sleeves she had rolled up to her elbows. Her apron was tied at her natural waist, with the bib pinned to the top of her dress, and she wiped her hands on it as she came off the side porch from the kitchen. Then she stopped and gazed at her daughter as if she were not sure what she was seeing.

"Kathy," she said at last.

The two women ran to each other and hugged.

"How did you get here?" Katie-Marie asked. "Look at you, and your hair. Oh, Kathy, darling, what did you do to your beautiful hair?"

"I just cut it, Ma. All the girls do in New York. They don't take you seriously if you don't."

Katie-Marie hugged her again. "Well, don't let me be nagging at you. I'm so glad to see you."

"I started packing the minute I got the telegram. How's Pa?"

"Fine."

"What?" Kathy's jaw dropped.

Katie-Marie laughed. "Dr. Scofield told me to wire you and Abraham yesterday when he was so sick. It was the pneumony. But the crisis came this morning and durned if the old cuss didn't face it down and keep living. He's been sleeping most of the day. But the fever's broke. Dr. Scofield says he ain't seen the like of it. We were all certain he was done for, and praying he'd hang on just long enough for you and Abraham to get out here."

"Then he's all right?" Kathy reeled with the relief. "Thank heavens! I was so worried. Oh, d—! I didn't have to get into that stupid plane after all."

"Plane?" Katie-Marie looked over and saw the biplane for the first time. "Lord have mercy, is that how you did it?"

"Yes." Kathy blushed. "My friend. It's his plane. Freddie. Um, Ma, this is Mr. Freddie Little. Freddie, my Ma."

Freddie walked up and took Katie-Marie's hand. "It's a pleasure, Mrs. Briscow."

"Well." Katie-Marie stepped back, surprised but pleased. "Mr. Little. Thanks be for that. I tell you, we've been wanting to meet you."

Freddie chose his words carefully. "Mrs. Briscow, perhaps you should be aware that there seems to be an ongoing misunderstanding among your relatives in New York."

Katie-Marie laughed. "I know all about that. But when my Kathy starts writing me about a gentleman friend, he's someone I want to meet." She put her arm around Kathy, who was blushing even more furiously, and took Freddie's arm. "Now, have you two been flying all night and all day?"

"Just since this morning, Ma," said Kathy.

"Have you had your suppers yet?"

"Now, Ma, don't go troubling yourself fixing up a lot of food."

"It's no trouble. We've plenty from ours."

Freddie paused. "Should I get my plane off the road?"

"There's no rush," said Ma. "But if it'll make you feel better, why don't you put it next to the barn there. Joshua, you come inside with us. Gideon, Isaac, Gammers, you help Mr. Little. Kathy, Joshua has someone inside you'll want to meet."

The someone was just putting away the last of the pots from dinner. Her hair was fair, as was her skin, and her figure was slender, with full breasts. Her simple peach dress was new, but she wore a faded brown full-sized straight apron with wide, scalloped edges over it. Joshua went proudly to her side.

"Kathy, this is Betty," he said. "My wife."

Kathy gaped, then turned to her mother. "Ma..."

"He didn't write us, either," said Katie-Marie, chiding but not unhappy.

"It sort of slipped my mind," said Joshua, with a sheepish chuckle.

"A year and a half and a baby, and it slips your mind." Katie-Marie shook her head. Kathy just barely caught the skeptical glint.

"A baby?" Kathy noticed the basket rocking

slightly in the middle of the kitchen table.

"Yes," said Betty, blushing and becoming red. She picked the infant up. It was wrapped in a blue cotton baby smock and matching bonnet and wore baby stockings up the length of its legs. "This is our son, Jacob Wallace Briscow."

"We're calling him Little J," said Joshua. "So as not to confuse him with Pa."

"He's beautiful," said Kathy, trying to sound more enthusiastic about the baby than she felt.

The infant was about two and a half months old, and promptly spit up. Betty wiped him up with a rag from the basket, while Joshua grinned as if the little beast had just said his first word. Kathy hoped she would not be invited to hold him. She'd done enough of that years before, helping to raise her younger brothers. Katie-Marie bustled about getting food.

While the kitchen was huge, it was a cozy place, with a large rectangular table in the middle covered by a red-checked oilcloth and surrounded by chairs. The cast iron wood-fired stove took up half of the back wall, with the new water boiler above it, and on the other half were two small wooden worktables flanking a gigantic washbasin. Red gingham curtains covered the base, and Kathy noticed that there were new water spigots over the deep, white porcelain sink. Cupboards with yellowed whitewash and a couple dark wood breakfronts lined the remaining walls, with an icebox tucked into the corner. An eight-day clock ticked peacefully over the icebox.

"Joshua, I can't believe it," said Kathy, looking around and absently noting that so little had changed in the years since she'd left. "What are you doing out here as it is? Don't you need to be in California with your oranges?"

"This time of year, the groves can take care of themselves." Joshua plopped into a chair. "I promised Betty a honeymoon, and this is the first chance we got. Figured what the heck, and packed her and the kid into the car and took off. Got here about a week ago, before Pa got sick."

"You drove from California?" Kathy gaped. "Were there even roads?"

Joshua nodded. "Most of the ways. We had plenty of gas cans, too. Only needed them once in the desert."

"I'm feeling slightly less adventurous." Kathy also sank into a chair. "How long did it take you?"

"Only two weeks. We took some time at the Grand Canyon. I tell you, Kathy. You got to see that. It is some sight."

The screen door banged open.

"Is he still jawing about that stupid Grand Canyon?" asked Isaac, coming in with Freddie, Gideon, and Gam close behind.

Gideon snorted. "You'd think it wasn't enough bringing home a new wife and baby he forgot to tell us about."

"Mr. Little, this is Betty," said Katie-Marie, pointing at the girl.

"The Mr. Little?" asked Betty, with a coy smile.

"Apparently so," said Freddie. "It's a pleasure."

"Ma, is there anything I can help you with?" Betty turned to her mother-in-law.

"That's just like you, Josh," hissed Kathy across the table. "Forget to tell us you're married, then she turns out to be a goody-two-shoes."

"What about your Mr. Swell?" Joshua hissed back. "An airplane, for crying out loud?"

"Ma?" asked Kathy. "When can I see Pa?"

"Gam, check on your father," said Katie-Marie. "Don't wake him if he's asleep." She turned back to Kathy. "I'm figuring he probably is. We'd have heard from him by now if he were awake. Isaac, go down to the root cellar and bring up some potatoes."

"Ma, we don't need a spread," protested Kathy.

"I'm not fixing a spread." Katie-Marie pulled a plate filled with chicken pieces from the icebox, then a bag of flour from the pantry. "Gideon, did you get the milking done?"

"Yeah, Ma. I always do."

Katie-Marie softened and smiled at him. "Yes, you do. Get some of the new cream in, and churn up some butter."

"Yeah, Ma."

"Ma, dinner won't be ready 'til nine," said Kathy. "You'll all be in bed."

"Don't talk nonsense, girl." Katie-Marie took a plate from the breakfront and set it next to the chicken, flour, cabbage, and radishes already on the table. "It's only seven-thirty."

Freddie pulled his watch from his pants pocket. It read eight-thirty. He looked up at the eight-day clock and laughed.

"Railroad time, Kathy," he said.

"Oh, that's right. I forgot." Kathy sighed, then noticed Freddie was still standing. "Freddie, go ahead and sit down. Around here, if you wait for an invitation, you'll be standing all night."

Katie-Marie whirled around. "Lord have mercy, is that why you were standing around, Mr. Little?"

"I don't like to presume," said Freddie, taking a chair.

"Well, we don't stand on formalities around here. Betty, start peeling the potatoes. Isaac, go back and get some peas and the shelling bowl. Josh, light a lamp or two." Katie-Marie went back to dredging chicken pieces in flour and bread crumbs.

"He's awake, Ma," said Gam, coming back into the kitchen as Josh put two kerosene lamps on the table and lit them with matches from his pants pocket.

The screen door slammed as Gideon came in with a small milk can that he was shaking vigorously.

"Ma, what do you want us to do with the suitcases?" he asked.

"Put Mr. Little's in the attic room," Katie-Marie said.

"He's not staying, is he?" asked Gam, disgusted.

"You better not have wakened your father, young man." Katie-Marie shook a flour covered finger at him.

"Naw. He was just waking up. Heard all the noise." Gam went to the far corner of the kitchen and leaned next to the icebox with folded arms and a sullen face. "I told him Kathy was here."

"Oh, you did!" Katie-Marie quickly wiped off her hands and got a bowl out from the breakfront. "You'd better get in there, Kathy, or he'll be upsetting himself. The doctor said he was to get complete rest, no upsets. Here, see if you can get him to eat this."

She ladled broth from the stock pot, simmering on the back of the stove, into the bowl. Kathy bounced up, and Freddie with her.

"Lord, it's getting warm." Kathy quickly unbuttoned the flight jacket she was still wearing.

Freddie's hands were already on her shoulders. Kathy blushed as he helped her off with it.

"You don't have to do that here," she hissed.

Freddie chuckled. "It's a habit, I'm afraid."

Kathy glared at the others, who were watching with amused grins.

"So the man was brought up with good manners," she snapped. "That's no reason to make out something that doesn't exist."

Fuming, Kathy got a spoon from the breakfront drawer, and went into the shadowed hall to the study.

It was a small room filled with books and a long couch. In times of illness, it was the sick room because it was so close to the kitchen, making it easier for Katie-Marie to watch the invalid. Chintz curtains graced the open window over the roll-top desk that was overflowing and seldom rolled down. The setting sun had left the room blanketed in blueish shadows. A corner jutted in that hadn't been there before. Kathy guessed it was the new downstairs toilet.

It was frightening to see her big, strong pa lying on the dark couch swathed in blankets, his normally tanned face looking white. He was an average sized man, with tough, wiry muscles and a full head of graying hair. Medicine bottles sitting on the lamp table looked like a crown over the pile of pillows on which Jacob Briscow lay.

"Pa?" asked Kathy softly.

"Kathy." His smile was weak, and his voice soft. But the life-spark in his eyes gleamed as strong as ever.

"Here, let me light the lamp." Kathy set the bowl on the lamp table and struck a match. She lit the kerosene lamp, and soft yellow light brightened the sick bed. "Ma says you have pneumonia."

"It weren't so bad." Jacob coughed. It was pretty ragged yet, but Kathy could tell it was better. "What did she go and wire you for?"

"The doctor didn't think you'd make it." Kathy knelt beside him and took one of the large, calloused hands. "He should have known you'd stand down the angel of death. Looks like God Himself is going to have to come down to get you."

"Now, don't be blaspheming, girl." Jacob smiled tenderly at her. "You cut your hair."

"I know. It's the style in New York." Kathy got the bowl. "Ma said to get you to eat this."

Jacob gingerly accepted a spoonful of broth. "Gam says you came here in a plane."

"Yes. My friend, Mr. Little, is a pilot, and when he saw how worried I was he insisted on bringing me." Kathy fed him another spoonful.

"Mr. Little, eh?" Jacob chuckled. "When do I get to meet the fellow?"

"Perhaps later. The doctor says we're not to excite you. You're still pretty sick, Pa."

Jacob snorted. "That fool doctor is worse than a mother hen."

He coughed again.

"Here, eat some more soup, then I'll let you rest." Kathy spooned in another mouthful before he could protest.

Jacob ate a couple more spoonfuls before yawning

and coughing again. Kathy would have been worried, but his forehead was cool, and he had the peaceful look of someone on the mend. She kissed his forehead, turned the lamp down low, and slipped out of the room.

She met Freddie in the hallway. He had shed his flying jacket, and Kathy realized she'd seen him in shirt sleeves three times in the past two days. Before that, she hadn't seen him without a jacket more than once or twice the whole time she'd known him.

"I hear he's going to make it," he said, smiling.

"He is." Kathy sighed with relief.

"Still wish you'd taken the train?"

Kathy chuckled. "No. I'm glad I got here when I did."

Back in the kitchen, Katie-Marie was still giving orders and cooking. Kathy got stuck setting the table, while Freddie was given peas to shell. After a quick lesson from Isaac, who had taken over the butter making from Gideon, Freddie managed quite well.

Soon the meal was ready. Upon Freddie's and Kathy's protests that there was quite a bit more food than they needed, Gam, Isaac, and Gideon each decided to indulge in a second supper. The yellow lamplight took over from the fading sun as they gathered around the huge table. Katie-Marie, Joshua, and Betty all drank coffee and snacked on the just-made biscuits and home-canned cherry preserves.

Even though the menu was simple, the freshness of the food made the meal quite unlike anything Freddie had ever eaten. He'd never tasted chicken that had been clucking that afternoon or peas that hadn't been hauled over miles of road. The only sauce was a rich, steaming, chicken gravy poured over potatoes mashed with the buttermilk left from the new butter made from cream that had only been milked hours before. The radishes and carrots were newly dug, and the cabbage for the slaw cut that day. Even the green tomato pie had its own special freshness, and it had been baked the day before.

Freddie did feel somewhat self-conscious, and a little shocked when he noticed that the others picked up and ate their chicken with their hands. He debated trying it, decided he couldn't, and continued neatly removing the meat from the bones with his knife and fork. Kathy's world was very different from his. He suspected he wasn't fitting in nearly as well as she had with his.

Gam and Isaac were sent to bed promptly at nine. Betty disappeared with Little J to feed him. Gideon yawned and said good night also. Katie-Marie distributed towels to Kathy, Freddie, and Joshua, and began washing up.

"It's a good thing you came when you did, Kathy," said Joshua.

"Young man..." warned Katie-Marie, glancing at Freddie.

"Oh, Ma, I already told Freddie you were having trouble out here," said Kathy. "What's been going on? It must be something pretty awful."

"It's just vandals," sighed Katie-Marie, without conviction. "One or two other places around here have had a bit of trouble with them, but they seem to be picking on us."

"Is this a recent development?" Freddie fumbled awkwardly with a wet plate.

"It started late last spring. Our well was fouled. Pa dug another, then it was fouled. We had some savings, so we got the indoor plumbing. But it didn't stop there. Someone set a fire in the west field. We got that out before we lost too much of the hay. Then Britches, you remember her, Kathy?"

"The brown jersey cow?" asked Kathy.

"She was stolen about three weeks ago. Found her two days later, up on Peterson's Road, shot. Couldn't even butcher her. The next night, someone broke into the barn and made a mess of it. Then Pa's horses were spooked, and he landed in the creek."

"Ma, didn't the dog let you know someone was on

the property?" asked Kathy.

Katie-Marie sighed. "He attacked one of the deputies when it started. The sheriff had him destroyed."

Joshua shook his head. "Can you believe it?"

Freddie pondered. "Is there anyone who has anything against your family?"

"I don't know," said Katie-Marie with a sigh.

Kathy looked at Freddie. "It doesn't have to be obvious. It could be any sort of imagined slight, don't you think?"

"I wouldn't say imagined, necessarily." Freddie ran the towel over a frying pan. "It would seem pretty obvious to the person slighted. The trick is in guessing who and why."

"I say someone wants to drive Pa off his land," said Joshua. "Or maybe even worse."

"Why?" asked Freddie and Kathy together.

Joshua stepped back. "All the vandalism. Everything that's happened is stuff that would make it harder to run the farm, and cost Pa money to do it. If it were just someone getting revenge, why not just try to hurt him?"

"We have had a couple agents come round," said Katie-Marie, shifting uncomfortably. "But you know your Pa. With three boys yet to get through college and on their own, he won't think of selling."

"Is there any way of talking to these fellows?" asked Freddie.

"No," said Katie-Marie. Her fingers slid on a plate. "They were fly-by-nights, here one day, gone the next. Land ain't been a real good business around here of late."

"I don't know," said Joshua. "I haven't been doing too badly by it. And with all the speculation that's going on in Florida, must be someone out here getting the bug."

"Nobody in their right mind," said Freddie. "That land option business is pretty risky. It'll blow up in their faces, mark me well."

Kathy's grin was wicked. "Is that why you don't have any real estate?"

"I have plenty of real estate," retorted Freddie. "I just don't have it in Florida."

"It's good business as far as I'm concerned," said Joshua. "That's how I got my spread."

"Mortgaged out to your ears, I'll bet," teased Kathy.

"Nope. I paid cash," said Joshua proudly. "Even made a cash investment in the packing plant. Started out building houses and selling them, and bought land out near Hollywood just in time for all the movie people to come out and start buying it. I still got a couple tenanted places in Los Angeles, but it was getting too crowded for me. And farming's in my blood, anyway."

But not in Kathy's, Freddie noted with some satisfaction. Although she did the work with an ease that meant a lifetime of practice, he could tell she wasn't doing it because she liked it. He found dish drying rather soothing, but doubted he'd like doing it every day.

Katie-Marie wiped off the table cloth quickly, then laid the wash rag over the sink's edge and wiped her hands on her apron.

"Does anyone want this last biscuit?" she asked. No one did. "Into the pig bucket with it."

She tossed it into a galvanized pail under the sink. Freddie had wondered why she'd scraped all the plates into it before washing them.

"Being from the city, I really don't know much about life on a farm," he said slowly. "I hope you don't mind if I ask a few questions."

"If you'll get to your point, I don't mind at all," said Katie-Marie as Kathy giggled.

"What's a pig bucket?"

"Slops for the pig." Katie-Marie picked up a coffee pot. "Any more coffee, anyone?"

Kathy smiled at the confused look still on Freddie's

face.

"Slops are leftovers," she explained. "What we don't eat, the pigs will. It's a cheap way to keep meat on the hoof."

"You wouldn't have us wasting all that food, would you?" asked Katie-Marie. "You sure you don't want any more coffee?"

"No, thank you, I'm quite satisfied," said Freddie.

Joshua yawned. "I think I'll be turning in."

"It's after nine already," said Katie-Marie. "Kathy, why don't you show Freddie to his room, and get him some water so he can wash up."

"Yes, Ma." Kathy beckoned Freddie.

He followed her upstairs. She stopped at a large, white armoire in the hall.

"I don't know how tired you are," she whispered, getting out a towel, and a white basin and ewer bearing a dark green print of lords and ladies and vines. "But if you're not ready for bed, go ahead and stay up." She looked around the hall. "There's the bathroom. I guess we're still cleaning up in our own rooms. I hope you don't mind."

"Not at all."

Kathy sent Freddie up the narrow stairway to the attic while she filled the ewer. When she got there, she found Freddie ducking the low beams of the slanted ceiling. It was a narrow room, with an old brass bed made up with a white cotton bedspread and a slightly battered, dark brown bureau decorated with a lace runner. The walls were papered in a faded rose pattern, and white curtains with brightly embroidered hems covered the window.

"Oh, dear," sighed Kathy. "You did get the only room in the house that hasn't got someone else in it."

"It's quite all right, Kathy," Freddie said, smiling. "It won't hurt me to rough it a little."

She set the ewer and basin on the washstand next to the bureau. "I hope it's not too uncomfortable."

"The bed is soft enough." Freddie put his valise

on the end. "And believe it or not, I can even manage unpacking by myself. Please, Kathy, don't worry about me."

"I guess I am a little embarrassed. I can't offer you a fine mansion with servants, or even a nice apartment."

Freddie laughed. "Instead, you provide a warm welcome and better food than I've eaten in a long time."

"And you get put to work for it, too. Freddie, you don't have to stay. I can take the train back home when all of this is over."

"You mean the vandalism."

Kathy nodded. "I really want to find out who is doing it, and put a stop to it before something really terrible happens."

"Won't the sheriff?"

"Wimberton? Not likely. His idea of chasing criminals is putting up a wanted notice at the post office."

"I thought that might be. Well. I won't stay if you don't want me, but we have gotten to the bottom of more than one mysterious incident. I'm sure that together we can do it again."

"Together?" Kathy's face lit up in a way that set Freddie's blood racing. "Oh, Freddie, I was hoping you'd say that. I thought I might be able to do it myself, but it will be easier with you." She paused. "Frankly, I'm pretty worried. Ma's not saying so, but I think everything's got her real upset. That's why I changed the subject and started teasing you and Josh about the real estate. You could tell she didn't want to talk about it. I think there's something worse going on here. Pa could have been killed when those horses spooked, instead of going in the creek."

"There's a great deal more to this vandalism than meets the eye, especially given how we were greeted this afternoon. Unless your family is in the habit of welcoming strangers with buckshot."

Kathy sighed. "I know. I was wondering about that, too. But asking won't do any good. If Ma had wanted to tell me, I would have heard about it by now."

"Kathy?" hissed Katie-Marie's voice from the bottom of the stairs.

"I'll be down in a minute, Ma." Kathy turned to Freddie with a guilty smile. "They're protecting me. Since Pa's sleeping in the study, I'm sleeping with Ma."

"I wonder if they realize that I'm the one who needs protecting from you," said Freddie with a chuckle as Kathy slid her arms around him.

"You must think of me as a terrible tramp," she whispered.

Freddie held her face in his hands. "No. I have always thought very highly of you. You're just a woman who knows what she wants, and will take the risks to get it."

The kiss was slow and soft, and no less passionate for it. Kathy had to tear herself away.

Chapter Three

It had been a long day for Freddie, but as darkness and sleep settled over the house, he felt restless. Taking his cigarettes, matches, and holder, he slipped downstairs. He moved softly, yet as he passed the study a board creaked.

"Who's that?" called a voice from inside.

"Just Kathy's friend," Freddie called back quietly.

"Come in here."

Freddie hesitated. Mr. Briscow was to rest, according to Kathy's mother, and the doctor had been very specific about no excitement. Still, Freddie had a feeling ignoring his host's request would cause still more. He went in.

The lamp left the steel gray-haired man with almost a halo. His shoulders were broad, and his face lean and tanned with years of hard work in the sun. Illness had left its traces, but this was not a man who would be claimed easily. He lifted his hand.

"Jacob Briscow," he said quietly.

"Freddie Little." Freddie shook his hand firmly, but with respect for the man's illness.

"Sit down, son. I expect you been hearing I been wanting to meet you."

"I've heard a word or two about it." Freddie pulled around the desk chair and sat down. "I thought at first it was exaggeration on the part of Kathy's uncles. But your wife says Kathy's been writing about me. I can't imagine what."

Jacob laughed, then coughed. "Not much. Just a passing mention every two or three letters, at first. Last few your name's come up once—in passing, you understand—every letter. Of course, in four years away at college, and in six years in New York, this is the first time Kathy's ever mentioned a man."

"I can see where one might draw a few conclusions from that." Freddie nodded.

"My brother-in-law says you can keep her comfortable."

Freddie chuckled. "I'm not about to make the mistake of trying to keep her. She keeps herself quite well, thank you."

"And you?"

"I'm well off."

"I'd guess so if you can take off and leave without getting into a scrape at the office." Jacob's brown eyes, so like Kathy's, watched him, searched him. "What do you do for a living?"

"I don't, actually." Freddie felt a little embarrassed. "My family has money. I've made some investments, in addition."

"You don't work?" It was as if Freddie had said he didn't breathe.

"I don't go to an office and put in time. I don't know how much Kathy has mentioned." Freddie paused. He still wasn't sure of it, but Kathy had insisted he was. And he did spend a good many hours at it. "I am a writer. My first book should be out soon, and I'm working on another."

"That's working." Jacob peered at him. "Why didn't you say so?"

"My livelihood is certainly not dependent on my writing." Freddie swallowed. "And most of my friends seem to consider it a queer sort of hobby."

Jacob chuckled. "It is, at that. But as long as you can support a wife and children, it don't matter to me how you do it, as long as it won't put you in jail."

Freddie felt the irritation rise. "Mr. Briscow, aren't we being a little presumptuous here?"

"That is your intention, isn't it?"

"At the moment, my intentions are moot. As I've explained before, your daughter has no intention of marrying me."

"That's what she thinks." Jacob coughed. "She's gone on you, son."

"I am well aware of her feelings for me." Freddie tried not to squirm. The interview was definitely covering dangerous ground, especially given what Kathy wanted for their relationship, and what Freddie wanted, and the fact that he had no idea how it would all fall out. "But the situation is, shall we say, delicate. I'm not about to press the issue. Furthermore, there is a great deal your daughter stands to lose by marrying me in terms of her own self-reliance, and the satisfaction she derives from it."

"We'll have to do something about that." Jacob nodded thoughtfully, then noticed Freddie's glare. "I ain't thinking what you're thinking I am. I'm probably more modern-minded than you. Problem is, Kathy keeps forgetting that a job is only half the battle. What time is it?"

Freddie shifted, getting the watch from his pocket.

"Just after ten o'clock."

Jacob coughed.

"Perhaps I'd better leave you to your rest," said Freddie.

"I was thinking you'd better get to yours." Jacob laughed. "I don't mean to be so hard on you, son. But just 'cause she's all growed don't mean I stop worrying about her. About any of my children. Like that fool, Joshua, knocking up that girl, then marrying her. I don't care what they're saying, they ain't been married no year and a half. It comes from my side of the family, you know. Briscows always been hot-blooded." He coughed again. "Well, be off with you."

"Good night, Mr. Briscow."

"'Night, son."

Freddie let himself out of the room. He could have gone to bed, but it still seemed so early. Even with the windows open, the house was a little stuffy. Freddie wandered out to the side porch.

There was a porch swing facing the barn. Freddie found a broken cup that could be used as an ashtray and set it with the cigarette case and lighter on the porch railing, then settled himself on the swing.

The tobacco was a relief. The blue light of the stars illuminated the yard, stilled by the night. It wasn't silent. Something scraped beneath him. A chain rattled from the barn. A small breeze whispered through the trees behind the house. Freddie sucked in another relaxing drag.

"What are you doing out here?" demanded Gam's voice.

"Thinking." Freddie blew out the smoke casually.

"In the dark?" Gam came out of the house, wrapped in a bathrobe and carrying the shotgun.

"I didn't want to wake anyone."

Gam looked him over suspiciously. "Aren't you going to ask what I'm doing out here?"

"Given your weapon, I would guess guard duty. But as this is your home, and I am a guest here, I didn't feel I had the right to ask."

"You sure talk funny." Gam backed himself to the other end of the porch and sat down cross-legged, holding his gun ready.

Freddie shrugged. "No doubt the result of too much education, too much time, and too little to do. Something tells me that you do not have that problem."

"I don't know." Gam shrugged. "Pa always says when I get into trouble it's because I didn't have enough to keep me busy."

"Get into trouble a lot?"

"Sometimes. When they catch me." Gam's eyes narrowed. "What you asking for?"

"Nothing, really. Just making conversation." Freddie blew a couple smoke rings.

Gam was impressed in spite of himself. "Golly, that's pretty swell. Can you do it again?"

"Sure." Freddie blew another three.

"Gee, even Maxie Whitecase can't do that."

"Smoking already?"

"Maxie's twelve. Got held back a year, so he's in my class." Gam looked at him again. "You must like my sister an awful lot."

"We're good friends."

"Did you really fly all the way from New York?"

"Mm-hm. Would you like a ride in my plane?"

"Yeah!" Suddenly fear creased Gam's face, and he looked at Freddie suspiciously. "No. No, I don't."

Freddie was puzzled. "As you like." He was about to apologize, then thought better of it. "Do you smoke?"

Gam shifted. "You gonna tell my Pa?"

"If he asks, I might. But I don't see why he should ask."

"You mean you'd tell him?" Oddly enough, Gam seemed more reassured than threatened.

"It depends." Freddie looked the boy over carefully. "If you asked me to keep a confidence, and it wasn't the sort of thing that would hurt you, I wouldn't dream of telling. On the other hand, I don't feel it would be right to keep something that might hurt you a secret, or if your father had good reason to know."

Gam thought this over. "Can I have a cigarette?"

"Certainly." Freddie held out the case.

Still hanging onto the gun, Gam swaggered over and made his selection. He tamped it down, obviously in imitation of someone, Freddie decided one of his schoolmates. Freddie struck the match. Gam sucked, then bent over choking.

"First time, eh?" Freddie smiled.

Gam nodded and handed the cigarette back. "Why do people do that?"

"It has its attractions," Freddie confessed. "But all in all, it is a nasty habit. I'd recommend avoiding it, or at least waiting until you're older before trying again."

Gam retreated to his corner. "I know, it'll stunt my growth. You know, you're the first person who's ever let me try, and didn't lecture me."

"I never listened to anyone who lectured me. I remember when I was roughly your age thinking that it was a singularly ineffective way of achieving an end." Freddie took the butt from his holder and put Gam's cigarette in.

"Did you like girls when you were my age?"

"Let's see, you are eleven?"

"Yep."

"At eleven, I was not interested. Girls were something I had to dance with at proper parties for young gentlemen and ladies. They were heavily chaperoned, and deathly boring."

"What's chaper...what's that you said?"

"Chaperoned. It means guarded by stuffy old ladies who think holding hands is taking liberties."

Gam laughed. "You mean sex stuff, right?"

"Something like that." Freddie smiled. "Does your friend Maxie know all about that, too?"

"What's to know?" Gam said with a shrug. "I know people don't do it like a bull mounting up, but it's sort of the same. I don't know if I'd like it. Maxie dared us to get Carol Ann Kepner to show us her pussy. Big deal. She'll show it to anybody for a nickel."

Freddie laughed.

"What's so funny about that?"

"I, too, knew a Carol Ann Kepner. Well, that wasn't her name. But she, too, would show us her pussy for a nominal fee." It was quarters, actually, but Mary Wilkins knew Freddie and his schoolmates had more pocket change. Freddie grinned at Gam. "Did you?"

"Did you?" Gam challenged.

"Of course."

"Me, too." Gam's face fell. "It wasn't anything, really."

"That's because there's nothing to see at that age. Wait until you're both older."

"I don't get it. Adults get all fussed about this sex thing. They won't talk about it, kind of pretend it isn't there, except when you're looking at a girl. They say you're thinking dirty thoughts. I can't see why they're all excited. It don't seem like much to me. What's so great about it?"

Freddie took a long, thoughtful drag. "Ever feel yourself go good and hard?"

Gam brought the gun up defensively. "No! I never did it!"

"Hold on." Freddie sat up straight. "I didn't mean anything by that. I was only trying to answer your question."

Gam looked away. Starlight picked up the glint of a tear on his cheek. Freddie sighed, almost certain he knew what was causing Gam's upset.

"Gammers, you don't have to tell me if you don't want to, but when I was at school, there were some older boys who would take the younger boys, and in a very nasty, uncomfortable way, use them as men generally go to women. Has that happened to you?"

"I ain't saying!"

But he already had. Freddie's lips pursed tightly. It seemed his and Kathy's worlds weren't so different after all.

"I get the feeling you're a little afraid of me sometimes," Freddie said softly. "I don't really blame you. But rest assured I'm not going to ask you to keep any secrets. You can even tell your parents, if you like."

"I can?" Gam looked at him.

"Even that I gave you a cigarette. I probably shouldn't have. But if it will make you feel better, I'm willing to take a lecture or worse."

Gam grinned. "Ma will give you one. She don't like

tobacco. She don't like liquor, neither. Not that there's much of that to be had around here. She made sure of that years ago."

"That's regrettable, at best."

"Why? Do you drink?" Gam's respect for Freddie grew.

"I've been known to take a nip or two."

"Golly, how do you get it?"

"It's very easy in New York. In fact, it's probably fairly easy to get it around here. One just needs to know where to look."

"Peter Dawson's pa has a still. But I sure didn't like the taste of it."

Freddie nodded. "It could have been bad hootch, or it could be because liquor, like cigarettes, is a taste that is acquired."

Gam shrugged, then stopped. "What's that?"

Freddie waited, listening. The farm was oddly silent, then there was a scraping sound.

"It's coming from that shed," Freddie whispered. "I take it that is not a normal sound."

"Nope." Gam put the shotgun to his shoulder.

"Wait," Freddie whispered. "Maybe if we sneak up on them we'll catch them, and find out who is behind all this. Let's pretend we're going in."

Gam grinned as Freddie stretched and gathered his cigarettes together. Gam stretched also. Freddie opened and banged the screen door shut, then dashed into the porch's shadows. Gam followed.

They slipped over the railing and around to the tool shed. Freddie took the gun from Gam, then rolled around to the door. He gently eased it open. He peeked into the opening, then rolled inside, gun to shoulder and ready.

The shed was black. Freddie fumbled for a switch, then remembered there wasn't any. He slid around the wall as silently as possible, which wasn't very silent at all thanks to all the various pieces of hardware that he tripped over. Still, Freddie was confident that whoever else was in there was tripping over the same things. Except no one was in the shed.

Gam watched the door, ready to jump anyone coming out. All he saw was Freddie as he emerged.

"Didn't you see anyone?" Freddie asked.

"Just you," said Gam, completely confused. "How could they have gotten out?"

"There doesn't seem to be a back door," said Freddie.

"Nope." Gam groaned. "The side window. They probably jumped out when we was coming over here."

Freddie ran for the road. It was deserted.

"How the hell...?" he grumbled.

"They probably went for the woods," said Gam, trotting up. "It's the best cover on the place."

Freddie nodded, then walked over to his airplane. The Curtiss was untouched, as far as he could tell.

"Maybe we ought to check the shed and see what they done," suggested Gam.

"Unless you've got a really good lantern, we might as well wait until morning," said Freddie. "With luck, they were scared off before any damage was done."

"Well, I'm gonna wait up and make sure they don't come back." Gam took the shotgun from Freddie.

"I think I'll have another smoke and wait with you."

Freddie gave Gam the porch swing and leaned against the house. Before he finished his cigarette, Gam had nodded over and was fast asleep. Chuckling, Freddie removed the shotgun from the boy's hand and picked him up.

Fortunately, Kathy had pointed out which room Gam was sleeping in. Freddie left the shotgun in the hall and put Gam in the one empty bed.

"Who's there?" asked a sleepy voice.

Freddie made out Isaac's profile in the dark. "Mr. Little. Gammers and I were out on guard duty, and Gam fell asleep."

"You and Gammers?"

"Sh. We don't want to wake him."

"Where's the shotgun?"

"In the hall."

Isaac laid back down. Freddie slipped out of the room. But before going up to the attic, he waited a moment. Sure enough, Isaac poked his head out of the room and slid out. Freddie smiled. At last, he knew why the vandals had not been able to inflict more damage.

Chapter Four

Freddie was used to the sound of people moving about his room when he was asleep. All his life, servants had slipped past his sleeping form, preparing baths, laying out clothes or other necessities, bringing in breakfast. Freddie ignored the sound of ceramic ware clattering and the soft curse until he noticed he was sleeping on worn cotton, with knobby French knots in colorful yarns decorating the edge of the pillow case.

He lifted himself and turned to gaze sleepily as Kathy struggled with last night's ewer and basin, and a fresh towel. She wore a faded, green, over-sized apron over her best blue dress.

"What are you doing?" he asked through the cotton fuzziness of waking up.

"Oh, drat. I was trying not to wake you." Kathy hitched the ewer and basin onto her hip. "I brought you some fresh water for washing up."

"Mm. I take it a bath is out."

"Only if you want a hot one. The boiler isn't that big, and everyone else needed to get ready for church. I had to heat this up on the stove."

"I thought you didn't go to church."

"Pa doesn't, and I don't except when I'm here."

Freddie nodded and rolled onto his back. "What time is everyone leaving?"

"In about fifteen minutes."

"Fifteen minutes?" Freddie sat up. Kathy gasped a little because his blue and white striped pajama top was unbuttoned and she could see his union suit underneath. "What time is it?"

"Eight."

"In the morning? Why so early?"

"Because Sunday school starts at nine, and Ma likes to be there early to talk to people."

"Damn." Freddie yawned.

"Everyone except you has been up since five," said Kathy, half chiding, half teasing. "There's some breakfast saved in the oven for you. But I'd get it quick before it scorches."

"I'll do what I can." Freddie yawned. "I should have had you wake me. I hate to ask, but do you think it would be terribly irritating to the rest of your family if you stalled them just a bit so that I might join them?"

Kathy shrugged. "They might wait of their own accord. Do your best."

She left. Freddie concentrated on giving himself the quickest shave he'd had since he'd left the army.

Outside, the old Model T truck's engine wouldn't turn over. Gideon's face was red from cranking the truck again and again, and sweat soaked his Sunday shirt. He and his younger brothers were all wearing white long-sleeved shirts with stand-up collars, and dark wool pants.

"We'll have to push it again," grumbled Katie-Marie.

"I know what's wrong!" yelped Gam, and he took off running into the house.

Freddie had just laid out his gray wool suit pants when Gam burst into the tiny room.

"Mr. Little! I know what they did last night," the boy all but yelled. His brown hair was just starting to dry and become untidy again.

"That's all very well," snapped Freddie. "But I'd appreciate it if you would knock first, in the future. And for the moment, please allow me to get into something besides my union suit!"

Gam stepped back. "I'm not stopping you. Oh. You mean, leave."

"Precisely."

Gam slipped out of the room, then yelled through the shut door.

"Mr. Little, the vandals last night. They did something to the truck. Gideon cranked and cranked, and it won't catch."

Freddie's irritation at not being left to dress in peace melted into curiosity. He reached for his flying pants instead. Minutes later he was down in the yard, giving the engine a crank himself.

"He likes playing with engines," Kathy explained to her mother. "His family is appalled, but all that grease and muck makes him happy as a clam."

Muttering and grumbling, Freddie propped open the hood. Gam danced attendance on him, running and fetching tools.

"It's like night and day," Katie-Marie told Kathy. "I haven't seen Gam this happy in months. He's taken such a shine to your Mr. Little. I like to have died when Gammers told me they'd been talking last night. I was so shocked, I didn't even fuss when Gam said Mr. Little had let him have a cigarette."

"And he told me he kept his vices to himself." Kathy shook her head.

"How long has it been acting like this?" Freddie suddenly asked.

"Past week or two," said Katie-Marie, the long hem of her Sunday dress fluttering around her lower calf. It was a green cotton dress with white linen trim and short sleeves and a more fashionable lowered waistline. Her white straw hat had a broad brim and a couple pink artificial silk flowers decorating the crown. "Not all the time, you understand. But when it don't start, we been getting it going by pushing it."

"That's one way of doing it." Freddie slipped under the truck.

A minute later, he scrambled out as if something had bit him. Getting to his feet, he walked quickly into the tool shed and examined the oil-caked dirt inside. He looked at something in his hand, then picked up several bolts lying on the ground.

"It's a good thing you didn't push it today," he said. "Someone tampered with your steering column."

"Lord have mercy!" Katie-Marie gasped, as Kathy put her hand to her mouth in fear.

"But didn't the vandals just make it break down?" asked Gam anxiously.

"Vandals?" asked Gideon. "Were they here last night?"

"We scared 'em off," said Gam proudly.

"Apparently not fast enough," grumbled Freddie. "Who would know how to sabotage your truck?"

"Almost anyone," Gideon said. "Everyone around here has some sort of Model T. And lots of folks fix them up to do all sorts of things."

"But are they people you know?" Freddie pressed.

"Of course, Freddie," said Kathy. "This is a small town. Everybody knows everybody."

"We'd best get the truck back in the shed," sighed Katie-Marie. She took a quick look at the truck and surreptitiously made the sign of the cross. "Joshua, Gideon, Isaac, Gammers, get the truck back, then hurry on to church. Except you, Joshua. You can drive us in your car, can't you?"

Joshua grinned. "Sure and I can."

"I'll get the horses hitched to the wagon," Gideon said. "It'll still be faster than walking."

"Good," said Katie-Marie. "Mr. Little, you'd best be cleaning up. We'll wait for you. I'll be getting you some fresh breakfast. Betty, come help."

She shooed everybody to their appointed tasks. Freddie was ordered to wash up in the kitchen sink while Katie-Marie went out to the hen house, which was attached to the back of the house. Kathy rescued the saved breakfast from the oven and put it into the pig slops, then put a fresh log in the stove. Betty played with Little J as she pulled the pans from the cupboard. Her Sunday dress was a yellow-flowered batiste, with a full skirt that flowed from the lowered waist, and gauzy, flowing short sleeves trimmed in ribbons. But she still wore her faded brown apron.

"Betty!" hollered Joshua from outside.

Betty went to the screen door. "What's the matter?"

The reply was gestured, but it seemed urgent. Betty groaned worriedly, then glanced around. Kathy had quickly sunk her hands into the flour sack. Little J's basket was elsewhere. Betty spotted Freddie drying his hands.

"Here, Little J, go to Uncle Freddie." She put the baby in Freddie's hands and ran out.

Kathy couldn't help grinning at the look of utter dismay on Freddie's face.

"What am I supposed to do with this?" he sputtered, holding the infant under its arms away from his body.

Little J smiled and cooed, then spit up all over Freddie's hand.

"Oh, for heaven's sakes!" he groaned. "Kathy, will you do something?"

"I'll get a rag." Kathy wiped off her hands on a towel and went over to the shelf next to the breakfront. "You might try supporting his head and back instead of letting him dangle like that."

Freddie shifted one hand to the baby's bottom and yelped again.

"It's wet!"

Laughing, Kathy came over and tickled Little J's stomach.

"So that's why you were grinning," she told the baby.

"Will you do something?" asked Freddie.

"We'll have to change him." Kathy wandered out

of the kitchen. "Bring him along."

"Aren't you going to take him?" Freddie followed more out of desperation than desire.

"Why should I make both of us wet?"

Freddie, upon thinking about it, would probably have agreed. But at that moment, he was too flabbergasted and annoyed to think beyond getting the wet, squirming little baggage out of his hands.

"This is getting ridiculous," he complained, as he followed Kathy upstairs. "The way your family presumes upon me. First, Gammers comes charging into my room without knocking."

"He likes you, Freddie."

"That is no excuse for such rude behavior."

"No, but he is only eleven." Kathy went into the room where Joshua and his family were staying and rummaged through the luggage.

Now the guest room, Kathy had shared the room with her sister, Teresa, back when the two were girls. The walls were whitewashed, as was the plain chest of drawers. A faded rag rug covered the floor, and chintz curtains billowed in with the breeze.

"I can't imagine you were any great paragon of protocol at that age," Kathy continued.

"I most certainly was. By that age I was well aware of what the expectations were, and I lived up to them."

"She's got to have diapers in here somewhere. Here they are." Kathy laid three out on the faded patchwork quilt covering the bed, then turned back to the luggage. "Put him there, and take off the diaper."

"How do I do that?" Frowning, Freddie laid Little J on the diapers.

"Unpin the safety pins and take it off. There it is." Kathy pulled a carton of cornstarch from the bags. "Just make sure you—"

Freddie's cry interrupted her. "Damn it! The little bastard almost got me in the eye!"

"They will do that." Kathy wrung out a cloth in the basin and tossed it at Freddie. "It's amazing what they can hit with absolutely no control. Then when they get it, they can't hit a thing." She wrung out another cloth. "The trick is to put your hand over the top of the diaper as you lift it."

"Why don't you demonstrate?" sneered Freddie. Wiping himself off, he backed away. The smell of the open diaper still reached his nostrils. He choked. "Good lord, I had no idea they smelled so bad."

"This is nothing," said Kathy, calmly wiping up. "Try changing a nine-month old's diaper first thing in the morning."

"I have no intention of ever doing such."

"And you will never be obligated to." Kathy's tone turned sour. "Nor will Joshua."

Freddie understood Kathy's chagrin but did not want to discuss it at that moment.

"What do you do with the dirty ones?" he asked instead.

"We used to rinse them out by the outhouses, then put them in a covered can until wash day." Kathy laughed grimly. "Speaking of something else that will water your eyes at thirty paces." She looked around the room. "I suppose we could rinse it out in the toilet..."

"Well, my dear Miss Briscow, you know that I consider the weaker sex a misnomer, so I will leave the operation in your capable hands."

"Coward."

"In this case, yes."

"Oh, no. Not again, you little beast."

Freddie paused outside the door and watched as Kathy again wiped the baby's bottom.

"I know," she grumbled to the infant. "You can't help it, and won't be able to for another two years. Well, all I have to say is that it won't be soon enough."

Sighing, he left. Kathy was indeed capable, and while she wanted nothing to do with the baby, she was not unkind. Freddie was fairly certain motherhood was not among Kathy's aspirations. But it would be all too likely, even without marriage. Surely Kathy was aware of what she risked that way as his lover.

When Joshua rolled his Packard Single Six touring car from behind the tool shed, Freddie couldn't help raising his eyebrows. Joshua caught the look and quickly signaled a request for silence. He waited just long enough to make sure Katie-Marie and Betty were both out of earshot.

"I know I'm doing well, but I ain't doing this well," Joshua whispered to Freddie, waving at his car.

Freddie couldn't help raising his eyebrows again. Packards were the kind of automobiles his set preferred.

"It's not my place to question," Freddie said, desperately hoping Joshua would explain nonetheless.

"A friend of mine gave it to me." Joshua winced. "Okay. I built him a hangar for his Sopwith Camel." Joshua lowered his voice still more. "He's a rum runner. He needed a false wall, you know?"

"Indeed, I do," said Freddie with a sigh.

"Ma don't know how fancy a car this is," Joshua whispered. "If she or Betty knew I'd gotten it from a rum runner..."

"I understand completely,' Freddie said.

As they rode along the dirt road, Katie-Marie told Freddie, with great pride, that the town had almost 5,000 people living there and was the county seat for Ellis County. Freddie's first sight of Hays, Kansas from the ground, however, did little to impress him. There were few buildings of any great size, although the courthouse stood out with its short cupula tower. Houses abounded, with yards of all sizes, and even a couple vacant lots. Coming from New York City, where there was next to no vacant land, Freddie couldn't help but wonder where the 5,000 people actually were.

Even in the car, they arrived in town about half an hour late for Sunday school. The other boys had just arrived, and while Katie-Marie made sure they got to their classes, plus found classes for Betty and Joshua,

Kathy pulled Freddie away.

"Services aren't until eleven," she explained. "So we can take a walk, or do whatever you like."

"There won't be much open, will there?" he asked. "Perhaps it would be better if we went to Sunday school. We'd at least meet some of the townsfolk."

"We can do that at services. Let's walk down to the creek. It'll be cooler there."

Freddie nodded. "That might be nice."

He offered his arm and Kathy took it, steering him down Chestnut Street toward the public school at the southern end. Houses of varying sizes dotted the mostly empty lots on either side of the street.

"Are you sure it was the vandals who tampered with the steering on the truck?" Kathy asked as they walked.

"Yes. Contrary to what Gammers believes, the vandals did not cause the entire crank mechanism to deteriorate and break down. That takes time, and it will need replacing, by the way."

"But couldn't the steering parts have just fallen out? When we had that other problem with your car last June, you said that sometimes happens."

Freddie winced at the memory. "It can. But usually, when bolts fall out, they land in the road. I found all three of the missing bolts on the floor of the shed, along with the pins. And if you want to disable a car, tampering with the steering can cause a very nasty accident. I almost wish we could have gotten the truck running. It would have been very interesting to see who was surprised to see it."

"That would. But could you have fixed it that fast?"

"The steering? Very probably. But I will have to order parts for the crank mechanism."

Kathy sighed. "Freddie, this is getting serious. Somebody could have gotten killed in that truck."

"I don't doubt things will get nastier. But who stands to gain anything by hurting your family this way?"

"I just can't imagine anyone wanting revenge." Kathy frowned. "Pa has always prided himself on being a good neighbor. He's always there when there's a need. The rest of the time, he keeps to himself. Ma gets about more, but it's all for charity and taking care of the family."

Freddie mused. "As I understand it, your mother was quite active in drying up this place."

"You mean liquor? Freddie, Kansas has been dry since eighteen eighty. Wait. There were some joints operating near the tracks when I was real little. Now that I think about it, Ma and Grandma ran the group that eventually ran them out. But that was still years ago, long before I left for college. Why would someone take revenge now? And besides, the way Sheriff Wimberton enforces the law, anyone who wants liquor can get it."

"Wait." Freddie stopped walking. "Didn't you once tell me about how your father took a teacher to task on your behalf? Something about how the teacher had made a mistake and your father went to school and corrected her in front of the whole class."

"Yes, but I wasn't even in high school then. Why do something about it now?"

"Might it be possible your father has gone to the defense of one of your brothers, and in so doing, offended someone?"

Kathy nodded. "That may be. I don't think the boys have done anything to cause this. It wouldn't be this serious. It won't be hard to find out, either. The funny thing is, I think Josh may have a point when he says someone is trying to drive Pa off his land. After all, the attacks seem to be more directed at the farm itself than anyone on it."

"But who would stand to gain anything by taking your father's land? The way farming pays these days, the only reason anyone is doing it is for the nobility of the man and the soil."

"What if someone wanted to consolidate all the

little farms, and make one big farm to cut down on the costs?"

Freddie shook his head. "It would be a terrible investment. The more they produce, the lower the crop prices fall. The cost of buying all that land would make the entire venture a complete loss."

"But if they got it cheaply because Pa was trying to get off."

"It wouldn't be that cheap, not for the small profit that could be expected."

"Well, you know more about that sort of thing than I do. I guess that leaves us with revenge for a motive."

"It's not a bad one, and it does give us someplace to look."

"That's true. I'll see what I can find out. I'd recommend you just keep your ears open, and don't ask questions. People can get a little suspicious about strangers around here."

"No doubt." Freddie looked ahead. "What's that?"

They had just reached the creek. Water flowed around a grove of trees between mossy banks. What little breeze there was blew cool and fresh. A heavy-set man wearing a broad-brimmed scout's hat and a tan uniform dragged a dog towards the water.

"Howdy, Sheriff!" Kathy called, letting her voice sound cheerful.

The man looked up, the sun catching the badge pinned to his shirt. "Well, I'll be. If it ain't little Kathy Briscow. I heard you wasn't s'posed to be here 'til this afternoon's train."

"I got in a little faster than I expected." She and Freddie slid down the slope to where Sheriff Wimberton was.

He gave Freddie a calculated once over.

"This is Mr. Little," Kathy said. "He's a friend of mine from New York. He escorted me out. Freddie, this is Sheriff Wimberton."

"How do you do, Sheriff?" Smiling lazily to hide the speculative interest in his eyes, Freddie offered his hand.

"How do." Wimberton shook it.

"What brings you out to the creek this morning, Sheriff?" Kathy asked, her tone also masking a less than casual interest.

"This dog." Wimberton shook the rope holding a large, long-haired mutt, covered by large black and tan spots. "Gotta destroy it."

Freddie held out his hand. The dog sniffed it.

"Why?" Freddie asked. "He seems friendly enough." He patted the dog's head, then scratched it. The dog leaned into the scratching.

"He's a stray," said Wimberton. "Can't have him running around loose."

"I suppose not," said Kathy. "But he seems like such a nice dog. Hasn't anybody claimed him?"

"Nope, and I'm fed up feeding him." Wimberton pulled his handgun.

"Here, here," said Freddie. "If nobody wants him, then there's no reason I can't take him."

"What the hell are you going to do with him?" Wimberton demanded.

Kathy wondered also but knew she didn't want the dog destroyed.

"I have a young friend who recently lost his dog," said Freddie. "This fellow seems just the ticket to ease the lad's grief. Let me have him. Please."

Wimberton looked Freddie over with even more suspicion than before.

"Who's your friend?" he asked.

"Gamaliel Briscow. Miss Briscow's youngest brother."

"Oh, Gam will be thrilled," gushed Kathy. "Freddie, how utterly kind of you. Poor Gam, he's been heartbroken since he lost his other. Sheriff, please can we have him? It would make my brother so happy."

Scowling, Wimberton holstered his pistol and handed the rope over to Freddie.

"Thank you, Sheriff." Freddie tipped his panama

hat genially. "You've done us a great kindness."

"There'd better not be any trouble with this one," growled Wimberton, and he stalked off.

Kathy waited until he had gone beyond the trees before glaring at Freddie.

"Now who's presuming?" she demanded.

Freddie knelt and ruffled the dog's neck. "Did you want him shot?"

"No."

"Then somebody had to take him. And I think having a dog on your parents' place is not a bad idea. Do you realize your brothers have been standing guard at night instead of getting their rest?"

"No, but I'm not surprised after the greeting we got yesterday."

"Nor is it entirely secure, as last night proved. A dog can hear things we cannot." Freddie stood and took the rope.

Kathy folded her arms. "You also forgot something. What are we going to do with him during services?"

Freddie paused, then smiled guiltily. "I suspect I shall have to risk your mother's disfavor and not go."

"We'd better get back. With luck, she might just accept your excuse."

Katie-Marie was thrilled with the dog, as were the boys. They gathered in the church's yard behind the sanctuary, surrounded by other church-goers heading to services.

"It is just a dog," Katie-Marie conceded. "But it seems a terrible shame to destroy the poor beast just because no one wants him."

"We do!" yelped Gam. "Please, Ma, can we keep him? Please?"

"Yeah, Ma," cut in Isaac. "I'll feed him. Every day, I promise. And Gam can help me give him baths. Can we, please, Ma?"

"You know, Ma, we could really use a guard dog," said Gideon.

"That we could," sighed Katie-Marie. "But services

are about to start. What are we going to do with him in the meantime?"

"I'll walk him home, Ma," said Kathy quickly.

The younger boys also volunteered noisily.

"Is there a problem?" asked a deep, gravelly voice.

"Reverend Macadam," said Katie-Marie. "It's good to see you. It seems we've got a bit of a problem with keeping this dog for the moment."

The Reverend laughed. In a confusion of voices, the boys told him how Freddie had saved the dog from the sheriff, and how they were going to keep him, only they had to decide who would miss services to watch the dog. The minister, who was somewhat shorter than Freddie but with broader shoulders and thick, muscular arms, sorted out the tale without questions. He dispatched the dog to his office behind the church, so no one would miss services. Kathy smiled, but Freddie could tell she was sulking.

"So, you're Kathy's Mr. Little," said Macadam, turning to Freddie. "It's some pleasure to meet you."

"Likewise, Reverend." Freddie shook hands, wondering who else in town knew he was Kathy's friend.

After services, Freddie found out his name was not unknown among several of the townspeople. He greeted everyone politely but was a little disquieted by how quickly they had learned he had brought Kathy home in a plane. As the flow of people from the church diminished, Freddie ambled slowly around the side of the church looking for Kathy, and for a place where he could light up a cigarette. Around the back of the church, next to the alley, he spotted several butts on the ground. He also spotted what looked like a foot behind a rubbish bin up against the back of the church wall. Freddie moved closer, pulling his cigarette case and holder out of his jacket pocket. After lighting up, he moved the bin back so he could throw away the match.

The boy hiding behind the bin was close to Gam's age, maybe a little older. He had hair the color of corn silk, and piercing blue eyes, but what Freddie saw first were the ugly bruises on his shoulders and arms, some new, others fading and yellow. The boy was shirtless and his dirty blue pants were too short but so big around the waist they were tied on with a rope. His ribs showed through and a brownish welt ran across them. He was terrified.

"It's all right," said Freddie soothingly. "I'm not going to hurt you."

The boy shook his head and took off running down the alley. Freddie watched as he slipped between a carriage house and a shed about three houses down. The worst of it was, Freddie recognized the finger-shaped bruises and knew that Gam was not the only boy in town being tortured. Sucking a final and deep drag on his cigarette, he snuffed it out, then went back to the front of the church.

As he entered the courtyard, Freddie noticed a portly man of nervous mien watching him curiously. Kathy had been pulled away by a group of women, including her mother. Joshua was still introducing Betty and Little J around. The other boys had long since gone home with the dog.

The man approached. He looked to be about Kathy's age, with dark brown hair under a neat black bowler hat. He wore a dark suit with a white pocket square and gold watch chain that should have made him look quite authoritative, but instead only emphasized his round belly and hunched shoulders.

"William K. Javits," he said, nervously offering his hand.

"Freddie Little." Freddie shook, ignoring the unpleasantly sweaty palm.

"I, uh, heard. I figured I'd better at least introduce myself, seeing as we're almost family."

"I beg your pardon?" Freddie asked, a little irritated.

"My—my wife, Teresa." Javits half-heartedly waved towards the church. "She's Kathy's sister."

Freddie looked around. "I don't believe I've had the pleasure. She doesn't seem to be around."

"She's on fellowship committee today. That's why she's not out here."

"Ah. Well, Mr. Javits, I don't know what your wife has told you, but there does seem to be something of a misunderstanding regarding the situation between your sister-in-law and myself."

Javits nodded morosely. "I said something like that, too. Now I got four kids."

Freddie debated explaining. Javits was certain Kathy would get her man, just like Teresa had gotten him. Freddie doubted Javits would believe that he, Freddie, was chasing Kathy, let alone understand him wanting to.

A chorus of greeting screams turned Freddie back towards the church. A woman not unlike Kathy in build and coloring was embracing Kathy happily. Nearby, Katie-Marie watched, holding another infant, and keeping a close watch on three very young children. Within a minute, the woman saw Freddie and swooped down on him.

"There you are!" she crowed, embracing him and landing a kiss on his cheek. "I am so glad to meet you. I just know you and Kathy will be so happy together."

Freddie disentangled himself. "Mrs. Javits, I presume?"

"Oh, just call me Teresa."

Freddie knew she would soon turn twenty-one, but she looked closer to Kathy's twenty-eight. In some ways, Kathy looked younger. Teresa's dark green linen dress was fairly fashionable, with its starched white collar, short sleeves and dropped waist. And she wore a light straw hat with a broader brim.

Freddie hesitated. "I don't wish to disappoint you, but you are making a gross presumption, Mrs. Javits, and no doubt embarrassing your sister."

"Bill said the same thing." Teresa patted his cheek. "Come here, children. Come say hello to your Uncle

Freddie. This is Ruth, she'll be four in September, and here's Daniel, he's two and a half, and this is Naomi, she's eighteen months, and the baby here is Rachel. Four months old, and she's about to get her first tooth."

Freddie tipped his hat. "It's a pleasure."

The children looked bored and dusty and sullen, and their Sunday clothes were already wrinkled. Daniel's nose was running, and the baby started screaming. Freddie smiled weakly at them and looked for Kathy to rescue him. Then he remembered Kathy was just as eager to avoid them herself.

Fortunately, Katie-Marie moved in.

"Now, Teresa, we still got Abraham to pick up from the afternoon train," she said. "Do you want to stay in town and bring him in? We can take the children."

"Mrs. Briscow, if I may be so bold," cut in Freddie. "But your daughter and I are both expecting luggage on this train. Perhaps we might stay here and meet your son, and hire a taxi, or something."

"Hire?" Katie-Marie looked at him as if he'd said steal a taxi. "Lord have mercy. What a waste. Teresa, you can take me and the little ones in your car, can't you?"

"That's perfect, Ma." She turned to her husband. "Bill, get the Chevy, honey." She grinned at Freddie. "'Less of course you want to borrow the hearse."

"Excuse me?" Freddie stepped back.

Teresa laughed. "Bill's the town undertaker. Didn't Kathy tell you?"

"As I believe I mentioned before, your sister and I are not on those sorts of terms."

"Ooo, don't you talk fancy. And fighting it, too." Teresa gaily shook her head and reached for her son's hand. "Come along, children. Ruth, get Naomi."

Naomi was tottering off after her father, who was meekly going after the car. Ruth ran after her sister and dragged her back. Katie-Marie gave Freddie an apologetic pat on the arm, then went after her eldest son and his family. Kathy stepped up to Freddie.

"Is she gone?" she asked.

"For the moment." Freddie smiled smugly. "Didn't you call me a coward earlier today?"

"And didn't you retort there are times when cowardice is justified?"

"Point conceded. Has she always been that way?"

Kathy nodded sadly. "She was the most demanding, cussed baby Ma had. Once she gets an idea in her head, even Pa can't shake it loose."

"Her poor husband."

Kathy snorted. "Bill Javits asked for it. His ma used to lead him around by the nose, and then when she died he went after Teresa, hoping she'd do the same. At least, that's what Ma wrote. I was in New York by then and had to miss the wedding."

"It sounds like a perfect match."

"I suppose. Bill was a year behind me in school. They used to say he was carrying the torch for me. Fortunately, I was never one to tolerate spineless fools."

Freddie chuckled. "And yet you tolerate me."

"Freddie, you are neither spineless nor a fool." Kathy ambled down the back alley. "Everyone thinks I'm so sweet on you just because I admit you've got some brains."

Freddie joined her and offered his arm. "And aren't you sweet on me?"

"Not in the way they're thinking."

She was looking straight ahead, but Freddie could feel her blood heating up much in the same way his was.

"And I thought you cared for me as a person," he said softly.

"You know I love you. That is precisely why the carnal desires are so intense. I just don't want to get married is all."

"I see. I take it you are aware of the current plan regarding this afternoon's activities."

"I heard it all. What were you trying to avoid?

Shelling peas or playing horsie with those miserable brats of my sister's?"

"Neither, although playing horsie sounds like a fate worse than death. I presume I would be the horse?"

"You presume correctly." Kathy stopped outside two private stables at the other end of the alley from the church, where Gideon had left the horses and wagon hitched. "You realize, of course that the afternoon train won't be here until two thirty. And here's a team and wagon at our disposal. We could make interesting use of it."

"If you are hinting at giving in to your carnal desires, then we are not going anywhere. I've told you before I will not take you as a lover, and especially not while we are staying under your father's roof."

Kathy's smile was wicked. "Afraid he'll get out his shotgun?"

"Not in the least. I merely think it is highly inappropriate."

"I suppose then I shall settle for a quiet drive along the creek."

"Now that has its attractions."

Chapter Five

Kathy got up off the bench at the train station, stretched, and wandered to the end of the platform. She gazed into the corner of the station depot building where the Western Union office was. The man on the customer side of the counter was still there.

His hair was white and gray, parted down the middle, and he wore thick mustaches and a pince-nez. He was well dressed, in a dark woolen three-piece suit with watch chain and fob. A matching homburg hat sat on the counter next to him. Kathy had been around Freddie long enough to know the suit's cut could have been a little better, but then millionaires were not as common as well-to-do businessmen. He certainly seemed to be taking his time ordering his telegram.

Freddie looked up from the volume of sonnets he'd rediscovered in his jacket pocket.

"Is he still there?" he asked.

"Yes." Bothered, Kathy strolled back along the platform.

"Perhaps he's waiting for a reply."

"Standing at the counter?" Irritated, Kathy looked back at the telegraph office. "It looks more to me like he's sending a whole bunch of them. I still say I know him."

"That's not surprising in this town." Freddie pocketed the book and got out his cigarettes.

"I just wish I could place him. It's so aggravating. And why would he be sending telegrams today?"

"I can think of a dozen reasons someone might want to send a telegram or two on a Sunday afternoon." His cigarette lit, Freddie picked up the book again.

"But he doesn't seem worried or excited or anything like that. People around here just don't send telegrams unless it's urgent or it's business, and it can't be business because it's Sunday."

Freddie chuckled. "It might, then again it might not."

"Nobody's died today, either, and we would have heard by now."

A train whistle sounded in the distance. Kathy went over to the edge of the platform and peered over the tracks.

"Here it comes," she said. "And it's about time, too. How late is it?"

"At the moment..." Freddie pulled his watch from his vest, "...eight minutes. That doesn't sound too bad for this far from civilization."

"Hmph!"

It was another five minutes before the train came whooshing and hissing up to the platform. Three other people got off, and then Abraham Briscow, wearing a dark suit and a straw boater on his head, and carrying a small valise. The station master and the train porter scrambled to unload trunks, parcels, and a sack of mail. The whistle screamed, and the train strained and puffed, and moved on.

Abraham, a slightly taller version of his brother Joshua, was already hugging Kathy. "How the hell did you get out here so fast? Good lord, Kathy, I was worried sick when I got off in Topeka and you weren't anywhere. They even said the New York train had come and gone, and after the early morning local had left. How's Pa?"

"That's the good news, Abe," said Kathy, pulling away. "He's all right. The crisis came yesterday morning, and the old cuss lived. He's still pretty weak, but the doctor says he'll make it."

"What was it?"

"Pneumonia. Did you get Ma's letter about him going in the creek?"

"Is that what did it? Good gravy, they've been having trouble."

"It's worse. But we'll get to the bottom of it."

"Bet you could use your Mr. Little around now. Well, hello." Abraham grinned as he noticed Freddie quietly standing by.

It had taken a surprise visit during the spring break in his studies, but Abraham had managed to catch Freddie and Kathy together to get an introduction to the mysterious Mr. Little. He'd gotten little else. Freddie had quickly excused himself that Kathy might visit with her brother, to Kathy's enormous relief.

"It sure is good to see you, Mr. Little." Abraham went over and vigorously shook hands. "Hey, this doesn't mean what I think it does."

"It depends on what you're thinking," replied Freddie genially, in spite of his irritation. "I'm here because I happened upon your sister in her distress Friday night, and offered to get her here more quickly than she could by train, by flying her here in my airplane."

"You flew?" Abraham gazed at Kathy in admiration. "That's crazy."

"Perhaps," said Kathy. "But wait 'til you hear this. Josh is here, and he drove all the way from California. Furthermore, he got married and has a baby. It sort of slipped his mind to write us."

Abraham started for the luggage pile. "No kidding. How long they been married?"

"He says a year and a half." Kathy smirked.

Abraham nodded knowingly. "I'll bet. How old is

the kid?"

"Two months."

"If he's been married longer than eight months, I'll give you five dollars."

"It could be as long as ten." Kathy looked over the trunks and parcels. "Freddie, there's yours."

"Thank you." Freddie stepped around the boxes. "And here's yours. Don't worry, I'll get it."

"You sent your trunks?" asked Abraham, bewildered by such a costly thing to do.

"It was Freddie's idea," sighed Kathy. "I was too upset to argue."

"My plane only has room for two small valises," said Freddie, setting down Kathy's trunk. "I thought it wise to be prepared for a longer stay, should it be necessary."

He went back for his trunk, then helped Abraham with his. It took two trips to get the trunks loaded onto the wagon. Kathy took the reins. Freddie and Abraham joined her on the seat.

Kathy trotted the horses back to the farm. Over the jostle and the rattle, Abraham talked about law school, of which he had recently finished his first year. He was at Harvard, where they had an uncle on their father's side who conveniently saw to providing scholarships. Abraham was to spend his summer working in Boston for a former classmate of their Uncle Mike's, from their mother's side, who was a lawyer in New York. A generous leave had been granted for the emergency, and Abraham saw no reason not to take advantage of it.

At the house, the kitchen was crowded with food preparation. Teresa's baby howled at full force. Abraham fled to the study to visit his father. Josh and Gideon hurried out to put the horses away, leaving Freddie without an escape. Bill ignored the noise. Little J was shoved into Kathy's hands, so Betty could help Katie-Marie. Teresa jiggled Rachel with one hand, stirred gravy with the other, and chattered non-stop, over the baby's cries, about Reverend Macadam's sermon.

"Don't you have something you could put in that creature's mouth?" snapped Kathy. Little J happily sucked on her finger.

"She's teething, Kathy," said Teresa.

Betty turned shyly. "Hate to suggest this, but Mama always said whiskey on the gums helps."

There was a pause, broken only by Rachel's screams.

"We don't hold with spirits in this house," said Katie-Marie finally.

"I don't either," said Betty.

"Can't we make an exception to shut the beast up?" asked Kathy.

"Where are you gonna get it anyway, Kathy?" asked Teresa, who considered the idea ridiculous.

Katie-Marie looked at Kathy in shock. "Kathleen, you don't have any, do you?"

"No," said Kathy, a little wary. "But I bet I know who does."

All eyes turned to Freddie, who shifted.

"Mrs. Briscow, in deference to your feelings, I have hidden my supply away," he said slowly. "But if it will quiet the child, I will gladly fetch it."

"I'm sure Josh and Abe have some, too," said Kathy, who had been thinking of them initially.

Rachel's screams redoubled. Sighing, Katie-Marie nodded her consent. Teresa shrugged. Freddie all but dashed upstairs.

The hip flask was given to Betty since she had suggested the operation. She soaked the corner of the towel and dabbed it on Rachel's gums. Rachel bit her hard for her efforts, but the cries faded, and soon the kitchen was quiet but for the ringing of everyone's ears.

Abraham wandered in from the study. "Pa wants to know how you shut the little brat up."

"Highly unorthodox methods," said Kathy.

"Hey, whose hip flask?" Abraham grabbed it and

took a belt. "Oh, that's good hootch."

Freddie sighed silently as he watched the few precious drops slide away.

"Abraham!" gasped Katie-Marie. "What, in the name of all the saints, do you think you're doing?"

"Ma, everybody drinks."

Kathy grabbed the flask back. "Well, unless you're prepared to share, that's all we've got to keep that beast from squalling."

"Will you stop calling my children beasts and brats?" snapped Teresa.

"You're dosing the kid?" Abraham laughed.

"We rub it on her gums," said Betty quietly. "It's soothing."

"I'll bet." Abraham grabbed for the flask.

Kathy dodged, then corked it and tossed it to Freddie, who caught it one-handed and placed it safely in his jacket pocket.

The screen door slammed open, and Joshua struggled in with a trunk.

"Where's Abe sleeping?" he asked.

"In with Gideon," answered Katie-Marie.

"Fine." Joshua wrestled the trunk around the table and all the people. "How did you shut the kid up?"

"Whiskey on the gums," said Abraham.

"Where'd you get—Betty!"

Kathy laughed. "I knew it! I knew it! And you all looked at Freddie."

"Lord have mercy!" groaned Katie-Marie. "Where did I go wrong with you boys? Joshua, Abraham, how much do you have? Out with it now."

Joshua and Abraham looked at each other guiltily.

Joshua spoke first. "I got a bottle of whiskey, and some bottles of Mexican firewater."

Abraham shifted. "A bottle of gin, and a bottle of whiskey. But it's not as good as Mr. Little's hootch."

"Mr. Little is our guest," said Katie-Marie severely. "And he can't be expected to know all of our house rules."

"Ma, for Christ's sake—" began Joshua.

"Watch your blaspheming, boy!"

"I'm not a boy," Joshua shouted back. "Damn it, both Abraham and I are over twenty-one. I'm married with a kid of my own. We have a right to make our own decisions."

"And I have a right to say what is kept under my own roof," Katie-Marie yelled back.

"Then we'll take it out!" Joshua hefted the trunk again and nodded at Abraham. "Come on, Abe. We'll put it in my car."

Katie-Marie sighed. "Somebody better be explaining to your pa what's been going on."

"I'll go," said Kathy.

She handed Little J to Bill and hurried out.

"Kathleen!" Katie-Marie called after her, then dropped it. "Fool girl ought to know better than to hand a baby to a man. Here, Bill, give him to me."

The yelling had left Freddie shaken. Voices were never raised in the world he called home. That was ill-bred and common. As uncommon as he found Kathy, Freddie had to admit she was of the common folk. But was his family any better for their well-bred distance? Watching the warmth even towards Betty and himself, the strangers to the unit, Freddie wondered what his life would have been like if his parents had bothered to extend some warmth towards him.

Even more curious was Bill's reaction. According to Kathy, he and Teresa had been married at least five years. Freddie couldn't believe this was the first outburst Bill had witnessed. Yet he had caved in and actually trembled. Even Freddie could see that it was but a brief storm, and quickly clearing.

The screen door was slammed again, this time by Gideon, carrying Kathy's trunk. Isaac and Gam were close behind with Freddie's, with the dog trotting along getting under their feet. As they passed through the kitchen, Freddie was startled by the sullen look on Gam's face. The boy had seemed happy when they had driven up.

Joshua came down and went into the cellar. He appeared a minute later with a huge basket of oranges, which he plopped onto the table.

"Brought this out for you and Teresa, Bill," he said. "Here, Freddie, why don't you take a couple?" He tossed the fruit at Freddie, who caught it.

"Thank you," said Freddie, with a quiet smile.

"They're just lovely, Josh," said Teresa. "Aren't they, Bill?"

"Very nice, Joshua," mumbled Bill.

Joshua took another orange and plopped into a chair, his fingernails digging into the bright orange skin.

"Freddie, you like investments," he said. "You ought to look into these. Crop prices have never been better. Everybody wants them. And in Florida, they're chopping down trees right and left for the developers. These little babies are gold."

Freddie chuckled. "I'll look into it."

"They're mighty fine eating. Bill, you ought to look into them, too. I'm telling you, they're a great way to make money."

"Bill doesn't need to throw his money away on chance investments," said Teresa with a sniff. "We're saving it."

"It doesn't need to be a chance investment," said Freddie. "There's always some risk. But your brother has a point. As long as citrus fruits remain something of a delicacy, the prices should hold, and given the relatively few areas in which they can be grown, the demand should remain greater than the supply. Of course, I would have to double check the operational costs, and any liens involved, before I put my money in. But it is definitely worth considering."

Bill just smiled weakly.

In the hall, Kathy stopped Isaac as he returned from putting Freddie's trunk away.

"Let's go into the living room," she whispered.

Isaac shrugged and turned into the room usually left unused except when the reverend, or any other important guest, called. Chintz curtains matched the two over-stuffed sofas. There was a fireplace on the one end, the mantle crowded with photos. A Victrola sat in the other corner, with a small shelf loaded with records. The front door featured a small window with etched glass.

"What do you want?" Isaac asked softly.

"I want to know if anybody in town is angry at Pa for any reason," Kathy replied, her voice equally soft.

"Naw."

"Are you sure?"

"Why do you want to know?"

"The vandals. Have your or Gam or Gideon gotten into any trouble and Pa had to stand up for you?"

"Gideon crashed into Mr. Wilson's car on his bike about two months ago. But the car didn't show no dents or anything. The bike was in worse shape, but Pa made Gideon apologize and he had to work it off."

"How did Mr. Wilson feel about it?"

"Pleased as punch. Gideon set in his entire crop of late beans."

"All right. Any rumors going around about land agents, or consolidating land?"

"Conso-what?"

"Making one big farm out of all the little farms."

Isaac thought. "Nope."

"Anybody in town acting a little strangely?"

"Nope."

Kathy sighed. "Will you do me a favor and ask around? Only don't be obvious about it. Your friends might have seen something you haven't. And tell only me what you find. Okay?"

"Okay."

Back in the kitchen, the conversation had rolled around to the current troubles. Abraham had been brought up to date and was racking his brain for legal precedents.

"I still say they're trying to drive Pa off," said Joshua.

"But for what purpose?" said Freddie. "Revenge seems unlikely, as we have no reason to believe that your father has done anything that would warrant sufficient anger."

"So we have to figure out who would want the land badly enough to go to the trouble of driving Pa off," said Abraham. "Teresa, you know what's going on in town. Who wants the land?"

Teresa shifted Rachel and thought. "Mr. Dreiser, he makes furniture in town, he's been wanting to cut into Pa's stand of oak for a long time. Pa won't let him because he says the trees are there to keep the air moist."

"That can't be the only stand of oak in the area," said Freddie. "Mr. Dreiser must have other suppliers, or he wouldn't be in business."

"But what if the other suppliers were falling through?" asked Kathy. "Then he might be desperate enough to try threatening Pa this way."

Freddie nodded. "That is a possibility. Do you want to talk to him, or do you think I might catch something?"

"It depends on how you do it." Kathy thought. "Everyone knows you're here with me. But he's always been very friendly. If you approach him as a customer, he might let something slip."

"That's worth a try. Why don't we go into town tomorrow? You can ask around all the places you want, and I'll talk to Mr. Dreiser, and maybe the garageman and telegraph operator also. I have to anyway to get the parts for the truck, and I'll probably be wiring Detroit to do it."

"Freddie...," Kathy warned.

"Your mother and I have already talked it over."

"Land sakes," said Teresa. "You two talk like you're detectives or something."

Abraham laughed. "Didn't Uncle Dan write you all

about how they brought those two killers in?"

"We heard all about it," said Katie-Marie, looking up from the roast she was basting. "And I don't think we need to hear any more. As for this detecting nonsense, I'll thank the two of you to keep out of it."

"But, Ma, somebody's got to find out who is doing this to the farm," protested Kathy. "I don't see Sheriff Wimberton asking any questions. I'll bet you haven't even said anything about it to him."

"Kathy, you know how much good that will do." Katie-Marie slammed the oven door shut. "There's nothing happening that your pa and I can't handle. I don't want you stirring up more trouble, or worse, getting yourself hurt. That's my final word on the subject. Now, call the little ones in for dinner. Betty, set out the plates. We won't all fit around the table. We'll have to serve in here and eat in the living room. Teresa, get the potatoes and the beans in bowls, and put the corn on the oval platter."

Kathy gave Freddie a wicked smile before leaving the kitchen. His face remained passive, but inside he was laughing. Kathy wasn't about to stop investigating, which meant neither was he.

Chapter Six

Dinner was over by six. Teresa declared she had to get her children home, and so missed washing up. For all everyone seemed to resent the timing of the departure, there was a general sense of relief once the children were gone. Gam and Isaac were given drying-up duty, anyway. Kathy helped for a few minutes, then noticed that Freddie had slipped out somewhere.

She found him behind the barn. There were still a good three hours before sunset, and the sun was lazily hanging in the western sky, waiting to make its descent into night. Freddie stretched lazily himself. His jacket and tie had been removed, presumably to his room, and his waistcoat was unbuttoned.

"You're darned near undressed," teased Kathy from the corner of the barn.

Freddie chuckled. "There are advantages to a more casual lifestyle. So, what do you make of our little mystery?"

"Me?" Kathy's grin grew even more wicked as she walked over to him. "Didn't you hear Ma? She doesn't want us involved."

"I know. But I seriously doubt that's going to stop you."

Kathy shrugged. "You have gotten to know me pretty well. As for the mystery, I haven't any ideas. Isaac told me that Gideon crashed into a Mr. Wilson two months ago, but it would appear that Mr. Wilson got the sweeter part of the deal. I'm somewhat inclined to put down Teresa's possible suspect just because I don't trust her. But as I pointed out, there is a possibility he is desperate. How we'll find out, I have no idea."

"It is a place to look, and nothing more. We seem to have so few."

Kathy folded her arms and sighed. Freddie's thoughts quickly focused on her. Her face grew softer in the quiet evening light. A gentle breeze plucked at her hair, lifting but a strand or two. She turned to him and smiled.

"You're not thinking about our mystery anymore," she said quietly, a soft smile playing about her lips.

Freddie smiled also. "No."

His hand brushed her cheek, then slid behind her ear. He bent. She reached for his mouth. They pressed together, happily drinking each other in. Then Freddie just held her, enjoying her warmth, as she enjoyed his.

At the same time, they both spotted the pile of hay lying against the barn.

Kathy giggled. "Come on."

"It looks itchy," said Freddie, following her.

"It's fun."

"Something tells me you know from experience."

Kathy pushed him into the hay. "So I did a little spooning in my youth. You can't tell me you never took advantage of a back seat and a dark night."

"A gentleman never tells about past liaisons."

"I thought a gentleman never asked about them either."

Freddie grinned as he pulled her down next to him.

"I wasn't asking."

He slid his arm under her head and pulled her next to him. She began kissing him almost immediately, even rolled underneath him. Freddie didn't care. Her lips were sweeter than any he'd known, and her hunger for him more delicious. Kathy squeezed him closer to her, reveling in the solidness of his weight on top of her. His kisses were the only ones she actually craved.

Gam, sulking in the hay loft above, noticed the movement below and became very confused. Quietly, he slipped out of the barn and ran into the house. Joshua noticed him heading for the study and followed.

"Pa, you awake?" Gam hissed.

"What's wrong, Gammers?" Jacob asked, his voice considerably stronger than the day before.

"It's Mr. Little." Gam came the rest of the way into the room and shut the door. "Darn it, Pa, I thought he was our friend. But I just saw him wrassling Kathy back behind the barn, and it sure looked like he had her pinned down pretty tight."

"He did?" Pa's eyebrows raised. "Damn that girl. Where's Joshua?"

"Right here, Pa." Joshua, chuckling, stepped into the room. "Want me to bring them in?"

"Right here, front and center. Gam, get the shotgun and bring it to me, then go with him."

Gam brightened. "You gonna fill his hide with buckshot, Pa?"

"I won't have to fill his hide. We'll see about your sister's. Now git."

By the time Gam made it back to the barn, Isaac, Abraham, and Gideon had joined Joshua in the hay loft. The dog waited on the barn floor below, ears lifted and tail wagging. Gesturing for silence, Joshua beckoned Gam forward. The wrassling was still going on below. Freddie had allowed his kisses to wander to Kathy's neck, and she wriggled with pleasure.

"She looks pretty happy, don't she?" Joshua whispered to Gam.

"They're spooning!" whispered Gam. "Boy, it sure looks like wrassling."

"It is, in a way. But we gotta put a stop to it."

"Or she'll end up like Betty," teased Abraham.

Joshua glared at him. "Are we ready?"

Gideon, Abraham, and Isaac nodded. They'd cut the wire on a bale of hay and spread it on a canvas. Together, the five boys lifted the cloth.

Kathy batted at the first few straws, then pressed her lips to Freddie's forehead. He lifted his head to kiss her mouth again, then found himself choking in a deluge of hay. Underneath him, Kathy was wriggling again, but not with pleasure.

"You bastards!" she screamed and coughed.

"Such language, big sister!" teased Joshua. "Don't you want to be a good example for your impressionable young brothers?"

The boys laughed.

"I'll example you!" Coughing, Kathy pushed Freddie off of her.

"What did they do?" Freddie gasped, wading through the mess.

"They dumped a bale of hay on us." Kathy tried to get to her feet and couldn't.

Freddie looked up and finally saw the loft. "Weren't you men supposed to be inside?"

"That's where Pa wants you," said Joshua. "Front and center in the study, right now."

"Oh, damn," groaned Kathy. She looked up. "All right. You delivered your message. Now get out of here, or I'll take the shotgun to all of you."

"Good luck catching us," hollered Abraham as he beat a hasty retreat.

Kathy sat back with a sigh as she watched Freddie pick hay out of his hair and clothes.

"I'm sorry," she sighed. "I forgot it's also a little dangerous around here."

Freddie chuckled. "The curse of younger siblings. Honoria has visited worse upon me, I assure you. We'd better get in."

"I guess. We don't want Pa any more upset than he is."

She kissed him quickly, then got up.

Between the sunlight and the lamp, the study was plenty bright when Freddie and Kathy presented themselves. Katie-Marie stood in the corner with her arms folded. The boys had been sent upstairs and were playing cards in Gideon's room, drinking Abraham's whiskey and listening for even the slightest sound from downstairs.

"Gam says you was wrassling behind the barn," said Jacob severely.

Freddie put on his most appeasing smile. "It was strictly a friendly match."

"Like hell. Kathy, you was spooning again."

"So what?" demanded Kathy. "It's not as though I were some blushing teenager. Pa, I'm a grown woman, and perfectly capable of handling myself with a man."

Jacob glared at Freddie. "And you. What about what we talked about last night? You still gonna try and tell me you ain't got intentions?"

Freddie swallowed. "I never said I didn't. I also never said I did. I believe I did say that the situation was delicate."

"What is all this pussyfootin' around?" Jacob sat up. "Damn it all to hell, I'm not getting any younger."

"Pa," warned Katie-Marie. "The doctor said not to get excited."

"I'm not getting excited. I'm getting my daughter married off to this young man."

Kathy gaped. "I'm not getting married!"

"Mr. Briscow, I firmly feel you are stepping out of line," said Freddie, equally angry and flabbergasted. "I am not going to marry your daughter at your demand."

"You will, even if I have to goose you all the way to the altar with this!" Jacob whipped the shotgun out from underneath the couch.

"Pa!" Kathy screamed, her face vermillion. "You can't do this!"

"Jacob," said Katie-Marie. "I don't know if this is such a good idea."

"I know what I'm doing." Jacob glared at Kathy. "And you can just quit your screaming because Wednesday night I'll see you a married woman, or you'll be tasting buckshot yourself. I most certainly can do this. I'm doing it, you hear?"

"Pa, please!" Kathy fell to her knees next to him, tears streaming down her face.

"You're not changing my mind, girl. Katie-Marie, take her now."

"Come along, Kathy." Katie-Marie picked up her daughter and shot her husband a worried glare.

Freddie waited just long enough for the study door to shut behind them. Tapping his fingers against his leg, he turned on Jacob.

"Mr. Briscow, this has gone too far."

"You should have thought of that before you got her in the hay."

"I'll confess to taking some liberties, but I assure you, it was not going to lead to a loss of virtue. I am well in control of my passions. This—this farce is completely uncalled for."

Jacob stashed the gun under the couch.

"It's what you want, isn't it?" he asked, casually, but knowing full well it was.

Freddie stepped back, startled. "Yes. But—but not this way."

"I happen to know it's the only way you're gonna get it." Jacob grinned as he settled himself on the couch. "Now, the doctor says I can take a short walk on Wednesday. I figure a walk up the aisle ain't too long."

"Mr. Briscow, however well-meaning your intentions, I do not know that they are in Kathy's best interest."

"Sit down." He waited as Freddie sat. "Freddie, my boy, I've known Kathy a good bit longer than you have. That girl is more stubborn than a forty mule team. Now, I know she don't want to get married, or that's what she says. The fact is, she needs to. That weren't the first time I pulled her from behind that barn. I told you last night, Briscows are hot blooded, and I think you got cause to know how hot."

"Only by inference, Mr. Briscow. I have not trespassed."

"Oh, fiddle dee dee. Don't get so het up and proper about it. I don't care if you have or you haven't. All I care about is that she's got her heart set on you, and there's going to be real trouble if she don't say 'I do' to you real soon."

"I understand. I share the same concern. But she does have several valid concerns about the marital state. I believe I can convince her to marry me. However, it will take some time."

"She don't have time if you want young 'uns. And even if you don't, you got 'til Wednesday to convince her, 'cause my mind is made up. Don't try arguing with me, son. You know as well as I do, buckshot is the only thing that'll get that girl to the altar, and I ain't afraid of using it."

"Then will you allow me some time alone with her that I might at least try to convince her to marry me happily? I think it would be better for both our sakes."

"You got 'til Wednesday."

Sighing, Freddie got up. "Thank you."

He left the study and went upstairs. He could at least make himself presentable while he thought out his strategy. He wasn't sure leaving would help. If Jacob Briscow truly had his mind made up, Freddie could go to the North Pole, and Jacob would find him. Oddly enough, there was a sense of relief in that. The only way out was exactly what Freddie wanted: Kathy as his wife.

Kathy was still sobbing on her mother's shoulder in the kitchen.

"How could he?" she gasped. "I've never been so humiliated in my life."

"I know, darling."

"Ma, I can't get married. I'll hate being married,

and I'll end up hating Freddie."

"Now, Kathy, darling, why are you saying that?"

"I don't want to be owned. Is that so terrible?"

"Of course not. But I'm a free woman, and I'm married."

"But you do everything Pa says."

"I've learned over the years there's times it's better not to argue with him."

"But he owns this whole place, he makes all the decisions."

"That's where you're wrong, darling. I make the decisions, too. He decides about the farm and money matters, and I run the house and the children. I don't know much about farming, never did. And he married me because he had no notion how to run a house. So we each do our bit, and together the whole place runs smooth as clockwork."

"He still gets to decide the important stuff."

"And your going to college wasn't important? I made that decision. It was your pa who backed me up. I decided to try and set Joshua's leg instead of amputating it. I decided a lot of things, and your pa's always backed me."

"Then why did you cave in just now? Why didn't you back me?"

"I didn't cave in. I just didn't argue. There's times it's better not to. And I've learned, when your pa says he knows what he's doing, he does, no matter how blamed fool an idea it seems. Just like he's learned to trust me."

"I'm not getting married."

"I'll talk to him, darling. Will you be all right now?"

Kathy sniffed and nodded. Katie-Marie patted her hand one more time, then left. Kathy got up. The house was silent. She slipped through the hall, stepping over the creaking board.

"Kathy?" called her father.

Angry, she went into the study and shut the door.

"Haven't you done enough to me?" she asked.

"It's what you want, ain't it?"

"No, it's not."

"Well, Kathy, I'm not getting any younger."

"I can take care of myself."

"Yes, you can." Jacob sighed and picked up the shotgun. "You do right well. And I really don't mind the idea of you being an old maid, except for one thing."

"What?"

"You're not a maid."

Kathy colored up. "Pa..."

"Kathleen, I know how it is. You done what you done. That don't matter and never did. The problem is I won't be here forever. And God forbid it, but if the worst should happen, you'll need some safe haven to come back to, and this farm's it. But if I'm not here, who knows what'll happen? I can't promise your brothers will be here to take care of you. It's not their place anyway."

"It doesn't matter. I'm careful."

"That don't mean you're safe."

"So what? It's my life. I have a right to decide what risks I'll take, and to be responsible for them."

"Yep. That you do. But let's be honest, Kathy. A corn cob only helps for so long."

"Pa!" Kathy felt her face coloring up even hotter.

"You're hot blooded, girl, just like everyone else in this family. And the only way to keep you people out of trouble is to see you married. Now get used to it. You're marrying Freddie on Wednesday, and that's final."

Kathy started for the door.

"Kathy?"

"Yes, Pa?"

"You're getting married on Wednesday, aren't you?"

Kathy took a deep breath and looked at the door.

"No," she whispered, and fled.

She ran upstairs. At the top, she could hear her mother riding roughshod over her brothers, and Betty soothing Little J. She went on up to the attic.

She knocked and slipped into the attic room.

"Freddie, you've got to leave," she said and turned. "What are you doing?"

Freddie stood before the washstand mirror, wearing only his pants over his sleeveless union suit, his chin and cheeks covered with soap. He smiled at her.

"I'm shaving," he said calmly.

"I can see that. Why now? Is this some weird calming ritual?"

"No." He picked up the razor and went to work. "It's just seven o'clock and time to dress for dinner."

"We already ate. This isn't New York. And you'd better get back there as soon as possible. You've got two hours of daylight. You can take off now, and spend the night in Topeka, or somewhere. Just anyplace but here."

Freddie didn't answer as he shaved his upper lip.

"Freddie," Kathy groaned. "Don't you realize he's serious?"

"Uh huh." Freddie checked for nicks and stubble, then shaved his chin.

"Then you've got to leave. Freddie, he'll make us do it. I can take the train home when I get this all figured out, but if you stay we'll end up married."

Freddie didn't answer, instead, he checked his chin, then the rest of his face, scraped a whisker off his jaw, then rinsed the razor.

"For crying out loud, Freddie. Will you quit acting as if nothing is going on?"

Freddie wiped off his face. "Kathy, did it ever occur to you that I want to marry you?"

Kathy sank back, her face white. "No, not you. How could you?"

Freddie saw the betrayal and sighed. "I phrased that badly. I'm sorry. What I want to propose is marriage, but different. I want us to be equal partners, no man's home is his castle, no little slaveries, none of that nonsense. Just two people coming together as equals, and promising their lives to each other."

"Why can't we be lovers then?"

"I don't want a lover. There's no permanence, no sharing. I want you for my life, Kathy, as my partner. We'll work together. I'll support you in your ventures, you support me in mine, as equals. So what if a minister blesses it? The promise is still there, in front of witnesses, that we are for each other for life."

"It will never work, Freddie."

"It will work. The only way it won't is if we don't make it work. We can do it, Kathy."

Kathy sniffed, searching for another escape. "It will be very hard for me to work. You know how conservative Mr. Healcroft is. I'll be lucky if I can keep my job, and I don't want to start all over again someplace else."

"That's the beauty of getting married out here in Kansas. Who in New York has to know?"

"I can think of a whole crew of aunts and uncles, for starters."

"We'll work that out with your mother. Beyond them, we don't have to tell anybody."

"How are we going to live? Mrs. Lynne won't let you upstairs at the boarding house, and the doorman at your place is sure to get nosy. And somehow I don't think I'd like giving a phony name at a hotel."

"We'll move, or maybe we won't have to."

"One of us will, and it's going to be me."

"If you want, I'll live in a boarding house with you."

Kathy had to laugh. "You'd do that, wouldn't you?"

"Yes. I think we'd be more comfortable at my place, but if you'd rather not give up your standard of living, then I'll abide by that."

"That's the one thing I wouldn't mind giving up." She looked at him, then sat on the far edge of the bed. "What about my name? Can I keep that?"

"Kathy, if we are equals, then I have no right to give you permission to keep your name, let alone deny it. That is your decision."

"You really mean it." She sniffed and the tears began again to fall.

Freddie handed her a handkerchief. "Here. It's clean."

"Of course. It always is." Kathy wiped her eyes and nose. "I must have at least eight of these. I keep forgetting to give them back. Do you want them?"

Freddie sat down next to her and folded her hand around the handkerchief.

"I want everything that I own to be owned by you also. And if you'll have me, that's how it shall be." He dug something out of his pocket. Kathy gasped at the size of the diamond. "Kathy, will you please marry me?"

Kathy trembled. "Freddie..."

She couldn't finish.

"Darling, I know you're afraid. I'll do my best to calm your fears. I don't know what else I can do to reassure you."

Kathy closed her eyes and swallowed.

"Freddie, take me. Now," she whispered.

"How?"

Kathy stared at her hands. "As..." Her voice grew even fainter. "As my husband."

Trembling himself, Freddie picked up her left hand and slid the ring onto her finger.

"I ought to get you one, too," she whispered, still in shock.

Freddie leaned in and kissed her lips. He felt her fear, then the passion ignited in both of them.

"Will you take me?" she asked softly.

"Given what you've just conceded, it's the least I could do."

He took her lips again, pushing her backward onto the bed. Her hands were everywhere, grasping and fondling. He pressed into it. His fingers found her breasts, and he caressed them as she writhed with him. She reached for his pants and slid her hand inside. Freddie put his hand over hers.

"I will not be rushed," he whispered.

"I know this household, Freddie. It will be rushed or not at all."

He got up. "Then we will take precautions."

He locked the door and removed the key, then tugged the curtains over the window.

"And now, my love, we will do all silently. If anyone comes knocking, we are not here. It won't be easy, but we will not be rushed."

He had barely unbuttoned the back of her dress when the first knock came. He clapped his hand over her mouth and continued nibbling the back of her neck. She took a breath and relaxed with the gentle motion of his lips.

The second knock, a minute later, startled her, but she did not bolt.

"Kathleen," said her mother's voice. "We all know you're in there with Freddie. Get out now. You're not man and wife yet."

Kathy turned. Freddie shook his head, and they waited.

"Kathleen, if you two are not out of that room in two minutes and downstairs, your pa is coming up with his shotgun, and he means it."

Kathy sat up and buttoned up her dress. Freddie grimaced.

"He'll do it," Kathy whispered. "He's sick enough. I can't take a chance on calling his bluff."

Freddie sighed but conceded. "We'll find another opportunity."

Chapter Seven

Freddie quickly re-dressed while Kathy waited in the hall. They found Betty and the boys sitting in the living room. Little J rolled on the floor, while the dog sat next to Gam, panting.

"Who's come calling at this hour?" asked Kathy, puzzled.

Freddie checked his watch. It wasn't yet eight, but he remembered they went to bed early.

They looked at the study. As if in answer, Reverend Macadam emerged, followed by Katie-Marie. The reverend grinned at Kathy and Freddie.

"Well, good evening to you," he said in his gravelly voice. "I hear congratulations are in order."

"Thank you," said Freddie pleasantly.

Kathy pressed her lips shut. The others, except Katie-Marie, looked at each other, wondering what was going on.

"We'd better get down to the planning, then," continued Macadam. "Your pa, Kathy, says that you folks gotta get back to New York by the end of this week, and figures with all the family here you might as well tie the knot on Wednesday night."

"That's the plan," said Freddie. "I hope the short

notice is not an inconvenience."

"Tie the knot?" asked Joshua, grinning.

"Pa is making 'em get hitched!" yelped Isaac happily.

"Making?" Macadam looked at Freddie, then his gaze settled on Kathy. "According to your pa, Mr. Little proposed this evening."

"As a matter of fact, I did," said Freddie.

The reverend lifted his eyebrow and waited for Kathy.

"He did," she said softly.

Macadam looked at Katie-Marie. "Mrs. Briscow, I told your husband that I was not going to perform a shotgun wedding, and something tells me that's exactly what he's up to, I don't care what tales he tells."

"Reverend, with all due respect," said Freddie. "I am aware that my intended father-in-law is somewhat anxious to see the nuptials transpire promptly. But if I did not want to marry Miss Briscow, I assure you, I have the means to take myself well beyond the reach of Mr. Briscow, and I would not be here now."

Gideon guffawed. "He sure talks a piece, don't he?"

Macadam returned his gaze to Kathy. "Are you doing this of your own free will, Kathy?"

Kathy hesitated. "Yes."

"Why do I have trouble believing that?"

"Because, Reverend." Kathy swallowed and took a deep breath. "I am not entirely happy about getting married. But Mr. Little has managed to convince me that marriage is in our best interests, and he is offering it on terms that are, at worst, bearable, and at best, more than acceptable. And Pa is right. As long as we are all here, and seeing as though Mr. Little and I do have to get back to New York, Wednesday night does seem to be the best time."

Macadam remained unconvinced. "We can talk about this privately, Kathy."

Kathy smiled weakly and shook her head. "Thank you, Reverend. I understand what you're trying to do.

But it's not necessary." She looked over at Freddie with a fond smile. "It's not Mr. Little that's the problem. I love him very much. It's just that at my age, I got used to the idea of not getting married. Spent a lot of time avoiding it, even. But I'm in love now, and I guess the only decent thing to do is marry him."

Freddie laid his hand on her shoulder, and Kathy squeezed it.

"Reverend," said Freddie gently. "It wasn't easy for Kathy to give in. But I am confident she did so of her own free will."

Betty sighed. "Kathy, you don't have to get married, do you?"

"Oh, I wish I'd had the chance," groaned Kathy. "But Freddie's too damned much of a gentleman to put me in that position."

"Kathy, such language!" gasped Katie-Marie, albeit more as a reflex than an actual admonition.

Macadam laughed. "It's good to know there's not a baby on the way. I've done enough of those weddings."

"So's Josh," teased Gideon.

"Hey, Josh, it looks like you and Freddie got a lot in common," said Isaac.

Betty's face was beet red.

"Come on, Josh," pressed Abraham. "How long you and Betty really been married?"

Joshua pulled his wife next to him. "We was gonna get married, even set a date."

"How long, Josh?" Gideon demanded.

"Nine months tomorrow," Betty said and giggled.

"I thought as much," said Katie-Marie. "Now, let that be a lesson to the rest of you. There are some things that are sacred to the marriage bed, and should be kept that way. Lord have mercy, I don't know how I did wrong by you."

"Mrs. Briscow, small mistakes aside, your family is a credit to you," said the reverend. "Now, we do have a wedding to plan."

Freddie grimaced. "I understand it's scheduled as

an evening affair. Wouldn't something so formal be a little difficult to arrange on such short notice?"

"Freddie!" groaned Kathy. She turned to Macadam. "You'll have to excuse him, Reverend. He's from New York. They do things differently there."

"Kathy, evening is not the proper time for an informal wedding," Freddie protested. "In Kansas or New York."

"Your folks aren't going to be there to protest," Kathy retorted. "Out here, nobody knows the difference."

"I do."

"You're not going to get written out of the Social Register. Nobody in New York is supposed to know, anyway."

"Nobody know?" asked Katie-Marie. "Kathy, what are you talking about?"

Kathy shrugged. "It's my job. My boss is real conservative, and he's not going to let a woman with a husband to support her take a job from a man."

Joshua frowned. "But I thought Freddie could keep you comfortable."

"More than adequately so," said Freddie. "But Kathy is proud of her independence, and I respect that. I'm perfectly happy to do what is necessary for her to keep her job, even if it means practicing an innocent deception on the good people of New York City."

"The whole city?" said Macadam. "That seems to be going a mite far."

"Not necessarily," said Freddie. "I am, unfortunately, subject to some publicity, which would, of course, alert Kathy's employer."

"I don't get it," said Gam.

"He means he gets into the papers," said Abraham.

"But Kathy, your aunts and uncles," said Katie-Marie.

Abraham shook his head. "Ma, you'd be surprised the lengths these society reporters will go to. And even if your brothers and sisters won't rat, there's even money one of the cousins wouldn't mind a fast five spot."

"They'll never forgive me," sighed Katie-Marie.

"Mrs. Briscow, it is getting late," said Macadam. "We do need to get certain plans settled before I leave tonight. The fellowship committee should be willing to help pull together a reception. We can use the church hall."

"That'll be good," said Katie-Marie. "But perhaps Mr. Spivens, at the Brunswick Hotel, will provide the refreshments. He's done it before on short notice."

Macadam shifted. "Mrs. Briscow, I don't know as that would be a good idea. I'll do the asking for you, but I don't hold much hope."

Katie-Marie nodded. "If it's money that's the problem, I can pay."

"Ma, what about the truck?" Kathy asked.

"Money needn't be an issue at all," said Freddie.

Katie-Marie laughed. "Freddie, don't be worrying yourself. I can give my daughter a wedding. It won't be any fancy city affair, but it will be fine enough."

"As you wish." Freddie retreated to the far end of the living room.

"So if the fellowship committee will help, we've got the reception settled, more or less," said Katie-Marie. "I suppose what's left is inviting the guests. I can call from Teresa's phone tomorrow."

"Oh great," grumbled Kathy. "I don't want to listen to her smug gloating."

"I'll speak to her," said Katie-Marie firmly. "Then there's the dress. We'll make do with what's in town. And the ceremony. But I suppose, Reverend, that's your business."

"Beyond the official witnesses," said Macadam. "That's up to the bride and groom. You'll also need to get the license sworn out. I'd do that tomorrow."

"I'll see to it first thing," said Freddie.

Kathy smirked. That probably meant noon, given Freddie's habits.

Macadam nodded. "Then it looks as though everything's settled as can be. Kathy, why don't you walk me out to my car?"

Kathy sighed, then thought of something. "Certainly, Reverend."

Macadam made his good nights, then Kathy took his arm and steered him out of the house.

"Kathy, I have to be certain," he said as soon as they were outside.

"I know." She sighed. "Pa did get out the shotgun, and it was his idea. But Freddie does want to get married."

"And you?"

"I don't want to get married. I do want Freddie, though, and he'll only have me with honor. He's pretty stubborn about that. I had half an inkling he was getting ready to propose last week, on Fourth of July."

"Would you have accepted him then?"

"I don't know. If he proposed like he did tonight, I might have. Anyway, I have now, and of my own free will." She smiled at Macadam. "He would never push it on me. He really is a true gentleman."

"Your family weren't joking when they said you was stuck on him."

"I am, I'm afraid, damn it all. Begging your pardon, Reverend. But to change the subject drastically, why are you so hesitant about Mr. Spivens supplying the refreshments? He's done it for other weddings."

Macadam sighed. "He's been good, but I'm afraid only when it serves him best. Of late, he's been less than charitable when your family's name comes up."

"Why? Has Pa done something to him or Ma? Did she run him in for a liquor violation or something like that?"

"Naw. It don't seem personal."

"Then what could it be?" Kathy's brow creased as she thought.

"Don't know." Macadam stretched.

"Reverend, when you talk to him, do you think you

could ask him about his feelings towards us? After all, if there's a grievance I think we have a right to know about it."

"We'll see, Kathy. You sure about this wedding, now?"

"No. But I'm going through with it." She shrugged. "He's going to get me to sooner or later. I may as well concede to the inevitable. At least I love him."

Macadam nodded and left.

The next morning, Kathy woke up feeling as though it had all been a miserable nightmare. The sun shone merrily through her mother's bedroom windows. Outside, the dog was barking cheerfully, the cows lowed over Gideon's clucking as he drove them out to the pasture. Birds sang, not yet silenced by the heat of the day. Gam teased the dog and banged the pig-pail on the way back from the sty. Downstairs, biscuits were baking, and the screen door slammed as Ma came in from the hen house.

Kathy washed up and dressed quickly in a green checked day dress, then combed her hair out in front of the bureau mirror. The sun's rays caught the engagement ring sitting in a small dish on the bureau top. Its fire glittered and danced. Kathy's heart froze. It was real, damn it. She hadn't dreamed it. She'd done it.

Katie-Marie scuttled in. "Oh, good, you're up. I'll be needing you down in the kitchen. Betty has to feed Little J, and we've got bread to bake, and I want to make a coffee cake for this evening. We'll be seeing visitors, I'm sure."

"Yes, Ma." Numb, Kathy set the comb down.

"Oh, that ring!" groaned Katie-Marie. "What was that fool boy thinking of? You'd better not take it off, girl. You don't want to be losing it."

"It's too big," said Kathy softly, glad that it was.

"All the more reason to keep it on you. We'll stop by the jewelers when we get to town this morning. Hurry along, now. I want to get breakfast over with and leave.

We've got laundry today, too. You'll be handling the diapers, won't you?"

"Why can't Betty?" Kathy snapped. "It's her baby."

"And she has to do them all the time. The least you can do is give her a bit of a break from it."

Kathy snorted as she slid the ring on her middle finger, grabbed her green apron and followed her mother out. Downstairs, she banged the pans as she tossed them on the stove. Katie Marie whipped eggs together, stopping every so often to stir the gravy for the biscuits. Kathy hacked slices of ham off the bone and set them frying, then sliced potatoes from the night before.

"Kathleen, why are you being so sour?" her mother asked.

"I resent it, that's all. Betty gets a break, but I don't." Kathy scooped lard into another pan, then swept the potatoes into it.

"I've been letting you slide. But you've always been my right hand, Kathy."

"And I hated it. Why do you think I went to New York?"

Katie-Marie sighed. "I don't know how I did wrong by you."

She set aside the eggs, then sliced the bacon.

Kathy turned the ham. "You didn't, Ma. Every girl has to learn to cook, and what better way to do it? You and Pa just also taught me that there were other things in this world besides marrying and having babies. It's not your fault I decided I liked those other things better."

"Well, you'll still be cooking up meals for Freddie soon enough." Katie-Marie took some oranges from a bowl and cut them into quarters. "And I've been meaning to ask you about this working thing. How are you going to keep his house for him and get his meals if you're at a job all day?"

Kathy suddenly realized something. She giggled.

"That's right," she said stirring the potatoes. "I

won't have to. Unless I want to, which I don't."

"And how are the two of you going to eat? Surely, you don't expect Freddie to do the cooking. You're not that much of a radical."

Kathy grinned. "Ma, Freddie has a cook and a housekeeper."

"I don't doubt, him being a bachelor. But once you're married, he isn't going to want to pay for services."

"Ma, he's rich. He's always had servants. He expects to have them. You should see the flock of servants his mother has."

"A flock? Kathy, you're exaggerating."

Kathy removed the ham and potatoes to plates, then poured the eggs into the potato pan and stirred.

"No, I'm not, Ma. He lives near Park and 67th."

Katie-Marie shrugged and poured the gravy into the gravy boat.

"67th? I don't recall much going up around there. Maybe a few mansions on 5th."

"Well, the Vanderbilts all live up there now, and the Carnegies, and the Astors, and the Littles."

"The Vanderbilts?" In shock, Katie-Marie sat down at the table.

The screen door banged open as Gam came in with the dog on his heels.

"What's got into Ma?" he asked, grabbing an orange section.

"The Vanderbilts, you say," Katie-Marie gasped again.

"Yes, the Vanderbilts," said Kathy, dumping freshly scrambled eggs into a bowl.

"What's so great about them?" Gam asked, grabbing another orange quarter. "Freddie said they're bores, and his family had money long before they did. Only I don't see what difference that makes."

"It doesn't unless you're from Freddie's set," said Kathy. "Were you and Freddie talking again last night?"

"Yep." Gam scraped the fruit from the peel and reached for a third piece. "I was saying how Jep, here, has a lot of fleas, and Freddie said he probably had more fleas than New York has Vanderbilts, and I asked what a Vanderbilt was."

"They're a very rich family, darling," explained Katie-Marie. "And if Freddie's family has had their money longer, they're very rich indeed."

Gam shrugged. "He's got to have something. Airplanes aren't cheap."

"I noticed you named your dog," said Kathy. She smiled as she got out plates and silverware.

"Yep. Freddie and me did last night." Gam rolled his eyes. "Freddie wanted to call him Cerberus, you know the dog guarding the gates of Hell in the mythology books? I said that was too long. Then Freddie said Sirius, after the dog star. But that weren't right. I said he should have a good guard dog name, and Freddie told me about this guy he knew in the army, always kept getting into trouble 'cause he liked getting put on guard duty, so Freddie put him on guard duty permanently. His name was Jepson, so we're calling the dog Jep."

Kathy laughed. "That's a good name, Gammers. Why don't you call everybody in? Breakfast is ready. And don't wake Freddie!" She turned to her mother. "Please don't treat him like visiting royalty now."

"Why would I do that?" Katie-Marie got up and set the table. "He puts his pants on one leg at a time, same as everyone else. I didn't know he was that rich, but it's a relief to know you'll never want for anything." Katie-Marie smiled warmly at her daughter. "I know you do well for yourself, darling, but that don't stop me from worrying. Over you, over Joshua and those fool oranges of his, over Abraham and his schooling. It's a sorry state, but I thank heavens Bill Javits will never want for business. It's something to me when I don't have to worry about your living at least."

"Hello?" Dr. Scofield tapped on the screen door. He

was the perfect image of a country doctor with dark hair and mustache, wearing a light brown suit and matching bowler and carrying his small black leather medical bag.

"Doctor!" crowed Katie-Marie. "You're here early. Come on in. Can I be getting you some breakfast?"

"I've had mine, thank you." Scofield shut the door softly. "How's my patient this morning?"

Katie-Marie laughed. "As cussed as ever. We had a bit of an upset last night, but he's in fine fettle this morning."

"So I hear." Scofield smiled at Kathy. "Congratulations."

Kathy blushed. "Good lord, is the news out already?"

Scofield laughed. "I heard the news from Reverend Macadam." He sighed. "He came over for Mrs. Schultz this morning."

"Did she pass at last?" asked Katie-Marie sympathetically.

"Yes. It was very quiet in the end."

Katie-Marie nodded. "Well, she deserved to go that way. A good, long life she led, and a fine woman. I suppose I'd better be sending around a casserole dish."

"That won't be necessary, Mrs. Briscow," said the doctor, setting his bag on the table and yawning. "Excuse me. Her children and grandchildren are there and managing quite well. They'll miss her, but they understand it was her time to go. They should be burying her tomorrow."

"I'll be heading over to Bill's this morning anyway. He can tell me when services are."

Isaac slammed the screen door. "Gam said breakfast is ready. Where is it? I'm starved. Howdy, Doctor."

"Howdy, son." Scofield grinned and picked up his bag. "At least this one's healthy."

"Ma!" bawled Gideon, slamming through the door. "Gam says it's breakfast. It's about time!"

"All my boys are healthy," said Katie-Marie with long-suffering patience.

The screen door slammed again as Joshua and Abraham came in, complaining about the tardiness of their meal.

Some time later, Freddie came downstairs to see Betty, in her peach dress and brown apron, put the last of the breakfast dishes away. Little J squawked from his basket.

"I'll get your breakfast in a minute, Freddie," said Betty as she picked up the basket. "Little J needs his diaper changed."

"Take your time," said Freddie, who was wearing his flying pants and boots, but with a crisp white shirt, tie, and tweed vest.

Kathy kneaded dough on the far end of the table. The kitchen was otherwise deserted.

"They're out doing their chores," Kathy said, not stopping. "And Ma's tending to Pa. You're up early."

"But still too late for breakfast." Freddie ambled up behind Kathy, slipped his arms around her waist, and kissed her neck.

"Freddie." Kathy blushed but didn't move.

"A good morning kiss for my betrothed seems permissible." He turned her chin to his and kissed her. "Your ma does keep you busy, doesn't she?"

"Idle hands are the devil's playthings."

"As well I know." He squeezed her playfully.

"Freddie, even if we live somewhere else besides your apartment, can we still have a cook?"

"My darling, every penny I have is yours. If you want a palatial mansion with a fleet of servants, just go out and get them."

"I could at least consult you."

Freddie thought. "I do suppose I would like to know my new address before I'm moved there."

He released her and squeezed her seat. Kathy looked at her ring and frowned.

"It's getting all gooey," she grumbled. "But Ma

says I shouldn't take it off."

"You've got it on the wrong finger."

"You got it too big for me. We're taking it into the jewelers in town this morning."

Another bowl of fresh oranges rested on the table. Freddie took one and sat down to peel it.

"Going to be there all day?" he asked.

"Not by half. We've got laundry to do." Kathy gave the dough an extra hard roll. "Betty will have to finish the bread."

Freddie chuckled. "I'd offer to take you away from all this, but you already managed that quite neatly."

"For the moment, I'm stuck with it." She sprinkled some more flour over the dough, then shaped it into a long strip.

"Such drudgery," Freddie observed.

"And I get to rinse all the diapers by hand." Kathy sighed. "Work, work, work. All the most despicable, tedious jobs. And they wonder why I don't want to get married."

Freddie sighed. "You're still not happy about that, are you?"

"The promise of servants mitigates it some." Kathy stirred brown goo in a bowl, then sighed. "But, no, I'm not. I am getting used to it, though. Slowly."

"Kathy, we don't have to do it. I've got plenty of time to make my escape."

Kathy studied the dough in front of her. "Will you meet me at the train in New York?"

There was a pause.

"I can't promise that," Freddie said quietly. "Kathy, you know how much I love you. But I am not a toy that you can pick up and play with and lay aside as the mood strikes you."

"I know. That's why I said yes."

Taking a deep breath, she spread the goo on the dough.

"What are you making?"

"Coffee cake. Ma is expecting visitors tonight."

Her voice caught. Freddie got up and took her in his arms, pressing her head against his chest. The board creaked in the hall. Kathy pulled away.

"I've got to get this rolled," she said quickly.

A minute later, Betty came in with the baby and basket.

"Kathy, Ma wants you to go get dressed for town."

Kathy laid a cloth over the cake. "I'll be right there."

She put the cake on a shelf, wiped her hands, then whipped off the apron. Betty went out to the screen door.

"Joshua! Your ma wants you to get the team hitched up," she called. She turned and smiled at Freddie. "I'll have your breakfast in a minute. Pa just gets mush, but would you like some also? I can get you bacon, eggs, and biscuits, too."

"Ma left some gravy in the ice box," said Kathy, hurrying out.

"That sounds delightful." Freddie smiled.

"Who's out here?" Katie-Marie hurried in. "Oh, Freddie, perfect. The doctor says Pa can sit up in the kitchen today. Will you help me bring him out? He's swearing he can walk, but he's so weak yet."

"It will be my pleasure." Freddie bounced up.

Leaning heavily on Freddie, Jacob made his way out to the kitchen, wrapped in a heavy brown dressing gown, growling and complaining and coughing. He collapsed in the nearest chair. Katie-Marie dropped a small afghan around his shoulders.

"Ma?" Kathy called, coming in with her hat in hand.

"I'm right here, Kathy," said Katie-Marie. "Are you ready?"

"Yes, Ma." She grinned when she saw her father. "Pa, you're up. How did you talk the doctor into it?"

"That fool man don't know good health when he sees it," growled Jacob.

Katie-Marie rolled her eyes. "Of course, Jacob.

Now, remember, just because you're healing fast don't mean you're recovered. I don't want any shenanigans. You can sit out here for another couple of hours, then see that one of the boys puts you back in the study. You hear?"

"I hear you. Now, git."

Katie-Marie turned. "Freddie, you'll find your own way into town?"

"I'll take care of it," said Freddie.

Kathy went over and kissed Jacob's cheek. "You take care of yourself."

"Don't worry. I'll be walking you down the aisle Wednesday night."

Kathy grimaced while her mother kissed Jacob also, then shooed her out. Jacob chuckled as they left.

"She'll do it, by gum," he chortled. He grinned at Freddie. "What did I tell you? If I hadn't stepped in, you'd still be hankering after her, and keeping your own self company nights."

Freddie cleared his throat. "Your influence has certainly been felt."

"I tell you, Freddie, there ain't much that'll put the fear of God in that girl, except me and a shotgun. Used to be I could do it with a leather strap."

"You struck her?" Freddie gaped in shock.

"Wore out a bit of leather on her hide out back behind the shed. Spare the rod, spoil the child." Still chuckling, Jacob took a long, speculative look at Freddie. "You got a fair bit of moxie yourself, lucky for you. You'll need it with her. She never could suffer fools, and neither can I. Your folks must have wore out plenty of leather on you."

"My parents never struck me." Freddie shifted. His parents never paid that much attention. "Nor did anyone else, for that matter, until I reached prep school. Even then, I rarely trespassed to the point of requiring corporal punishment."

"No fooling. You don't seem the type to take it on the chin."

"I don't. However, when I was young, there were certain standards and expectations. I knew what they were, and lived up to them. It's how things were."

"Gee, that sounds strict," said Betty from where she was stirring the mush.

"You gonna wire your folks to come out for the wedding?" asked Jacob.

"I think not."

The screen door banged again. Gam trotted in with the dog close behind.

"Hey, Pa, you're sitting up," he exclaimed.

"That I am, Gammers. Finish your chores?"

"Yep. Freddie, you wanna come down to the creek later? We can go swimming."

"I do have to go into town, but perhaps after that."

Betty put bowls of oatmeal mush in front of Freddie and Jacob. She set a platter of eggs and bacon next to Freddie, and a small plate of biscuits, swimming in gravy, on his other side. As soon as her back was turned, Jacob glanced at the bacon. Freddie nodded. Jacob swiped a strip and nibbled. Gam also got permission to snitch.

"Maybe you, me, and Isaac can toss a ball around, too," Gam continued.

"Now, Gammers, you got chores to keep after, remember," warned Jacob.

"I know. But Josh has been doing an awful lot of them, and now Abe's here, and he's doing 'em, too."

The dog whined. Jacob slipped a piece of meat under the table.

"Pa!" groaned Betty. "You're not supposed to feed the dog under the table. Ma was very firm about that."

Gam snickered as Freddie slipped the dog another tidbit. As it happened, Freddie was the one who'd inspired the lecture the night before on not feeding the dog at mealtimes, a lecture that turned out to be as well heeded as the Eighteenth Amendment.

The baby squawked and began to cry.

"Take care of your baby, Betty," ordered Pa.

He waited until Betty ran off with the basket. "Fool women. Never could understand why giving scraps to a pig is all right, but not to man's best friend."

Freddie nodded. "I suppose it can be a nuisance when guests are present, however, I can't imagine entertaining with a dog present."

"You grow up with a dog?"

"Not really. My grandfather keeps them on his estate in Long Island."

"What's an estate?" asked Gam.

"A big house with a lot of land around it," said Jacob.

"Boy, we got one of those," Gam crowed.

Freddie laughed. "In a way, I suppose. But the house is usually larger than this one, and much finer."

"You mean like the Brunswick Hotel?" Gam's eyes grew round. "That's the finest place around. Pa's even been inside, haven't you, Pa?"

"It's right nice." Jacob's demeanor cooled considerably.

Freddie looked at him curiously. "Something wrong with the service there?"

"Oh, Mr. Spivens is just a snob," said Gam. "He's the owner. Ain't he, Pa?"

"Mr. Spivens is doing well by his business, and has a right to be proud of it," growled Jacob.

"But you and he don't seem to get along," said Freddie.

"Well, Freddie, that's between us."

"If it's affecting the farm, Mr. Briscow—"

Jacob sat up straight. "What's this Mr. Briscow nonsense? Landsakes, you're marrying my daughter in two days."

Freddie swallowed. "I apologize for the offense. I didn't want to presume is all."

Jacob laughed. "Well, I'll be. A bit of respect, eh? That's a damn sight finer thing than I'd expected from a son-in-law."

"You earn the respect, Mr.—" Freddie stopped.

"Just treat me like you treat your own pa."

Freddie shook his head. "I wouldn't be talking to you then. With my father, one listens in respectful silence and that's about it."

"Shucks," said Gam. "We always talk to Pa. Don't we?"

"There are no secrets between me and my children."

"A wise philosophy," said Freddie, with a quick glance at Gam.

Gam looked guilty for a second, then fed the dog some eggs.

"Well, I'm sated," said Freddie, laying his silverware neatly across his plate. "I've a few of my morning rituals to finish, so if I might be excused?"

"Just git if you want to go," said Jacob, taking the last piece of bacon. "We don't stand on formalities around here."

"I'm making an effort to remember that. However, old habits are not easily broken." Freddie got up.

"Can I go with you?" Gam asked.

Freddie was about to deny him, then thought better of it.

"Yes, Gammers. I think that would be an excellent idea."

Chapter Eight

"Kathy, will you co-operate!" Katie-Marie hissed.

"Yes, Ma." Kathy sighed and looked at the wedding gown once more. It was a lovely dress, but Kathy couldn't help feeling that the blushing bride who wore it should be a fresh young beauty, and not two years shy of thirty.

"This jagged edge hem is all the rage," said Mrs. Geisel, who ran the dress shop just north of the railroad tracks.

Kathy struggled to remember what Honoria had said the last time Freddie's sister had dragged her out on a shopping trip on the pretext of providing company. Kathy's taste was excellent, but it was something she had to work at and study, and given her ambivalence towards marriage, wedding dresses were not her idea of something she wanted to study. She looked at the white dress and tried not to sigh over the innocence it represented, an innocence she'd lost years before.

"It's lovely," she said with all the small enthusiasm she could muster.

Mrs. Geisel's round face fell. "Well, I do have another over here. It's stunning, and such lovely lace."

"I don't look very good in lace," said Kathy. "I'm

sorry, Mrs. Geisel. Any simple frock or suit will do."

"But, darling, this is your wedding." Mrs. Geisel frowned, completely puzzled. The elderly, tall woman had never seen a reluctant bride before. Reluctant grooms aplenty, but never a reluctant bride.

Katie-Marie shook her head. "Now, Mrs. Geisel. You'll just have to take Kathy with a grain of salt. Poor thing's terribly nervous."

"Oh," Mrs. Geisel looked over at Kathy. "The suddenness, I suppose."

"That's it, exactly." Katie-Marie bent over closer. "And all those years being thought of as an old maid, she came to believe it herself, poor thing."

Mrs. Geisel smiled. "She's not exactly a child bride, is she? Maybe I do have something a little more dignified."

The frock was simple, short-sleeved, dropped waist, but still trimmed in lace and gauze. Kathy felt ridiculous in it. She didn't want a veil, but Katie-Marie and Mrs. Geisel both looked so disappointed, Kathy gave in. The hat was a simple cloche, with the veil draped over it.

"Isn't she just a vision of loveliness?" sighed Mrs. Geisel.

Kathy thought she looked absurd. But she tried not to frown at the reflection in the mirror. Movement in the background caught her eye. She turned and looked out at the street through the shop window. The strange man from the day before was again heading for the telegraph office, only this time it was the Western Union at the freight depot, rather than the passenger depot.

"Kathy?" asked Katie-Marie.

"Ma, who is he? That man going into Western Union. I know him, but I can't remember his name."

"That's Mr. Tipton, the banker," said Katie-Marie, a little coolly.

Mrs. Geisel frowned at him also.

"He sure sends a lot of telegrams," said Kathy.

"Oh, he's quite the businessman, Elias is," said Mrs. Geisel sourly. "Always talking about his great investments, and how they're going to build this town. Hmph! When my Henry and I wanted a small loan to build this place up a little, he said no. Said we were not a good risk. We've been here forty years! And this town is growing, too."

"That it is," said Katie-Marie.

"I guess I just don't understand business," Mrs. Geisel took the veil and hat as Kathy took it off, casually hanging on every word. "He keeps saying farming's the town's business, and gives the farmers mortgages right and left to buy equipment, and the crop prices just keep going down. That don't sound like a good risk to me, but I guess if the farmers don't have any money, their wives won't be buying dresses."

"We're buying this one," said Katie-Marie. "Kathy, you think so?"

Kathy took a deep breath. "I guess so."

As they left the dress shop, Elias Tipton was still in the telegraph office, waiting at the counter. Kathy wanted to go in and investigate, but her mother pulled her on towards the jewelry store.

The droning started softly, but quickly grew louder. A minute later, a biplane's roar split the air over the town. Kathy's heart stopped. Had Freddie decided to leave after all? And in spite of what should have been relief, she felt hurt and angry.

But the plane doubled back over the town, climbing until it was almost upside-down, then banked sharply to the right. It shot away, then climbed again, this time rolling to the left. Then it pulled up and climbed until it was almost a speck. It circled twice and nosedived. Terrified, Kathy grabbed for her mother's hand. Katie-Marie took it, her eyes glued to the falling plane. With only feet to spare, it seemed, the plane pulled out of the dive. A minute later, it buzzed the town, almost scraping the rooftops. It circled and buzzed again, dipping low near the railroad tracks and a group of boys.

It finally landed on West North Main, just north of the passenger depot. Kathy ran, followed closely by her mother. Freddie's tall form bounded out of the rear cockpit, then helped a smaller, bouncier form out of the front.

"What do you think you were doing?" screamed Kathy as soon as she was within striking distance. "My god, you scared me to death!"

"Gamaliel!" yelped Katie-Marie. "What in the name of all the saints were you doing in that death trap?"

"It was fun, Ma!" Gam grinned, completely unrepentant. He was almost swallowed up in Kathy's flight jacket and helmet. "We did Immelmanns, and that death drop, that was swell! We even buzzed my friends over the railroad tracks."

"I was in perfect control the whole time," said Freddie.

"But why?" groaned Kathy.

"And did you have to do such stunts with my boy in the plane?" snapped Katie-Marie. "Flying's bad enough, for all you say it's safe."

Freddie took her arm reassuringly. "Mother Briscow, I realize that it looks risky, but those were truly basic maneuvers, ones I am more than qualified to undertake. After all, I spent the war teaching them to the army pilots."

Katie-Marie snatched her arm away. "I still don't like it."

"Well, I'd better get back and give Isaac his turn," said Freddie.

"No, you won't!" snapped Katie-Marie. "You're not taking another one of my children in that infernal noisemaker again. You've got business in town as it is. Gamaliel, take that jacket and that ridiculous hat off, and get back to the farm."

"Ma!"

"You heard me."

Sullenly, Gam trotted back down the road. Freddie took off his jacket and put the flying gear in the plane, replacing the leather with a tweed riding jacket.

"I apologize, Mother Briscow," he said quietly. "I didn't see any harm."

"There's been enough said on that," said Katie-Marie. "Kathy, give me the dress box. I'll be at your sister's. You go to the jewelry store and the courthouse for the license. I'll meet you back at the stables at two o'clock. Don't dawdle. There's laundry waiting for us."

"Yes, Ma." Kathy turned and stalked off.

Freddie scrambled after her. "You're not angry at me, too, are you?"

"I don't know," Kathy snapped. "At first, I thought you were leaving, and then you did all those insane stunts. I thought for sure you were going to be killed, and with Gammers in the plane."

"I was just trying to show the boy a good time. We did have your father's permission, I might add. I just didn't think it would be terribly diplomatic to say that to your mother."

"That's enough, Freddie."

"You're overwrought."

"I've just had a terrible morning, that's all. Poor Mrs. Geisel. She did her best. But I hated everything, and the worst of it was I knew I was supposed to be happy and gay, and I could barely manage a smile."

"Well, it is a bit of a shock, going about it this way. What's at the jewelry store?"

"I've got to get my ring fixed."

"Rings, you mean. I've got the band with me."

"Oh, damn." Kathy stopped and blushed. "This is so embarrassing. Freddie, you wouldn't happen to know how I could get some money from my bank account in New York, would you?"

"You could cash a check at the bank."

"I don't have checks."

"There's always Western Union," Freddie said. "How much money do you need?"

"Enough to buy you a wedding band."

"Me?"

"Well, you expect me to wear one."

Freddie grinned. "Actually, I like the idea. But, darling, can you afford it?"

"I have plenty of savings." Kathy held her chin up proudly, then sighed. "Not that it makes any difference now. So, I suppose I might as well buy you something nice. That is, if I can get my money."

"Do you know your account number?"

"Of course."

"Then we'll wire your bank and have them send it. It shouldn't take more than a day or two, at worst."

Kathy nodded. "And how much do you think I'll need?"

Freddie nodded at the nearby storefront. "Why don't we go in and find out?"

Prieman's Jewelry Store was not a busy place as a rule. But there were enough weddings and graduations in town for the store to make a fair living selling rings, watches, and fine pens, and the odd necklace or two to a particularly lovesick swain. Old Man Prieman, wearing black covers over his sleeves and a green visor with a brown vest, was bent with years of stooping over watch and other fine repairs, including the clockwork on more than one child's beloved toy.

He looked at the engagement ring, looked at Freddie, got out a loupe, looked at the ring again, and really looked at Freddie.

"All is in order, I assume?" asked Freddie.

"Yes." Prieman gazed at the diamond again. "Band, too?"

"Right here." Freddie handed.

"They need to be made smaller," said Kathy.

Prieman looked Kathy over. "Shouldn't take more than a day or so."

"If you can get it before Wednesday evening, it would be a help," said Kathy.

"Indeed." Prieman nodded. "Ralph!"

"Yeah, Gramps." A man Kathy's age, also in a brown vest, sleeve covers and visor, backed out of the back room, carrying a tray of small gears.

"Got a ring sizing for you."

Kathy swallowed and braced herself.

Ralph Prieman turned. "Kathy, Kathy Briscow! I heard you were back in town. Golly, got your hair cut, too. Getting hitched, huh?"

"Yes," said Kathy.

"Getting the ring from us?" Ralph took the rings from his grandfather. "Holy Toledo! That's some diamond."

He whipped a loupe into his eye, examined it, then looked Freddie over, and whistled.

"This is my intended," said Kathy awkwardly. "Mr. Freddie Little. Freddie, Mr. Ralph Prieman, a friend of mine from high school."

Ralph shook Freddie's hand warmly. "Sure is a pleasure to meet you, Mr. Little." He gave Kathy a slightly lecherous grin. "Didn't figure it'd take Kathy this long to get married."

"It's fortunate for me that she did," said Freddie, a little puzzled.

Although Kathy was blunt about her desires, Freddie had no reason to believe she was experienced. If anything, he had every reason to believe she wasn't. Experienced women were considerably more subtle, and quite capable of seduction. Kathy was anything but seductive, even if she was exceedingly desirable. Yet her father had hinted at a less than chaste past, and now her former schoolmate was hinting at the same.

"Get on those rings, son," said the old man.

Ralph winked at Kathy. "Excuse me, Mr. Little, might I have a word with your fiancée privately?"

"You'll have to ask her," said Freddie.

"Come on back, Kathy."

Kathy sighed and went back. The room was littered with papers and magnifying glasses. Ralph sat on the edge of a table.

"You know how good a stone this is?" he asked, chuckling.

"Quite good, I would imagine," said Kathy. "Freddie's not one to settle for less than the best."

"The man's got money."

"I am well aware of that, Ralph." Kathy looked at him severely. "Is that why you got me back here?"

"No." Ralph sighed. "I did wait for you to get out of college."

"I know, Ralph. But you knew I wasn't coming back."

"I was the only one who did and the only one who held out, too."

Kathy snorted. "Don't be ridiculous, Ralph. What you wanted from me had nothing to do with marriage."

Ralph chuckled lasciviously. "It had something to do with marriage, just not the marrying part. We had some good times, Kathy."

"We did." Kathy smiled softly.

"I would have married you."

"You were the only one, Ralph." Kathy shook her head. "But I didn't want to get married."

"The modern woman. You always were way ahead of the times." Ralph put his hand on hers. "Is it true what they say about New York and all the radical thinking there?"

"What kind of radical thinking?" Kathy watched him carefully.

"About free love."

"In certain parts, you find it."

"Where you live?"

Kathy paused. "Ralph, you're married."

"So are you, almost." His hand gently caught her chin. "I always wondered what it would be like with you."

Kathy softly took his hand from her chin and squeezed it.

"I can't say the same thought never crossed my

mind," she said. "But it wouldn't be fair to your wife, or to Freddie."

"It depends on what he's expecting to bump into on his wedding night." Ralph grinned at her. "Or is it going to be an easy, painless undertaking?"

Kathy's grin grew wicked. "I guess you're not going to know, are you?"

Laughing, Ralph led her out to the front.

"Mr. Prieman, I do have one purchase I'd like to make," Kathy said as she went around to the front of the counter.

"Yes?" The elder Prieman waddled around. "A gift for the groom?"

"Precisely," said Kathy. She glanced nervously at Freddie, who smiled.

Prieman nodded. "A fine watch, maybe. A fountain pen."

"A wedding band."

Prieman's eyebrows shot up. "A wedding band. Very old world, isn't it? But not bad for business. Wedding band..."

As Prieman bent over the cases, Kathy reached out and nervously took Freddie's hand.

"You don't mind, do you?" she whispered.

"I bought you one, and I told you I liked the idea."

"I've got two." Prieman pulled them out. "Some of the immigrants like them. What do you think? A little narrow, but good gold."

Kathy looked at Freddie. "Well?"

"I had the audacity to decide what you will wear."

"You're no help." She turned to the rings. "This one looks nice. I'll take it. Freddie, you'd better try it on for size."

Even though his manner was casual, Freddie's heart pounded as he slid the ring on. It was a little tight, but Prieman assured him it could be made larger without trouble. Freddie struggled a bit getting it off and gave it to the jeweler.

After Kathy got the price for the ring and the

sizing, she and Freddie left the store and headed for the freight depot and the Western Union telegraph office there.

"I don't think that they'll be able to tell us anything," Kathy said. "But Elias Tipton, he runs the Farmer's Bank. The one at Chestnut and Juniata. He was the man who spent so much time sending telegrams yesterday. He was sending another today. According to the woman who owns the dress shop, he makes mortgages to the farmers, but not the townsfolk. Says they're a bad risk, and that farming is the hope of the town."

"That's interesting," said Freddie, gazing across the tracks toward the Farmer's Bank. "Not entirely surprising, given his bank. And I suppose if the farmers go broke, the town's businesses will dry up."

"That's what Mrs. Geisel said."

Kathy stopped at the door to the telegraph office and swallowed.

"Freddie," she whispered. "I have no idea how to wire my bank. I've never done anything like this before."

Freddie patted her hand, which still rested on his arm. "It's quite simple. I'll help you write it, if you'll just wait for me to get my telegrams out. They are rather urgent."

"Your family?" Kathy asked, swallowing again.

"My sister and Lowell Winters. I believe the good reverend made some mention of official witnesses, in which capacity I think my dearest friend has a right to serve, and even if I don't care that my parents witness the nuptials, I thought it might be nice if some member of the family did. Besides, Honoria might prove useful if we decide to make our home in my apartment."

"She's more likely to plan it all out for us," said Kathy with a rueful laugh.

"Come along."

It didn't take long to order the telegrams, and Freddie insisted on paying for all of them. Kathy was appalled by the expense.

"You're sending novels," she exclaimed as they left the office.

"This is one time where clarity justifies the expense," Freddie said, in spite of the fact that he had not been at all clear about why Honoria and Lowell should drop everything to come to Hays. "In any case, we'd best hurry on to the courthouse. You've got to meet your mother, and I've got a garageman and a furniture man to talk to."

The licensing process was a bore. Then Kathy got a terrible case of the shakes as she signed the form. She just barely managed to swear to the information she'd given. Freddie was sympathetic and held her until she calmed down, then took her to the nearest drug store soda fountain.

"Two vanilla ice cream sodas," he ordered.

Kathy sniffed, wiping her nose with another of Freddie's handkerchiefs.

"I feel like such an imbecile," she sniffed.

"There's no reason to," said Freddie.

"Kathy Briscow," said the soda jerk. "I didn't recognize you with your hair cut."

"Steven Billings?" Kathy frowned, hoping she was right.

"Yep. I took over from Mr. James when he died." Billings rubbed the counter proudly.

"Oh. I didn't know he'd passed," said Kathy, sadly.

"Four years ago. His widow sold me the place and went back to Topeka to live with her sister." He nodded at Freddie. "So is this the lucky man you got to marry you?"

"Freddie Little," said Freddie, holding out his hand.

Billings shook it. "Steven Billings. Hey, Kathy, you okay?"

Kathy had started weeping again. Freddie put his arms around her.

"It's been a rough morning," he explained. "Neither

of us anticipated everything happening so quickly."

"Well, a bride's entitled to a few tears, I say." Billings put the two sodas in front of them. "But I'm awful glad to see it. Figure it'll take your folks' minds off all the trouble going on at their place."

"What do you know about that?" asked Kathy, wiping her eyes.

"Everybody knows about all the vandalism they got going on."

"I guess they would," sighed Kathy.

Billings smiled apologetically. "They're still doing a darn sight better than most folks around here. It's been awful rough the past few years. Mayor Standling's standing up for growth, but he's getting a little nervous. I figure that's why him and Mr. Spivens were cussing out your pa the other week or so."

"They were?" asked Kathy.

Freddie feigned interest in his soda.

"Oh, it weren't nothing serious," said Billings quickly. "You know how the farmers tend to respect your pa and all. And he likes to do things slow. I figure Mayor Standling thinks your pa won't support him next election, and Standling sure do like being mayor."

"I didn't know him that well," said Kathy.

"Well, everyone knows how much Mayor Standling likes being mayor. So does Jackie Meyers. She used to be Jackie Standling."

"Jaqueline." Kathy dredged up the memory. "She was a snob. It would stand to reason her pa isn't much different. Meyers... Which Meyers did she marry?"

"Mervin. He was six years ahead of us. Went to Lawrence University, then to law school. Now, he's the public prosecutor for the county. Though there's not too much to convict around here."

"It's pretty quiet," agreed Kathy.

"Well, I'll let you two lovebirds enjoy your sodas."

Billings moved off into the store, while Kathy quietly groaned.

"Why don't you act like a lovebird, for a change,"

said Freddie softly, as he dug inside his jacket. "And move a little closer to me, and I'll render these god-awful confections drinkable."

"Freddie." Kathy blushed and bent over the sodas.

"I find it interesting that there is someone in this town who has a grievance against your father." With practiced skill, Freddie spiked the sodas and slipped the flask back into his jacket.

"But it's so amorphous. Why would Mayor Standling think that vandalizing my father would help him in an election?"

"Maybe that's not Standling's purpose."

"No, maybe not." Kathy swallowed nervously. She glanced at Freddie's jacket. "You didn't empty that hip flask, did you?"

"Wary lest your sister visit that creature from hell upon us again?"

"Rachel's just teething. It's hard on babies."

"Well, fear not. There is relief. My good man, Roberts, saw to the inclusion of fresh supplies of restoratives in my trunk."

"You know, it also occurs to me that Mr. Spivens has been known to be less than kind regarding my father. But what could he possibly stand to gain?"

"The satisfaction of revenge for a real or imagined grievance. I'm afraid I shall have to do business with him, too. He does own the best hotel in town, and I am not taking you back to the attic Wednesday night."

"What's that got..." Kathy's eyes caught his. His smile was rich with anticipatory splendor. Her own heart raced, and she felt herself warming. Under the counter, his hand clasped hers. They were in a public place. He would never kiss her. But he could make her want to be kissed, to be touched, to feel all of him.

Kathy closed her eyes and turned to her soda. The inherent injustices and slaveries of society's preferred arrangement for men and women, and Kathy's fear of them, seemed to diminish for her as she considered the one great privilege insisted upon by the arrangement.

Freddie's curiously spidery, gentle fingers held hers while he sipped innocently. Only a few times had those wonderfully promising hands begun to show their promise. But Wednesday night, if not sooner, she would have him all, and for the rest of their lives.

Chapter Nine

The smell of grease and gasoline pleasantly tweaked Freddie's nose. The world of garages and mechanics had been a foreign one to Freddie until his college years when Lowell Winters had first introduced Freddie to the glories of the internal combustion engine. While Lowell, in spite of his competence, had always preferred to let someone else get up to their elbows in grease, Freddie had found he thoroughly enjoyed it.

Many an afternoon they'd spent by the side of some road, broken down, Lowell drinking and telling Freddie what to do. Then Freddie became adept on his own, and as often as not, the breakdowns would result in hilarious battles, because Freddie would also be drinking, and often disagreed with Lowell regarding the nature of the problem.

"Help you, sir?" asked the garageman as he came out of the back.

"Yes. I'm looking for a replacement cranking mechanism for a nineteen eighteen Model T truck."

The garageman was tall, somewhat chicken-necked, and covered with grease. He looked at Freddie thoughtfully.

"You're new in town," he said. He looked at Freddie

again, this time suspiciously. "You that Little fellow s'posed to be marrying their oldest girl Wednesday?"

"I am he. Freddie Little, at your service. And you are?"

"Jeb Carson."

"It's a pleasure to meet you, Mr. Carson." Freddie shook hands.

Carson grinned then looked at the black grime on Freddie's otherwise immaculate hands. Freddie laughed and slid out of his jacket.

"It's perfectly all right, Mr. Carson. You'll find no aversion to grease in me."

"Yep?" Carson looked puzzled, trying to figure out what Freddie had said.

"I'm very fond of engines." Freddie stepped around to the back and stopped in front of a large one. "What's this? A Packard Twin-Six. Let me guess, nineteen-nineteen?"

"Yep." Carson grinned. "That there engine works pretty good."

"They're lovely beasts. They stopped making them two years ago, and it's getting difficult to get parts." Freddie grinned. "This wouldn't happen to be for sale, would it?"

Carson shrugged. "What you offering?"

"One hundred dollars cash, now."

Carson chuckled and shook his head.

"Plus another hundred dollars cash upon delivery to the Briscow farm."

Carson scratched his chin. "Mister, you got yourself a deal."

"Thank you. Now, about that cranking mechanism."

"Don't got it." Carson pulled a greasy bandana from his back pocket and blew his nose. "Could try wiring to Topeka."

"Well, if we can't get it from there, I'll have to wire Detroit."

"Yep."

"How soon before we know?"

"This afternoon."

Freddie sighed. "If I can get the mechanism at the Briscow place by tomorrow, I would be willing to make it worth your while."

Carson scratched his chin. "I figure I can do that."

"I'll look forward to seeing it, and my engine, at noon, then." Freddie handed over several bills, the two shook hands again and Freddie left.

The furniture store was crowded with basic sofas and end tables, beds, bureaus, and wardrobes, all jammed into a room the size of the Briscow living room. An older man, presumably the Dreiser whose name was painted on the windows, watched Freddie with considerable suspicion.

"New in town?" he finally asked as Freddie looked over a rolltop desk.

"Just visiting," Freddie replied, and straightened. "Freddie Little."

"Matthew Dreiser. Ain't you supposed to be marrying the Briscow girl?"

"On Wednesday." Freddie smiled. "Thought I might see about furnishing a new home for her. I do like good oak furniture."

"Got plenty of that."

"Do you do specialized work?"

"Depends."

Freddie looked over the room. "Then let's start with a new bed. As you can see, my height makes ordinary beds somewhat uncomfortable. If I could give you the correct dimensions, do you think you would be able to make one to my specifications? In oak, of course."

Dreiser looked him over. "For a price."

"That's neither here nor there. My concern is that I'd heard a number of rumors of a lumber shortage."

"Nope. Plenty of oak in the lumber yards here. Costs a bit, though."

"Indeed." Freddie smiled with sleepy geniality. "That shouldn't be a problem."

Then he promptly dickered the price down to

considerably lower than what he'd seen in New York. Dreiser didn't seem unhappy. To ensure it, Freddie bought a couple other pieces and arranged for Dreiser to send it all to a small mountain shack Freddie owned in the Adirondacks. Keeping the coming engine and auto parts in mind, Freddie wrote a check.

"Feel free to wait until it clears at my bank," said Freddie. "I doubt my bride and I will be moving to a new place immediately."

Dreiser smiled. "Well, thank you very much, Mr. Little. Pleasure doing business with you."

"Likewise." Freddie nodded pleasantly and left.

It hadn't been all that unpleasant, but it hadn't yielded much information, either. At most, Freddie was reasonably sure Jacob Briscow's stand of oak was not behind the vandalism.

The town's biggest and most respectable hotel was The Brunswick. The Walz was too close to the tracks to be considered, and The Mulroy was simply too small. Hence, The Brunswick was as much a meeting place and a restaurant as it was a place for travelers to stay. These were mostly salesmen, with the occasional land agent or government worker. Still, it was the most elegant place in town, and few of the farm folk had ventured inside.

Freddie found it somewhat frumpy, like a grande belle grown old and tired in her former splendor. But it was clean, and the woodwork was of good quality. He rang the bell at the desk and was greeted by a thin, balding man somewhere in his forties in vest, sleeve covers and visor.

"Room?" asked the man.

"Not for tonight," said Freddie. "I'm Mr. Freddie Little. You, no doubt, have heard that I'm to be married on Wednesday. I also have two guests arriving for the event. I'd like to make arrangements for their stay, as well as a suite for myself and my bride. You are...?"

"Thomas Spivens. I own the place."

"And it's quite a fine one. Will you need a deposit?"

"These guests of yours. Will they be paying for themselves?"

"Of course not. I'm to be billed for everything."

Spivens looked Freddie up and down sourly. "It'll be five dollars a night for the suite, and three dollars for a room."

"I'll need two separate rooms for my guests, and three dollars is acceptable."

Spivens got out a card and pen. "Names?"

"Mrs. Honoria Wentworth and Mr. Lowell Winters."

"One room apiece. I'll need payment in advance."

Freddie got out his billfold. "Here's five dollars for the suite, and five and..." He dug a silver dollar out of his pocket. "One for the two rooms."

"Wednesday night only?" Spivens looked up at him.

"That remains to be seen."

Spivens shrugged and slid the money under the counter.

"You will, of course, mark paid on that card?" Freddie asked.

Slowly, Spivens took out a rubber stamp and stamped the card.

"Thank you very much, Mr. Spivens." Freddie offered his hand. Spivens shook it. "I look forward to my stay."

Freddie left, wondering how much of Spivens' coolness was a reflection on how the man felt about Jacob Briscow, and how much was directed at Freddie personally. It was odd. Everyone in town had seemed friendly enough when Kathy was around.

He had one more errand. He could have wired his bank for some money at the same time Kathy had wired hers. On the other hand, there was the odd behavior of Mr. Tipton, which meant there might be something to be learned from the bank, instead. Freddie had two more checks in his pocket and some more in his trunk.

The bank had three teller windows, but only one

was open. An elderly, heavy-set woman in a straight, dark blue woolen dress and brimmed straw hat waited on the public side while the teller went about his business. Freddie stood at the tall customer table and wrote out his draft. Two other tellers, one wearing sleeve covers, the other his full suit, worked at their desks behind the teller windows.

Mr. Tipton came out of a door at the back that presumably led to his office.

"Weidner," he snapped. "Did my reply from Levitt and Solomon come?"

"Yes, sir." The teller wearing the suit grabbed the yellow envelope from his desk and handed it to Mr. Tipton. "It's right here."

"Good. Get the boys' home in Topeka on the line. And tell them I need a boy who won't run away."

"Yes, sir."

Freddie glanced up. Mr. Tipton was headed back to his office, telegram in hand. Weidner was shaking his head as he picked up the candlestick phone and rattled the switch.

"Another runaway?" the woman asked the teller she was working with. "Isn't that the third one in a year?"

The teller, a short pale man, shrugged. "They're orphans, Mrs. Schmitt. Guess they don't like staying in one place too long."

"I suppose not. Well, thank you, Mr. Hurt. Good day." Mrs. Schmitt bundled herself off.

Freddie stepped up to the counter. Mr. Hurt was startled by the size of Freddie's check and scurried back to Mr. Tipton's office for several minutes. When he returned, it was with the news that it would take two days to prepare the draft.

"That's acceptable," said Freddie. "As long as I have my money by Wednesday afternoon."

"Yes, sir," Mr. Hurt said.

Freddie left the bank, his mind whirling. Mr. Tipton's reply telegram had come from a brokerage house that Freddie knew fairly well, one that specialized in real estate purchases. Then there was Mr. Tipton's request to call a boy's home and the image of a boy with those too familiar bruises on his shoulders and corn silk hair. Freddie couldn't do anything about the boy and had no reason to do so beyond an odd feeling that the runaway and the boy he'd seen were the same. But the brokerage house, that he knew what to do about. He returned to the telegraph office, confident that Kathy would be even more horrified at the length of this latest telegram.

Freddie landed his plane on the road outside the Briscow farm again. He parked it out of the way near the barn, but away from the road. Kathy, back in her work dress and wearing a red checked extra-large apron with huge pockets, was in the yard behind the house, cranking the agitator on a wooden washing machine. It was a tub made of barrel staves set up on four sturdy legs. The top held two heavy metal gears, with the crank on the side pushing the gear flush with the lid. A large galvanized pail stood next to the washing machine, in the puddles made from all the laundry going in and out of the tub. A wringer was clamped to the top of the machine, ready to wring out the freshly washed laundry, and Kathy had set a clothes basket on top of an old crate to keep it out of the mud. The basket sat ready for the wringer.

"How old is that thing?" Freddie asked.

"Don't know. I think I was around seven when we got it. It may even have been new. Ma was ecstatic. I remember that much. She's not anymore, though."

"Your family could use a modern washing machine," said Freddie.

She glared. "Do you see any electricity on this place to run it?"

"Perhaps as a wedding gift, I shall present a generator to your father."

"This is not a good time to be mentioning that."

She stopped cranking the tub and undid the crank. Before Freddie could help her, she lifted the heavy gear off the top of the tub and set it aside.

"My apologies, darling." He glanced around, then bent and kissed her cheek.

"If you're going to do that, you could at least hit the mark."

She lifted her face. Freddie obliged.

"Did you discover anything?" she asked, reaching into the water in the tub.

"Yes, a beautiful Packard Twin-Six, twelve cylinder, six point nine-liter engine, which I am having delivered here tomorrow. I'll see to shipping it to New York, eventually."

Kathy wrung out a diaper, set it into the wringer and started cranking. "I was hoping you'd find out something that will lead us to the vandals."

"So was I. However, the staff at the telegraph office was reasonably polite, but not enlightening. I did happen to overhear at the bank that Mr. Tipton has been communicating with a New York brokerage that specializes in real estate, so I sent a wire to my brokers inquiring about it. But I seriously doubt that will amount to much. Mr. Carson, the garageman, didn't have much to say but was quite happy to take my money. Mr. Dreiser, the furniture man, had no qualms at all about making an oak bed to my peculiar specifications. When I suggested rumors about a wood shortage, he said that there was plenty of wood in the local lumber yards, but that it would cost, which I promptly disproved with some canny bargaining."

"My god, you're actually capable of it." She set another diaper in the wringer. "Don't just stand there. Crank."

Freddie grimaced. "This is indeed a ghastly business. As for the rest of my afternoon, I did speak to Mr. Spivens, and cannot figure out for the life of me why he took such an instant dislike to me. The same goes for the rest of them, too."

"You're a stranger in town, Freddie." Kathy dropped another diaper into the waiting basket, then got another from the tub. "They don't trust you."

"Dreiser trusted me enough to take a check for the bed and a couple other items I'm shipping to my place in the Adirondacks."

"He won't send a thing until it clears the bank, and I didn't know you had a place out there."

Freddie waited for Kathy to set a diaper into the wringer before cranking again.

"It is a manly retreat that I mostly use during hunting season, and I had no intention of bringing you out there because we both know what would have transpired."

Kathy's smile went wicked. "Does this mean we get to go out there and let it transpire now?"

Freddie grinned. "Perhaps in the near future."

"Last one." Kathy grunted and took over cranking the wringer from Freddie. "And not a moment too soon. Will you at least keep me company while I hang these? It's a dismally tedious job, but it doesn't smell."

"I'll gladly stand by. I'll even find something pleasant to chat about."

"You'll talk my ear off, that's what you'll do." Kathy hefted the heavy basket over to the clothesline, already loaded with the family's clothing. She smiled at him fondly. "But it's not without its own distracted charm."

Pa managed to join the family for supper, although he ate only soup and some bread. The meal itself was cozy and warm, and very filling. Freddie, who was accustomed to seven-course dinners, was surprised to find himself feeling overfull.

As expected, the callers arrived just as the last of the supper dishes were put away. Isaac and Gam got sent out to slop the pig and were told to keep the dog tied up outside, then to come in and wash up. The visitors were mostly neighbor ladies who gossiped non-stop, but not about anything that would lead to the vandals. Three brought presents: embroidered pillow cases, crocheted antimacassars, and an afghan. Kathy thanked them, while Katie-Marie made notes for Kathy's thank-you letters.

"People are getting married around here all the time," Kathy explained to Freddie as the sun finally drifted past the horizon. "The ladies do the needlework and crocheting in their spare time, and usually have extras lying around for gifts when needed."

"It was certainly kind of them," said Freddie, looking over the handiwork. "If pointless."

"We'll find some use for them." Sighing, she turned towards the fireplace mantle.

Freddie put his hands on her shoulders. "Of course, we will, darling. You seem to be feeling a little better about this."

"I guess." She took a deep breath and let it out. "Freddie, will you hold me? It doesn't seem so awful when you do."

He gathered her up, kissing her hair and rocking her. A minute later she loosened her grip and looked up at him.

"I'll be all right now," she whispered.

"Good." He smiled at her, but out of the corner of his eye something else caught his attention. He reached out and picked up the framed photograph off the mantle. "This is you."

Kathy blushed. "My college graduation picture."

"You did have nice hair before you cut it."

"Oh, no. You'll be wanting me to grow it out now. Well, it's not going to help. I'd have to wear it all put up, and that won't be any fun for you."

Freddie put the photograph back and gazed at the other frames.

"Let's see, this is your father's family?" he asked pointing to the old daguerreotype.

"Yes. Guess which one is Pa."

"This one." Freddie touched a tough looking lad of

twelve.

"Nope. That's Uncle Jonah. He's the one who went to Harvard and became a professor there. Pa's this one. He was only three. The baby is Uncle Jedediah. He was more like Grandpa, always wandering. It was Grandma who got Grandpa to settle when they came here with the railroad. Grandpa sold dry goods to the railroad men, and then lumber to the farmers after he had staked out the best spread here."

"One of the founding citizens."

"That's right. They named the town after the fort, which was built to protect the railroad and named after a Civil War hero. It was a pretty rough place for a long time. That's why Grandma got so strong on the Temperance Movement. Pa was the only one who wanted to stick around, so he got the farm and the house."

Freddie picked up a double oval frame. "Now these are your parents as young people."

"Yes." Kathy beamed. "These are the actual pictures Ma and Pa sent each other before they met face to face. Pa wouldn't get married for the longest time. He said he didn't like the local girls. So he sent out for an advertisement in the New York Times looking for a woman with good intellect and not afraid of hard work. Ma was one of the ladies who answered. They wrote back and forth for a year. Ma's family were getting afraid she'd bolt on them, so Uncle Mike got assigned to keep an eye on her, and she gave him the slip. She and Pa were married in Topeka in the morning, then he brought her home to this house, she made dinner for him, and they went to bed. She was eighteen years old."

"And your Pa was?"

"Thirty-one. I told you, he's no spring chicken."

"And baby pictures. Don't tell me. Let me guess." Freddie pointed to each. "This must be Gammers. It's the most recent. Isaac?"

"Yes."

"Gideon?"

"Right."

"Screaming like that, that has to Teresa."

"Very good."

Freddie frowned. "These last three are confusing. Abraham, Joshua and you."

"Nope." Kathy re-arranged the frames. "This is Abraham, this is Joshua, and this is me."

"I see some high school pictures here, and this is Teresa's wedding. Bill looked like a jellyfish even then."

"Oo. He did."

"I don't see anything in between."

"Pictures are expensive, Freddie."

He sighed. "I never thought about that. This is your high school picture. Who are these people with you?"

"That's the honor class. I graduated at the top. But I didn't get to be valedictorian because I was a girl and because my morals were questionable."

Freddie looked at her. "They were?"

"Didn't know you were marrying a tainted lady, did you?" Kathy's wicked grin faded. "I let boys kiss me. A lot of the other girls were doing it, too. But because I was the smart one, they always expected more out of me. They never caught me, you understand. It was all based on rumor."

Freddie chuckled. "Your pa mentioned last night wasn't the first time he'd caught you out behind the barn."

Kathy shrugged. "I like kissing."

"So do I," Freddie whispered.

An untimely entrance by Isaac separated them temporarily. They found each other later on the porch swing.

"Kathy?" called Katie-Marie.

Kathy moved away from Freddie. "Out here, Ma."

Katie-Marie looked through the screen door. "Are you coming to bed?"

"In a little bit, Ma. Freddie and I want to talk for

a while."

"Don't be wandering off. And don't stay up late. There's a lot to do tomorrow."

As soon as Katie-Marie was gone, Freddie pulled Kathy over next to him on the swing. She snuggled in against his chest and put her feet up along the seat.

"I suppose we should be discussing theories regarding the vandals," she said softly.

"I suppose we should. But it's like you said today. It's so amorphous. We have a few motives, but nothing firm to grab a hold of."

"That's what's so frightening about this whole thing. At least we haven't had any trouble since Saturday night." Kathy suddenly giggled. "If we'd been here a lot longer ago, we might have a motive for Ralph Prieman."

"What did he want to talk to you about?"

"That's abnormally direct for you."

"You don't have to answer." Freddie lit a cigarette.

"You're still wondering."

"What do you expect? I'm naturally curious in general. I'm guessing he was an old flame hoping to rekindle."

"Not quite. But he was one of the boys I used to kiss."

"As long as it's past tense."

Kathy paused. "So you're going to insist on fidelity."

"Well, yes." Freddie stopped. "Now that I think about it, that was a gross assumption."

"Are you going to be faithful?"

Freddie sucked on his cigarette. "I must be honest, Kathy. I never thought about it one way or the other. My father always had mistresses, but then he and my mother didn't share a bed as far as I knew. They didn't even share a room. It's entirely possible my father touched my mother only twice in their entire married lives."

"I don't believe that. Your mother can't have been

that cold."

"It wasn't my father. He's a fairly active man that way. I remember when I was fifteen, I came home unexpectedly one day. I think I'd decided not to go to some tea dance I'd been scheduled to attend. As I was walking upstairs, I heard this strange grunting in one of the bedrooms and went in to look. He was on top of her, her legs were in the air."

"Your mother?"

Freddie snorted. "Heavens, no. The upstairs maid. I stood there, and Father kept on going. They must have been close to the end, because she cried out and he cried out, and then they noticed me."

Kathy snickered. "You must have gotten a beating for that."

"I got exactly the opposite. My father got up, pulled up his pants, and smiled at me. He said it looked like it was time I became a man. And he patted my shoulder. He'd never done that before. A week later, he took me out on an outing, and we ended up at this hotel. On the way, he explained all the protocols of keeping a mistress. In the suite, he made the introductions and left. It turned out she'd been one of his mistresses, and they'd remained friends after he'd moved on."

"How utterly ordered." Kathy had to laugh even though she felt a little repulsed. "I would have thought you'd have found your way during a youthful grope session gone too far in the back seat of some car."

"I won't say that hasn't happened. But I learned pretty quickly the resultant tears and carrying on generally weren't worth it. Worse yet, one could get stuck getting married that way. If I hadn't been a lad of seventeen, I would have been forced to marry her." Freddie shuddered.

"Not to your liking."

"No substance whatsoever, but pretty, which was how the necking started. After her, I stuck to mistresses."

"Which is the way it is done. But what about us?"

Freddie sighed. "The hard part is that while I do not question taking a mistress for myself, I do not foresee a desire to. But perhaps more importantly, I am truly committed to making our union that of equals, and if I am truly honest, the thought of you with another lover is very upsetting. Ergo, in all justice, I cannot take a mistress."

Kathy snuggled in closer. "Good. I tell you, Freddie, it's not fair. It's expected that you come to the altar with sexual experience. But if I do, then it's a terrible disgrace."

"I know. That's one of the reasons I didn't marry. It was understood. The good girls were the keepers of purity and the home, and those you married. But the bad girls you didn't, because they were fun. I didn't see any reason to bother with a home and family, so I stayed with the bad girls."

"What if I'm a bad girl, Freddie?" she asked softly.

"You're not, darling." He kissed her hair.

"What if I am?"

"Then since I've spread my oats about, I have no reason to object to your having spread yours. But I really wish you'd stop talking about yourself as if you were some sort of slut. You're not, by any stretch of the imagination, I don't care what you say you've done."

"How can you say that after the times I've thrown myself at you?"

Freddie chuckled. "I'm to object because you gave into a tremendous passion for me? And how many times has it happened? No more than four times in over six months. Otherwise, you've been perfectly circumspect. You're merely passionate, and you have some slightly radical views on men and women. That hardly constitutes a slut. Now, I don't want to hear any more about it."

Kathy sighed. The truth would be known soon enough, and Freddie would be faced with making good on his word. Hopefully, he wouldn't find it too bitter. She felt herself slip, and let her breasts slide under

Freddie's hand. He laughed softly, and toyed with them.

"Freddie, why are you so open to taking me now?"

"Fair play, I suppose. You agreed to marry me because that's what I want. I will become your lover at the first opportunity because that's what you want. And speaking of, it is finally quiet out here. It could be a little awkward, but I have reason to believe we will not be disturbed."

"Ma is waiting for me."

"She'll wait." Freddie pulled her into his lap, and softly began kissing the back of her neck.

And the dog growled. A car passed on the road. The dog barked furiously. Kathy sat up straight, sniffing.

"Fire," she said, then scrambled out of Freddie's lap, and yelled. "Fire!"

Freddie looked around. "The barn."

"The hay pile!" Kathy banged on a bucket next to the door, as she ran for the kitchen sink. "Joshua! Abraham! There's a fire behind the barn! Freddie, get the blankets in the pantry."

"I've got them." Freddie was already out the screen door.

Kathy yanked the full bucket from the sink. Joshua ran in wearing only his pants and union suit.

"What's going on?" he yelped.

"Fire!" yelped Gam and Isaac from upstairs.

"The hay pile behind the barn," said Kathy, heading out. "Get the shovels, quickly."

Abraham and Gideon came running through. Behind them, Isaac and Gam stumbled, another bucket between them. Katie-Marie, wearing a wrapper and boots, and Betty, wearing just a nightgown, came out, each carrying another bucket. Kathy pulled Betty back as she dashed toward the flames.

"Don't go near!" Kathy yelped. "You'll catch yourself in that thing."

"Kathy, Betty, let the boys do the flames," ordered Katie-Marie. "Help me get the animals out. Gam, Isaac, get the paddock open."

The flames were already licking at the back wall of the barn. Inside, the air was thick with smoke and the stamping of panicking animals. The horses reared, neighing in terror. Kathy dodged the hooves, and scrambled to get a blindfold over the lead horse's eyes.

"Easy boy!" she crowed. "Easy now."

She yanked down hard on the tie rope, and grabbed the bridle. Talking to the beast in a low, soothing voice, she led it out of the barn. Katie-Marie beat back some tongues of flame, then got the mare blindfolded and moving. Outside, Gam grabbed the lead horse, and threw his whole weight on the tie rope. Isaac had opened the gate on the paddock near the house, and Gam rushed the lead horse into the small fenced area.

Behind the barn, the flames danced and grew in intensity. Joshua and Freddie beat at them with the blankets, while Abraham and Gideon tossed dirt as fast as they could.

"Get some water on the blankets!" Joshua yelled.

Freddie grabbed one of the buckets and doused the smoldering wool.

In the barn, Betty struggled with one of the cows. The smoke grew thicker.

"We'd better untie them all," she cried.

"They'll stampede," called Katie-Marie. "I'll take this one. You get the heifer."

Kathy untied another cow. It decided it was not going to move. Kathy yanked and tugged, then finally kicked its hindquarters. The cow lowed in panic and started to run. Kathy skidded in the manure.

Gasping and coughing, Katie-Marie returned for the third cow. Isaac took Kathy's cow from her, and she ran back in for the fourth and final cow. Betty slid through the manure to the pig sty and got the sow. The yearling ambled along behind.

"Betty, I'll take the pig," said Kathy, grabbing the rope lead. "Get the buckets and start filling them again."

Kathy grabbed a bucket and ran back inside the barn to wet down the back wall from the inside. Katie-Marie joined her.

"You get outside and start refilling buckets," Katie-Marie ordered. "The boys'll need more."

"Ma, you need help in here!"

"It's too dangerous! Now, git!"

Kathy sent Gam and Isaac to fill buckets, then rejoined her mother. Isaac and Betty ran back and forth between the kitchen and the barn with bucket after bucket, while Gam dodged between the blankets, pouring water on them and stomping out stray sparks.

Slowly, the flames died down. The inside of the barn stayed soaked. Kathy climbed up to the loft to be sure no embers lurked there, and wet down the hay for good measure.

"It'll mold," groaned Katie-Marie.

"We'll spread it out tomorrow," said Kathy, coming down. "Josh says the far fifty is due for cutting anyway."

Outside, the men were taking turns resting and turning over the cinders to be sure they were out. They wet it down thoroughly, and slowly stumbled into the kitchen. Betty already had the washcloths and salves out. Jacob grumbled from a seat near the door.

"What in the name of all the saints are you doing up?" Katie-Marie scolded. "All you'll do is get yourself sick again."

"I'm all right," growled Jacob, and coughed. "What's the damages?"

"Just the hay pile, and the back wall's charred," said Joshua, falling into a chair. "Looks like there won't be any spooning back there for a while."

"The animals are all in the paddock," announced Isaac.

"Josh, you're burnt," cried Betty.

"So's Freddie." Kathy grabbed salve and applied it liberally.

They were all burnt. Joshua had it the worst. But Abraham's eyebrows were singed, and Gideon's fingers were bright red and cracked. Gam had a long sear mark along his cheekbone, at which he gazed in pride in the pantry mirror. Everyone's muscles were sore, and soft groans rippled through the kitchen whenever someone moved.

"Shouldn't we be getting the animals back in the barn?" Freddie asked, rubbing his shoulders.

Jacob shook his head. "It won't hurt to stay out tonight. And they won't go in while it smells of smoke."

Freddie nodded. It took an effort, but everyone slowly made it upstairs to bed except Jacob. He watched the rest of the night, waiting to go back to the study until he heard the first sounds of waking upstairs.

Oddly enough, Freddie was the first up that morning. Stiff and sore, he forewent shaving, and after washing up and dressing, went straight out to the back of the barn. Gam and Isaac soon followed to do their chores, as did Gideon, Abraham and Joshua. The cows didn't give much milk that morning, and Gideon drove them straight to the pasture from the paddock.

In the kitchen, Katie-Marie, Betty and Kathy all had breakfast going when Freddie wandered in.

"Didn't you sleep?" Kathy asked, worried.

Freddie yawned. "Excuse me. Yes. I just decided to get up early."

"Why?" asked Kathy.

"Because I wanted to get the first look at the damage." Freddie put a charred whiskey bottle on the table. "I found this."

"Were those boys drinking back there?" snapped Katie-Marie.

Freddie shook his head. "It's charred on the inside, too. It was used as an incendiary device."

"A what?" asked Betty.

"A fire bomb," said Kathy.

"Precisely," said Freddie.

Chapter Ten

The stench of charred wood covered the farm like a blanket of tension. Yet everyone tried to ignore it as they went about their chores and other tasks. Freddie went to work right away on the truck, as the parts and his engine arrived first thing. Kathy helped her mother and Betty in the kitchen. Betty tried to mention the fire once, but the scowl on Katie-Marie's face was enough to silence her.

Kathy was not so easily cowed.

"Ma, what exactly is going on here?" she demanded after the breakfast dishes were done and Betty had scurried away to feed the baby.

"It's just vandalism, Kathy." Distracted, Katie-Marie gathered together the ingredients for ice-box cookies. "Probably some young hooligans."

"What young hooligans?"

"Kathleen, I have no idea, and I'm not going to go gadding about, putting my nose where it don't belong."

"Ma! Somebody is attacking this farm. We have a right to find out who it is and put a stop to it."

Katie-Marie turned on her. "Knowing who it is won't necessarily put a stop to anything."

"Ma, you know who's doing this." Kathy advanced

on her mother.

"No, I don't." Katie-Marie pulled a mixing bowl from the cupboard and all but slammed it onto the counter. She turned to Kathy. "I promise you, Kathy, I really don't know."

"But you have your suspicions."

"None that'll do any of us any good." Sighing, she bent to measuring sugar and butter. "It ain't Mr. Spivens, or Mayor Standling or anybody else in town, but it seems that way sometimes. I get to thinking that maybe the whole town is against us, but I know that can't be. There's no reason for it at all." The older woman sniffed and shook it off. "It's just me being foolish and fearful."

"But, Ma, what if it is coming from town?"

"Well, it isn't the whole town, Kathy. That's ridiculous. Besides, we've been good neighbors. If that ain't enough, then there ain't a thing we can do about it. We've got our land, and we'll stand firm on it and protect it as best we can."

"That's what I'm trying to do."

"You'll do nothing, young lady." Katie-Marie advanced on her daughter, her eyes blazing. "I won't have you involved in this foolishness and risking your neck over it. There's only one thing I know about this vandalism, and it's that whoever's behind it ain't playing around. They mean business, girl, and I won't have you getting hurt over it. Do you understand me? You are not to play detective, nor is that man of yours. Is that clear?"

"Yes, ma'am." It was perfectly clear, but Kathy had absolutely no intention of obeying her mother, and it was quite probable that Katie-Marie knew it.

"All right. There'll be no more talk about it. We've got work to do."

Later that afternoon Kathy slid a cake into the oven, and checked the eight-day clock on the wall.

"The trouble with this whole business is that there's nothing concrete that points to anybody," she complained to Freddie, who had washed up and shaved after fixing the truck.

Freddie looked at the long whirl of peel he was removing from a potato.

"There was that car last night," he said. "Which direction was it coming from?"

"From town, but that doesn't mean anything." Kathy plopped down at the table and shelled peas. "There are all sorts of little roads and by-ways leading to farms and townships all around. Hell, they could even have cut across a field or two."

"And all the attacks seem to have occurred before midnight."

"Of course, this is farm country. People are in bed with the sun and up earlier. You'd stand a much better chance of getting caught at two a.m."

Freddie frowned. "It was a direct hit, too, as if they were aiming for that hay pile."

"It's the most logical place. You saw how fast it went up. If you and I hadn't been out there we could have lost the whole barn, and maybe even the rest of the place."

"But there's the problem. On one hand, the trouble seems to be directed by someone who knows this place intimately. Witness the direct hit on the hay pile. Yet, there is so little that is atypical here, that one could almost come from any farm and expect to be successful."

"And I'm the least suspicious of our neighbors." Kathy nibbled on a shell. "I can't think of anybody who hasn't called since Sunday night. We're even receiving presents."

"How many so far?"

"We got five delivered before lunch, and one just after. And I found out from Ma that it's the neighbors that are putting out the spread for the wedding dinner. Obviously, we're making some things. But the wedding cake, the meats, all the neighbors are bringing."

"How odd."

"That's just it, Freddie. It isn't. They've always

gotten together for group suppers. And past few years, with things getting so rough, they've started to do it for weddings, too. Didn't you hear Mrs. Tesch last night? Ma was so kind for her Muriel, and brought the chicken and dumplings."

"In other words, the neighbors have the least motive, but are the most able to vandalize the farm." Sullenly, Freddie rinsed another potato and took the knife to it.

"What in the name of all the saints?" Katie-Marie scuttled in and stopped. "Kathy, what are you thinking of, girl, putting poor Freddie to work like this?"

"I offered, Mother Briscow," said Freddie grinning amiably. "I am testing the theory of the dignity and nobility of woman's work. If it is so dignified and noble, it shouldn't diminish me to do it."

"Radicals, both of you." She picked up a peeling. "Nice and close."

"I got a lot of practice in the army."

Kathy giggled.

"I thought you'd be working on the truck still." Katie-Marie got out a roll of dough from the ice box.

"I finished about a half hour ago," said Freddie, picking up another potato. "And cleaned under my nails. I reassembled the steering this morning and tightened up the gear box. It may be a little stiffer than you're used to when you shift, but it will be better than falling out on the road. And I installed the cranking mechanism."

Katie-Marie gave him a hug. "Oh, Freddie, you're an angel of mercy. I hate to think what Jeb Carson would have asked to fix the blamed thing."

"It starts like a charm now. Even Gam can crank it."

Kathy eyed him. "You weren't letting him drive, were you?"

"His feet don't reach the pedals." Freddie focused on his peeling, hoping Kathy wouldn't ask if he'd let Isaac behind the wheel. Freddie felt it was only justice;

after all, Isaac had been grounded before his turn in the plane.

Katie-Marie cut slices of dough and put them on sheets.

"Ma, weren't you supposed to go to Mrs. Schultz's funeral today?" Kathy asked suddenly.

"It's tomorrow morning," said Katie-Marie. "Bill asked to put the viewing ahead 'til tonight. Guess he wanted to take some extra time with her. Is the cake in the oven?"

"Yes. It should come out in... twenty minutes. I'm done with the peas." Kathy set the bowl aside and dumped the shells into the pig bucket.

"And that's the last of the potatoes." Freddie dropped the peeling onto the newspaper.

Katie-Marie smiled. "Looks like we're a bit ahead of things. Why don't you two go off and spend some time by yourselves?"

Kathy grinned. "I think you might be able to convince me."

Chuckling, Freddie seductively pulled the tie loose on Kathy's apron. Kathy giggled.

"There'll be none of that now," warned Katie-Marie. "Or I'll be sending Gammers with you."

"No need for that, Mother Briscow," said Freddie, pecking her cheek. "There's no more hay pile."

He swept Kathy out of the kitchen before Katie-Marie could reply. Kathy made a point of walking apart.

"It's just until she can't see us anymore," Kathy said. "I don't particularly want Gammers around."

"We seem to be heading towards the woods."

"Mm-hmm. The hay pile wasn't the only spot good for spooning on this place."

Under the cool shade of the trees, Kathy took off her shoes and stockings. Freddie watched, amused.

"My, you are a brazen woman," he teased.

Kathy dumped them at the foot of a tree. "Shocking isn't it? I spent most of my summers barefoot. Get a little closer to the stream, and the mud is wonderfully oozy and cool, and a perfect delight between the toes. It's not very lady-like, but I think that's when I began to realize lady-like was a dreadful bore. You do realize, men get to do all the really interesting things."

"Given how boring my life's been I'd be inclined to argue, but then I understand, I'm not typical."

"In no way, shape or form, luckily for me."

They ambled along the stream for a bit. Kathy splashed in the water, even splashed Freddie until he caught her and threatened to dump her full in.

"That's not very gentlemanly," she complained, laughing.

"It's not very manly to let you take unfair advantage of me, and I don't care to get wet at the moment."

She rinsed her feet, then dashed off through the trees. Freddie scrambled to follow. He nearly bumped into her when she stopped abruptly.

A long knotted rope hung down from branches, balancing a plank floor.

"Josh's tree house," said Kathy. She took the rope. "Looks like Gammers and Isaac have moved in."

Suddenly, she hoisted herself up.

"Should you trespass?" asked Freddie.

"I've had to many a time before. Josh used to kidnap my dolls and hold them for ransom." She glanced down at him. "Are you looking up my dress?"

Freddie grinned. "I have good reason to believe you'd be disappointed if I didn't."

"Come on up."

"If I must."

Taking a deep breath, Freddie struggled up the rope. To his surprise, the tree house was spacious and without a roof. Kathy pulled up the rope and let down the trap door. She nodded at the two bedrolls and pillows.

"Looks like the boys have been camping out here," she said.

Freddie poked one, and smiled. "You realize, of

course, we are quite alone."

Kathy smiled back. "With little likelihood of interruption. It's getting close to milking time, and there are afternoon chores to be done."

"It's not the softest of bowers."

"I don't mind."

Kneeling, Freddie reached over and kissed her mouth, one hand on her shoulder, the other slipping up the sleeve of her work dress.

"Then, my dearest Kathy, it is now our time," he whispered.

They kissed again, as she opened his shirt, and he lifted her dress. Ever, the gentleman, Freddie rolled back, letting her use him as a cushion. The magic, the tenderness was there as they played and explored. Kathy rolled under the deliciousness of his hands, easing her kisses down his neck to his chest, unbuttoning the front of his union suit. Freddie purred, and pressed her body closer to his.

Kathy hesitated.

"Is something wrong?" asked Freddie.

"Nothing." Laughing, Kathy kissed his lips and sighed as his hands found her breasts. "I just keep thinking I see someone watching us through that knothole."

Freddie slid his hand inside her camisole. "Is there?"

Languidly, Kathy kissed him behind his jaw, then looked and yelped.

"What?" Worried, Freddie scrambled around and looked through the knothole in the floor.

Below was the naked body of a young boy with corn silk hair, his skin a bluish deathly white, with ghastly brownish bruises around his neck and older bruises on his shoulder. Someone had smoothed down the death swelling, and tucked the tongue back in, but the blue eyes still stared. Freddie groaned, his heart in his throat.

"We can't ignore this," he grumbled.

Kathy had her face in her hand. "No. We can't."

Freddie kissed her forehead. "Let's go."

The boy was in the bracken on the far side of the tree, which was why they hadn't seen him before. Kathy shut his eyes.

"We can't let Gammers see this," said Freddie, suddenly concerned.

"I suppose not. It is pretty ghastly. I've never seen him before. Maybe Isaac would know."

"I say we don't let him look. I wonder if this is Mr. Tipton's runaway."

"Runaway?"

"Yes. I heard him order one of his workers to call the boys' home in Topeka to send another. And the woman customer there ahead of me said this was the third runaway in a year."

"But this boy didn't run away. It looks like he was strangled," Kathy said.

"Yes, it does." Freddie held his breath, hoping she wouldn't remark on the shoulder bruises.

"We'll have to send for the sheriff, and get Bill," Kathy said.

"Let's go, then. He'll be all right for the moment."

They hurried back to the farm house, stopping only to get Kathy's shoes and stockings. Gideon saw them first, and called the others.

"You two look awful," gasped Betty.

"We found a body in the woods," said Freddie.

Gam's eyes opened wide. "Really? Can I see?"

"No!" Freddie grabbed him and held him back. "Gammers, why don't you run into town and get Bill Javits and—"

"No!" Gam screamed and ran into the house.

Freddie gazed after him, shocked, and suddenly aware of who Gam's tormentor had been.

"Gamaliel!" cried Katie-Marie.

"Let him be," said Freddie quietly.

"Isaac, you go into town—" started Kathy.

"No," snapped Freddie. "Gideon, you go. And get

the sheriff, too."

"I'll take the mare," said Gideon.

Abraham trotted after. "I'll help saddle. It'll be faster than cranking."

"We've got to keep Gammers out of that woods," said Freddie softly.

"If it's just a dead body," began Katie-Marie.

"It's a boy, Ma," said Kathy.

"A boy?" asked Isaac. "I ain't heard of anybody missing."

Gideon ran the mare out of the barn at a gallop, running across the fields towards town.

"The body's pretty cold, too," added Kathy. "We would have heard something by now."

"It'll keep," said Katie-Marie. "Let's get you two set down and some hot coffee in you."

By the time the sheriff's Model T chugged into the farm yard, Freddie and Kathy were both recovered from their shock. They led Wimberton straight to the treehouse, with Abraham and Joshua on their heels. Gideon trotted up on the horse.

"Bill's not there yet," he announced. "Teresa says she'll tell him as soon as he gets in."

He swung himself off the mare and led her through the trees. As they neared the treehouse, the horse shied and whinnied. Freddie's head shot up.

"I thought I heard a car," he said.

Kathy shrugged as Wimberton glared.

"Can we get this over with?" he demanded.

"It's right this way," said Freddie.

But it wasn't there. Kathy gasped.

"It was right here." She looked up. "There's the knot hole. That's how we spotted it, through the knot hole."

"What were you two doing up in the treehouse?" asked Gideon.

"What do you think?" said Abraham as Joshua snickered and Freddie and Kathy glared.

"I don't see nothing," Wimberton grumbled.

"Sheriff, it was there," pressed Freddie. "It was the body of a young boy. He'd been strangled."

"Uh-huh." Wimberton was not convinced. "I've got half a mind to run you in for getting me out here on a wild goose chase."

"Sheriff, you can't do that," said Abraham. "Gideon made the call, and it was on good faith."

"I don't see a body."

Abraham folded his arms. "Then you have no habeas corpus, which means there is no crime here, and no willful intent that you can prove. Furthermore, the horse shied as we got close, and I can see signs in this bracken that something was here, and it's not mashed enough to have been those two. You run Mr. Little in, and he'll be able to bring suit against you and this town for false arrest."

Wimberton snarled, and stalked off back to his car.

"I knew there was something to be said for attorneys," said Freddie as soon as the sheriff was out of earshot.

"But what about that body?" groaned Kathy.

"Are you sure that's what you saw, Kathy?" asked Joshua.

"We're very sure," said Freddie. "And it was definitely dead."

The mare nickered nervously. Freddie looked around the ground leading to the stream.

"Something's got the mare spooked," said Gideon.

"I think it was a body," said Abraham. "But why dump it here, and why take it back so quickly?"

"Somebody probably wants to discredit us," said Kathy.

"Who?" asked Joshua. "And why?"

"Why is easy," said Kathy. "The next time we report something to Wimberton, he won't come out quite as quickly."

"He weren't breaking any land speed records this time," grumbled Gideon.

Several paces away, on the other side of the stream, Freddie bent to the ground. Tire tracks.

"Chevrolet," he muttered. He couldn't be sure, but he was willing to put money on it. He looked down the path, then turned back to Kathy and her brothers. "Gideon, let me take the horse."

"Sure, if you want."

"Freddie, do you know how to ride?" Kathy asked, as he took the reins.

"Four years of dressage and jumping in prep school." Freddie mounted up. "I'd damn well better."

He kicked the horse into a run, ducking under the branches.

"He looks like he knows what he's doing," said Joshua.

"Wonder where he's headed," said Abraham.

Kathy thought. Someone had smoothed the death swelling from the face.

"I think I know." She turned and headed back towards the house. "I'm going into town after him."

She rinsed her feet off quickly in the kitchen sink, and put on her stockings and shoes as Katie-Marie protested about immodesty and getting in the way of supper preparations.

"I'm taking the truck," she announced, as she banged through the screen door.

"Kathy, you don't know how to drive," scolded Katie-Marie as she hurried out after her daughter.

"Yes, I do." Kathy opened the tool shed. "Freddie taught me last spring." She got behind the wheel and stopped. "Drat. He has an electric starter."

"I'll crank it," said Katie-Marie.

Freddie had no reason to believe he'd catch his quarry, but he did run him to earth in town. The Chevrolet was still parked in the alley behind the funeral home. Freddie found a hitching post at the corner, and tied the horse up. He went straight through the front of the funeral home with its heavily curtained windows, past the viewing room where Mrs. Schultz was set up, into Bill Javits' office at the back. Bill sat cowering at his rolltop desk.

Teresa held Rachel, who was screaming again, and ordered Bill out to the farm.

"I talked to the sheriff," Bill protested weakly.

"If Gideon says there's a body out there, there's a body out there," snapped Teresa.

"But Sheriff Wimberton says it was a hoax," whined Bill.

"It may have appeared so to the sheriff," said Freddie. "But it was no hoax. And I think I know where that body is."

"Freddie!" Teresa suddenly broke into a grin. "I told you, didn't I? Congratulations, darling."

"Thank you, Teresa. Now, I'd like to have a word with your husband."

Bill quaked. Either Teresa did not notice, or it was his usual reaction to being confronted by almost brothers-in-law.

"Go ahead," she said, not moving.

"Alone," said Freddie firmly.

Teresa nudged her cowering husband.

"N-now see here," stammered Bill. "You can't order my wife around."

"I can strongly recommend that she leave." Freddie folded his arms, his glower threatening.

"I'd better check on the children," said Teresa, escaping to the house across the yard.

Silence slowly filled the room.

"I want to know about that body," said Freddie. "Someone had prettied it up, and you're the only one in the neighborhood."

"I—I know." Shaken, Bill swallowed and looked around frantically. "Of course I worked on it. It—it was a charity case. A foundling come upon hard times and a tragic accident, I guess. Sh-Sheriff Wimberton brought him in, and took him away, I guess. I didn't take him from the shop."

"Wimberton took him away?"

"Of course. He always sees to the burying. It's all done very discreetly. Can't upset the town, you know."

"Heaven forbid."

"It—it—it must have been stolen from the sheriff. He wouldn't say anything. Would look too foolish, losing a stiff."

"True. But in this case, the stiff is a boy, a naked boy."

"I hadn't dressed him yet."

"Be that as it may." Freddie bore down on him. "There is another boy in this town, and I've got a bad feeling you've been working on him, too. Only he's alive, and what you've been doing I wouldn't wish on a dog!"

Javits went white, and he slumped in his seat. "I didn't do it. I don't care what the little beast said. I didn't touch him, honest."

Tears fell down his cheeks. Freddie yanked him out of the chair.

"How do you know who I'm talking about, then?" he yelled.

Javits squeaked and twisted out of Freddie's grasp.

"I didn't do it!" he cried, running for the front. "I didn't touch him. I didn't. I didn't!"

Freddie chased after and almost caught him. Javits slipped free and darted out the front door. Freddie pounced and slammed him back first against the windows of the shop. He braced his forearm across Javits' neck.

"Don't lie to me, Javits," he said softly at first. "I've seen things, I know the signs. If you ever touch Gamaliel Briscow—"

Javits squeaked in terror. Freddie half-smiled grimly.

"I know you did it to him," Freddie growled.

Javits whimpered and nodded.

"If you ever touch him again," said Freddie, his voice rising, "rest assured I will know, and you won't have to worry about buckshot, because I will come here and wring your neck bare-handed."

Still furious, Freddie released the whimpering man and shoved him back into the funeral home. Turning, he saw the shocked stares of an older woman and her not so young daughter.

"My apologies, ladies," he said, nodding. "Just a family matter." He smiled weakly. "A little threat can do wonders."

He stepped around them, still shaking with anger. The mare waited patiently. Freddie took a deep breath. A ride would be relaxing.

Chapter Eleven

Kathy found Bill Javits just inside the outer door, curled up next to a coffin, and sobbing.

"Bill, what happened?" she asked, kneeling next to him.

Javits sobbed and shook his head.

"I'm not going to hurt you, Bill."

He wouldn't respond. Kathy left him, and ran across the yard to the house next to the funeral home.

"Teresa, do you have any smelling salts?" she asked, going into the kitchen.

"What for?" grumbled Teresa, busy making dinner for the whining children at her feet.

"Your husband. He's just inside the funeral home door, practically catatonic."

"Oh my god!" Teresa turned on Kathy. "What did Freddie do to him?"

"He's already been here? How did I miss him?"

"He's been here all right. Insulting Bill, ordering me around."

"You? Take someone else's orders?"

"And if something's wrong with Bill, Freddie did it to him."

Kathy groaned. "Where are the smelling salts,

Teresa?"

"In Bill's desk. And in the viewing room. We keep them for the mourners. What are you going to do about Freddie?"

Kathy stomped to the door. "I'm going to find out what happened, first!"

She hurried across the yard to the clatter of Teresa taking pans off the stove and slamming them onto the counter. Kathy found the smelling salts on the desk in the back office, then went to the front. Javits was still sobbing.

Kathy held the bottle under his nose. He jerked.

"Feel better?" Kathy asked.

"No," sighed Javits. "I'm ruined."

"Bill, that's ridiculous," said Teresa coming in, without Rachel in tow for once. "Freddie Little can't do a thing to you."

"He's not going to do anything in the first place," groaned Kathy. "Just because he's not from this place doesn't mean he's some sort of monster."

Javits trembled. "The boy, he died yesterday."

"Boy? The body!" Kathy lifted Javits' head. "Bill, what do you know about that?"

"There's nothing to know," said Teresa. "It came in yesterday. Bill does charity cases all the time. Sheriff Wimberton brings them in, maybe once a year or so. Sometimes Mr. Tipton does. We just keep it quiet because they're all vagrants and the like. No point in alarming the town with how bad the situation is."

"Bill, is that true?"

"Of course it's true," said Teresa.

"Shut up, Teresa!" roared Kathy. She turned back to Bill. "Bill, did somebody take the boy? Maybe they broke in, and you didn't want to frighten Teresa. What happened to it?"

"Wimberton took it, I think." Javits sniffed. "It was gone this morning. I went looking for it. Kathy, I didn't kill him. I didn't."

"Did Freddie think you had?"

Javits sobbed and shook his head.

"Then who killed that boy?" Kathy asked gently.

Javits started to speak, then stopped. "I don't know. I really don't know."

"But you think you know."

"I don't know," Javits sobbed. "I don't know."

"Kathy, that's enough," snapped Teresa. "I don't know what you hope to achieve by browbeating him like this, but I won't take it anymore."

"I'm trying to find what's happening to Ma and Pa's farm," said Kathy angrily as she got up.

"And what about Freddie?"

"What about him? He's trying to find the same thing."

"He didn't have to come in here and beat up on my husband like a bully."

Kathy's temper snapped. "Freddie is no bully. He would never strike anyone unless he was attacked. I don't see any signs of it on Bill."

Javits sobbed, and Teresa flew to his side.

"Don't worry, darling," she cooed. "She just has to stand up for her man is all."

"I'm going to be sick to my stomach," growled Kathy. "Good-bye!"

She left the shop and looked around the street, hoping to find some sign of Freddie. He was gone. She hadn't seen him on the road to town. Perhaps on the road to Ellis. She cranked up the truck and got it going without too much difficulty. She'd been a little surprised at how different it was from Freddie's Cadillac, but the principles remained the same. She backed up, turned, and headed out.

She spotted the lone rider on a small dirt path heading towards her parents' woods. She braked quickly, tried to turn, let out the clutch too fast and stalled the truck. Cursing, she squawked the horn. At least the rider looked up and turned.

She primed the engine hard, then scrambled around front to crank it. It didn't catch. She primed it again and went around front and cranked, with no luck. Freddie stopped her as she started for the driver's seat for a third time.

"Easy," he teased. "You've flooded it."

"Stupid machine." She kicked a tire.

Freddie shook his head. "It will start in a minute or two."

"Where have you been?" she asked, sitting on the running board. "And what did you do to Bill?"

"I've been taking a restful ride in the country." Freddie sighed. "I was forced to raise my voice with Bill, and I find it a very unsettling experience."

"Is that all you did?" Kathy rolled her eyes. "Teresa swears you laid hands on him and beat him to a pulp."

"I did have to catch and pin him, but no blows were struck."

"Did you find anything out about that body?"

"He worked on it as a charity case, and assumes it was some unfortunate vagrant boy."

"He told me he died yesterday." Kathy stood up and straightened her dress. "He seems to think Wimberton took it."

"Apparently he sees to the burials of these cases."

"Oh. But guess what else. Tipton, the banker, also brings them in."

"Tipton?" Freddie grimaced. "Could the boy not have been a runaway after all?"

"It's possible. I asked Bill who killed the boy. He said he didn't know, but I'm pretty certain he thinks he does. I couldn't get him to say before Teresa got over-protective."

"So we've got exactly what we had before. Nothing."

Kathy looked him over fondly. "Why don't you ride on home?"

"Perhaps I ought to take the truck." Freddie brushed her hair gently.

"I'll kick you."

Freddie made it to the farm well ahead of Kathy, but stayed in the barn unsaddling the horse and otherwise hiding until she arrived. They entered the kitchen together under the suspicious glare of Katie-Marie. The family was already eating supper. Freddie apologized as they sat down.

"Where have you been?" asked Katie-Marie.

"We went to talk to Bill and Teresa," said Kathy sourly. "You knew that."

"All this time?" asked Katie-Marie.

"I did go look for Freddie afterwards." Kathy glared at her brothers, who were snickering.

"Nothing untoward happened," said Freddie testily.

"I wouldn't bet on that," chuckled Joshua.

"If it did, do you think we'd be in such rotten moods?" snapped Kathy.

"She has a point." Abraham leaned over to Joshua. "That is not the look of a satisfied woman."

"How would you know, Abraham?" asked Joshua.

Abraham cleared his throat. "I have very reliable sources."

"That's enough of that sort of talk at this table," said Katie-Marie firmly. "We've got plans to make for tomorrow, and I don't doubt we'll be having visitors tonight. Now, Freddie, what time did you say your guests will be coming in?"

"I believe the two thirty train."

Katie-Marie nodded.

As anticipated, there was a flood of visitors and gifts which Kathy dutifully oohed and aahed over, and for which Freddie mentally made space in his Adirondack cabin. It was late by the time everybody left. Katie-Marie made it clear there would be no talking on the porch swing that night.

"The boys are watching, and you've got to get up early, Kathy. You need your rest."

"As if I'll get any," sighed Kathy, when she was at last given a minute alone with Freddie.

"If it's any comfort, I'm beginning to get a touch of the nerves myself."

"Are we doing the right thing?"

Freddie lifted her chin and looked into her eyes. "Yes. I'm certain of it."

She smiled softly. "Then I shall trust you."

He pulled her into his arms...

"Kathy! Are you coming?"

"Just a minute, Ma!"

Freddie chuckled. "Tomorrow night they won't be able to stop us."

"I'll try and concentrate on that, then."

She reached up and they kissed.

The next morning was not particularly good for anyone, but especially not for Freddie or Kathy. Freddie borrowed the Model T truck to drive his trunk into town, got Kathy's money from Western Union, picked up the rings, then struggled to get his room checked in at the hotel. Then Teresa caught him and lit into him again. He ran to where he'd parked the truck and hurried back to the farm.

Meanwhile, at the farm, it was generally acknowledged from the moment anyone spoke to her, that the best way to deal with Kathy that morning was to keep one's distance. Even Jacob couldn't match her for cussedness, and voluntarily remained in the study.

The question of who would meet the train got reopened in light of Freddie's confrontation with Teresa. The decision was made, but a trifle late.

The train was early. Honoria Wentworth, almost as tall as her brother, Freddie, and dressed in a green silk travelling suit that set off her hazel eyes, looked at the little platform and station building and back at the conductor. Her matching cloche hat covered up most of her light brown hair.

"You're sure this is it?" she asked, giggling.

"I been running this route twelve years, ma'am."

"It's too charming," she said.

"It's a backwater and a hellhole," snarled Lowell Winters, behind her. He was of average height but very stout, especially about the middle. His hair was dark, thick, and wavy and his moustache was thick and full. "Are we getting off or has common sense actually taken root in you, and we're fleeing this pockmark called a town?"

"This is where Freddie said to get off." Honoria exchanged a look of long suffering patience with the conductor, who understood. He'd been listening to Lowell since Topeka.

They exited the train with a couple of obvious salesman. Down the way, a mother greeted her grown son.

"I don't see any porters," said Honoria.

"Good God, woman, this is Kansas!" growled Lowell. "A desolate, barren wasteland of wheat and farmhands. Poor Freddie is certainly suffering the worst of fates here."

"Second only to having you as a traveling companion." Honoria giggled and got out her cigarette holder and a cigarette. "I think it's perfectly charming. Do you have a light, Lowell?"

"I wouldn't smoke that around here, not unless you want to be considered competition for the local whorehouse."

"I never met a ruder man." Honoria nonetheless replaced the smoking equipment in her purse. "I wonder where Freddie is."

A battered Model T truck chugged up to the station. The two young men that jumped out were obviously brothers, of average height and not unattractive, Honoria noted with pleasure. They left the motor running. There was something slightly familiar about them, but she couldn't quite put her finger on it. Then again, there was something significant about Hays, Kansas, too, and she couldn't quite connect it, either.

"Are you Mrs. Wentworth?" asked the younger of the two new arrivals.

Honoria smiled. "Yes. And this is Mr. Winters."

"Pleasure to meet you folks," said the slightly older

one. "Freddie asked us to come get you. I'm Joshua Briscow, and this my brother, Abraham."

"It's a pleasure to meet you!" Laughing, Honoria turned to Lowell. "I told you this had something to do with Kathy." She turned to Joshua and Abraham. "The last time my brother was seen in New York he was escorting Kathy Briscow away from her boarding house, and neither of them have been seen since."

"It's his new book, Honoria," grumbled Lowell. "He was having trouble with it."

"Not enough to take him to Kansas." Honoria smiled at the boys. "You're related to Kathy Briscow, aren't you?"

"She's our sister," said Abraham.

"This is too exciting! We got the most mysterious telegrams from Freddie Monday, telling us to get out here, or we would be certain to regret it. He must have found the most intriguing investment or something. I can't wait to find out what the surprise is."

Joshua and Abraham looked at each and just barely contained their laughter.

"Uh, Freddie said to take you over to the hotel and get you checked in, then Ma says you're to come out to the house," said Joshua. "You got trunks?"

"Over here," snarled Lowell.

"You'll have to forgive Lowell," explained Honoria. "He's a journeyman curmudgeon. Liquor him up a bit and he will mellow, though."

"You got some New York hootch?" asked Abraham eagerly. "I tell you that stuff Freddie had was the best I'd tasted."

"Oh, dear, is it a bit dry out here?" asked Honoria.

"Blasted state has been dry since eighteen eighty," snarled Lowell.

"And Ma's a temperance lady," sighed Joshua as he carried Honoria's trunk to the truck.

"Just don't let her know you got it," said Abraham. "Or anyone else. Plenty of people around here drink, but they get real funny about strangers, especially city folk."

"Further confirmation that my decision to leave the farm was pure inspiration and not to be regretted," said Lowell as he followed Joshua and Abraham to the truck.

"You a farm boy, Mr. Winters?" asked Joshua.

"Iowa born and raised, and mercifully rescued from by our senator, who saw that I was not fit for a plow and sent me packing to Harvard University."

"Let me help you up, Mrs. Wentworth," said Abraham, suiting action to word. "Sorry it's not a real fancy rig, but it's the best we got."

"It's too charming." Honoria smiled as she settled herself into the truck's front seat.

Joshua climbed behind the wheel.

"Hey, I can drive," said Abraham.

"I'm older. Get in the back with Mr. Winters."

"Wait 'til Betty hears about this."

"Your lady friend?" asked Honoria pleasantly.

"His wife," put in Abraham. "They're newlyweds, and they got a two-month old baby."

Joshua gunned the motor and backed out. "Freddie said he's sorry he couldn't come get you himself. But my sister came after him today. Followed him all the way around town, and gave him a tongue lashing he won't soon forget."

"He probably got fresh again," said Honoria.

"Not in a month of Sundays," laughed Joshua. "He hates Teresa."

"Teresa?"

"My other sister. She's younger. Kathy's at the farm. Anyway, Freddie gave Bill, that's Teresa's husband, what for yesterday, and Bill was so upset he barely pulled himself together to lead Mrs. Schultz's funeral this morning."

"Freddie gave somebody what for?" said Lowell. "It's about time."

"It probably wasn't much," said Abraham. "Bill's a rabbit. Look at him wrong and he shakes. But Teresa's hell, and Freddie figured he'd better not go back to town until he had to."

"What's this Bill doing leading a funeral?" asked Honoria.

"He's the undertaker," said Joshua.

"He's not strange, like you'd think," said Abraham. "Just chicken."

Joshua stopped the truck and cut the engine. "Here we are. Best place in town."

"That does not bode well," grumbled Lowell. "Unfortunately, I am all too familiar with what to expect."

"It's perfectly charming, Lowell," said Honoria.

Abraham hurried around to her side and helped her out. He and Joshua got the trunks inside. Honoria rang the desk bell. Mr. Spivens appeared, took one look at Honoria's lean, stylish figure, and smiled.

"How can I help you, ma'am?" he asked.

"I'm Mrs. Honoria Wentworth," she said, smiling warmly. "And that cur over there is Mr. Lowell Winters. I understand we have rooms reserved for us here at this perfectly charming inn."

"You're Mrs. Wentworth, eh?" Mr. Spivens was taken aback, not sure whether to be irritated because of the connection to Mr. Little, or captivated by the charmingly flirtatious young woman in front of him. "I had figured on someone a little older."

Honoria laughed. "Embarrassing, isn't it? But I'm a war widow, dear, and married young at that. Our rooms?"

"Yes. Eh, right away. Just sign here, please."

Honoria scribbled. "Lowell, your turn."

Lowell signed without a snarl, strangely enough, and retreated. Spivens handed over the keys and even called for bellhops. Abraham and Joshua looked at each other and sniggered.

"Uh, Mrs. Wentworth, we gotta run one more errand," said Joshua. "Why don't you and Mr. Winters get settled and meet us out front in five, ten minutes?"

"Sounds perfect. We will." Honoria turned with a little wiggle for Spivens' benefit and followed the bellhops.

Joshua and Abraham left the hotel, sighing.

"Freddie has some sister," said Abraham.

"No fooling." Joshua glanced back at the hotel. "Are all those big city girls like that?"

"A couple. The kind with a lot of money. But even there, she's got a few tricks up her sleeve. She's a lot like Freddie that way. You know, acts really carefree and kind of simple, but real smart. That kind is dangerous."

Joshua nudged him. "I hear you like playing with fire."

Abraham grinned. "Yeah. Didn't Freddie say she's only a year older than me?"

"Something like that."

They laughed lecherously, and headed for the bank. Once there, Joshua went to one of the tellers and asked to see Mr. Tipton. Mr. Tipton appeared, decidedly out of sorts.

"What is it?" he demanded.

"I'm Joshua Briscow. Mr. Freddie Little tried to cash a check Monday and you needed a couple days to clear it. He asked me to pick the money up for him."

"This is highly irregular," snapped Tipton.

"I got a note here from him." Joshua handed it over. "He couldn't make it himself. He's marrying my sister tonight. He'll know how to catch me."

"I'm not in the least concerned about that, Mr. Briscow." Tipton glared at the note. "It seems in order. Mr. Pomfret, have you prepared Mr. Little's draft?"

"Right here, Mr. Tipton." The teller held up a paper envelope.

Joshua took the envelope and met Abraham just outside the door.

"How much is there?" asked Abraham.

"Shit!"

"What?"

"He's got five hundred bucks here!"

"Let me see." Abraham rifled through the bills. "Shit. Wonder where he's taking Kathy for the honeymoon."

"They could go to Europe on this." Joshua put the envelope in his front pants pocket. "Better keep this next to the valuables."

Some minutes later, the truck was cranked and Honoria seated up front with Joshua driving and Abraham and Lowell in the back.

"I got my car at the farm," said Joshua. "But it broke down this morning. Freddie's fixing it now."

"Oh no, not the grease again." Honoria laughed. "He's a perfect fiend for it, isn't he, Lowell?"

"Among other things."

"How's the hotel?" Abraham asked.

"Abysmal," said Lowell.

"It's too charming," said Honoria. "Pity there isn't anyone to unpack. I hate that dreary little chore. But roughing it won't hurt me. Obviously, you gentlemen are in the know as far as Freddie's little surprise. Would you mind enlightening me?"

Abraham laughed. "We absolutely mind. We like surprises, and if Freddie can stand up to Teresa, we don't want to stand up to him."

Honoria giggled. But Joshua and Abraham were on to her, and refused to divulge a whisper.

Kathy was sorting out linens in the living room when she heard the truck returning. She looked out the window and groaned. The dog also announced the new arrival. Gam peeked around the house and ran for the tool shed.

"Freddie! They're here!" he called.

Freddie was cleaning himself off in a bucket of freshly heated water.

"Great," he said through the soap suds, and ducked his head into the water.

Sudden doubts rippled through him, as they had

all morning. But something about Honoria and Lowell knowing what he intended made the whole weird spectacle a reality for the first time. He swallowed, then toweled off.

"This is too charming!" Honoria announced as Abraham helped her from the truck.

Freddie walked up. "Hallo, Mrs. Wentworth."

"Freddie!" Honoria quickly gave him an affectionate buss. "What is going on? I'm dying to know."

"Let me say hello to Lowell first." Freddie stepped around and took Lowell's hand.

"Freddie." Lowell shook and stepped back. "Far be it from me to agree with this wench here, but you've kept us on pins and needles long enough."

"Well..." Freddie took a deep breath and noticed Gam. Isaac and Betty were coming out from the henhouse, with Gideon coming out of the barn. The screen door banged as Katie-Marie came out, holding Little J. "Gammers, why don't you go get Kathy?"

Gam grimaced. "Do I have to?"

"Kathy?" called Katie-Marie. "Come on out. Freddie's guests are here."

There was a tense silence as the whole yard waited. The screen door creaked, and Kathy stepped out. She tried not to frown at the crowd in the yard. Freddie had obviously not told Honoria or Lowell yet, damn him. Taking a deep breath, she walked over to the new arrivals.

Honoria was puzzled. Something very strange was up. Kathy was not happy about it, either. And she moved so stiffly, too, as if she were forcing herself. Yet she and Honoria were reasonably close friends.

"Hello, Honoria," said Kathy, softly brushing Honoria's cheek with hers. "Nice to see you again, Lowell."

"I wish I could say the same, Briscow," snapped Lowell, rhyming her name with cow, as he always did. "Freddie's got us all up in the air about something, and it's getting ridiculous."

Isaac laughed, and clamped both hands over his mouth. Kathy glared at him.

"Freddie, have you made the introductions yet?" Kathy asked nervously.

"I was waiting for you," said Freddie, feeling very nervous and not at all sure how to break the news.

"I don't see why." Kathy's smile was forced, and Freddie knew he'd better break the news, or Kathy would make him regret it.

"Are you sure you don't want to explain?" he asked hopefully.

"They're your guests, Freddie."

"Yes." He swallowed, at last without hope. "Well, Honoria, Lowell. I asked you out here to witness a very special event tonight."

"Event?" asked Honoria, completely confused.

"No, damn it!" groaned Lowell. "Freddie, you fool, you didn't."

"I did, I'm afraid, Lowell." Freddie took Kathy's hand. "Tonight, Kathy and I will be joined together in wedlock."

Kathy's face burned, and she took her hand back. Honoria's mouth fell open.

"The world is certainly coming to an end," complained Lowell.

"You're getting married?" Honoria all but shrieked. "Freddie!"

Gideon guffawed. "Pa got the shotgun out."

Honoria laughed. "That's too perfect! Especially for you, Freddie. I wish I'd thought of that years ago."

Joshua laughed even louder. "Pa got it out to get Kathy down the aisle!"

"Joshua!" groaned Kathy. "Freddie, will you please make the introductions? I've got to get back inside. Excuse me."

She hurried off.

Freddie sighed. "She's a little nervous."

"Nervous?" Abraham snorted. "She's touchier than a mean horse with a burr under its saddle."

Freddie ignored him, recovered himself, and made the introductions, continuing inside to the study to meet Jacob. Katie-Marie quickly shooed everyone out, although Lowell stayed behind to complain and generally shoot the breeze with Jacob. In the hallway, Honoria noticed Kathy sitting in the living room. Letting the crowd cover her, she slipped back into the room.

"Hello," she said softly.

Kathy sniffed and dabbed at her eyes with one of Freddie's handkerchiefs.

"Hello," she answered even more softly.

"You seem a little put off by all this." Honoria wound her way through the boxes and sat down next to Kathy.

"It was a little sudden."

"So I heard. I just met your father. He doesn't quite seem the type."

"He is." Kathy sniffed. "No, he's not. He only got the gun out because he knew Freddie and I wanted each other, and we weren't going to do anything about it without a good push. At least, I wasn't."

"You do love Freddie, don't you?"

"Yes. Very much. It's not him, Honoria. Believe me, it isn't."

"It's getting married. I'm so glad I did it on the spur of the moment. No chance to think about it, because if I had, I don't think I would have done it."

"Did you love your husband?"

Honoria smiled. "For someone I hardly knew, yes. It was so strange. There we were, doing all these terribly intimate things that I'd never even heard of. I didn't know how babies were made until my wedding night, and Henry had to tell me, and he was barely more than a total stranger."

"I wonder how well I know Freddie. I keep thinking I do, and then he does something that completely surprises me."

"If it will make you feel any better, he does it to

me, too, and I've known him all my life."

"I wanted to be his lover, Honoria, not his wife."

Honoria shook her head. "That's not Freddie. He won't leave you that vulnerable."

"I know. That's why I'm marrying him." Kathy started to cry. "It's so awful. I'm damned if I marry him, and damned if I don't. Freddie didn't tell you in the telegram because if anyone in New York finds out we're married, I'll never be able to work. I've fought so hard to get as far as I have. I don't want to toss it all. The sad part is, I'd run the exact same risk as his lover. I'll get fired just as easily, and won't be able to get another job. And Freddie's right. At least as his wife I'll be able to get something back if everything goes sour."

"Do you want me to help?"

"We'll have to make some arrangement. Freddie and I aren't even sure where we're going to live after we get back. If you'll just avoid planning it out for us, it would be a help. Freddie doesn't always like what you come up with, but he would never say so."

"I usually weasel it out of him sooner or later. In any case, I and my apartment are at your disposal. I don't even mind moving, if you think it's necessary. Or I'll stay put and cover for you. Whatever." Honoria put her hand on Kathy's. "I'm glad it's you that's marrying him. Of all of Freddie's girlfriends that he's had, I've always liked you best. Even out of the couple mistresses I've managed to meet. Of course, he'd never marry them."

"No. He'd never do that."

"I've tried, Kathy." Honoria shrugged. "But you have to admit, he does have very modern ideas for a man."

"Very modern." Kathy managed a smile at Freddie's desire to make their marriage one of equals. It was impossible, of course. But at least he wanted to try. All in all, it really wasn't a bad compromise. "Thank you, Honoria. You're very encouraging."

Chapter Twelve

"I just love weddings!" Honoria crowed a few minutes later in the room Kathy was sharing with her mother.

Kathy smiled indulgently as she opened the box that contained the wedding dress.

"It was the best they had," she explained timidly.

"Kathy, it's perfect. It's too charming. It's just right for you."

"I feel so foolish in it."

Honoria laughed. "That's just like you, Kathy. Is it because you're an old maid? Goodness, darling, you're not fifty. You're not even thirty. If anyone wants to fuss at you for marrying so late, tell them you waited for the rich man."

"I don't think Freddie would appreciate that." Kathy chuckled herself.

Downstairs, a baby howled.

"Oh no," groaned Kathy. "Rachel."

"That's not that cute little dickens of your brother's is it?"

"No. Rachel is my sister's beast. She's teething."

Honoria frowned. "That's right. That's supposed to be hard on them, isn't it?"

"It is on Rachel. I guess Teresa couldn't get rid of her for the evening. At least Ma's already sent Freddie to the hotel. You wouldn't happen to have a flask with you, would you?"

Honoria opened her purse. "I'm never without one."

"Let's pretend it's Freddie's." Kathy took it. "It's a little trick of the mothering trade. Put whiskey on the gums of teething babes, and it shuts them up. Or it shuts Rachel up. Let's go."

Teresa was in the kitchen, still complaining about Freddie over Rachel's screams. Katie-Marie was trying to ignore the complaints and the screaming. Betty was taking advantage of all the men being gone to the church already, except for Jacob, who was hiding in the study. She sat comfortably breastfeeding Little J at the table.

"I've got Freddie's flask," Kathy announced, coming in.

"Thank you," sighed Betty.

Teresa looked Honoria over once. "Where'd she come from?"

Kathy took Rachel.

"New York," Honoria replied, not visibly perturbed. "Mrs. Honoria Wentworth. Kathy and I are very dear friends. I was so glad I was able to make it out in time. And you are?"

"Mrs. William Javits. Anyway, Ma, poor Bill is still completely terrorized. He spent the whole day shaking, and groaning that he's ruined. I don't care what Freddie says he did or didn't do. He completely thrashed my husband."

"What did Freddie do?" asked Honoria eagerly, sitting down at the table.

Rachel choked and then quieted. Kathy handed her to Katie-Marie.

"He brutalized my husband," said Teresa, sitting also.

"He did? Did they come to blows?"

"Teresa..." warned Katie-Marie.

"Freddie says they didn't," Teresa continued. "But poor Bill was completely bowled over. I'm certain he was pummeled."

"Oh, of course," said Honoria.

Teresa smiled. "Have you met Freddie?"

Betty and Kathy both bit back their laughter.

"He's a complete brute, isn't he?" said Honoria.

"An animal. How he could have done what he did to my sweet, sensitive, little husband."

"He's positively diabolical." Honoria looked over her fingernails. "But then, brothers are like that, I suppose."

"Brothers?" asked Teresa.

Honoria smiled sweetly. "Freddie's my brother."

Teresa gaped. "And you think...?"

"No. Actually, I find he's a perfect lamb. I don't think I've ever seen him strike anybody. There was... No. He just escorted the gentleman out. Didn't even push him. And you say he hit your husband? Dear me. That's not Freddie, is it, Kathy?"

"Not the Freddie I know," said Kathy.

Teresa snorted. "Well, Bill was still terrorized."

"Leave it alone, Teresa," said Katie-Marie. "If you don't like it, you don't have to stand up at the wedding, you know."

Teresa thought it over. "Maybe I won't."

"Then who?" asked Kathy, trying not to panic. She turned. "Honoria, would you mind? I hate asking on such short notice."

"How could you have asked before?" Honoria sparkled. "I'd absolutely adore it, Kathy. This is too wonderful. I knew this was going to be too much fun the moment I got Freddie's wire."

Kathy smiled, and slid her hand into her dress pocket. Freddie's ring was still there. She'd have to remember to give it to Honoria. No one else would think to. Possibly Freddie might remember. She wondered if he was as nervous as she was.

He was. He opened and slammed the tiny drawers in his trunk furiously, puffing quickly on a cigarette.

"Where are they?" he groaned. "I know I put them in here when I packed this afternoon."

"Where are what?" asked Lowell, who was lounging contentedly nearby with a bottle cradled in his arms.

"My lapis cufflinks. I can't have left them behind. I always wear them with this suit."

"They're on the bureau. You put them there before you took your bath."

Groaning, Freddie went to the bureau. The cufflinks were there. Freddie sighed and put them in his sleeves. The jacket to his dark blue suit lay on the bed and his vest was unbuttoned. The air was warm, almost stifling.

"I don't seem to remember you being this nervous on your wedding day," he told Lowell. "And you had more cause."

"Want to share my secret?" Lowell held out the bottle.

Freddie took it. "I might have known."

"I was completely sedated from the night before, and never let myself get any closer to sober. Barely delivered that night."

Freddie, who was about to pour some whiskey into a glass, suddenly shook his head and capped the bottle.

"You may have it back," he said snubbing out his cigarette and lighting another. "I don't think sedation will help me any."

"Neither will smoking too fast." Lowell took the bottle, uncapped it and took a sip. "Try some nice, smooth, even drags. That might calm you down."

"What will calm me down is getting this over with."

Lowell chuckled. "It's going to be quite a treat seeing you tied up with old Briscow. The two of you bullying each other back and forth. Freddie, you old fool, you have finally met your match."

"I'm only two days older than you."

"But you are not a veteran of the matrimonial battlefield." Lowell grunted as he pulled out a handkerchief and mopped his forehead.

"Poor Kathy." Freddie gazed out the window. "She's only marrying me because I want it."

"Poor Kathy?" Lowell coughed in amazement. "My god, the fat settlement that girl's going to get from you. The judge is going to look at your pile, and give her an alimony that will make even your eyes spin."

"That is assuming we divorce." Freddie turned to his old friend. "Alas, Lowell, there is such a thing as happily ever after. If I didn't think Kathy and I stood a reasonably good chance at it, I would have taken her as my lover and been done with it."

"And you think Briscow would have gone for that?" Lowell laughed. "I know you tell me not to make judgments about her based on her sex, but I have yet to meet a woman that wasn't going to settle for a wedding band, or a luxury apartment and plenty of furs."

"That was the way Kathy wanted it, to be my lover, with no claims on me whatsoever."

Lowell groaned. "Freddie, you fool! How could I have been so blind to this woman's charms? I could have stolen her away and made her happy."

"You can barely deliver, remember?" Freddie began buttoning his vest.

"For a woman who will not make claims, I'd find a way." Lowell's forehead was once again glistening with sweat and he mopped it away distractedly. "Good God, Freddie, don't you realize what you could have had? And you're the one that insisted on being honorable. Or was that just her father's shotgun? Please, tell me it was, Freddie, or I swear I shall lose faith in the entire male sex."

Sighing, Freddie pulled his watch from his vest. "It's almost five thirty. I believe we're supposed to be at the church by quarter 'til."

Lowell stood and put his hand on Freddie's shoulder.

"I wish you all the happiness in the world, Freddie," he said seriously. "I mean that. True, my experience has been bitter, but I am free of her, at last. And we did have some good times. Your Briscow is a remarkable woman. I suppose even I would take the fatal plunge rather than chance losing her."

Freddie smiled. "Lowell, I have almost always taken your advice, when seriously given. I remember you told me to hang onto this one editor at all costs."

"I didn't mean marry her. Of course, we thought she was a man then, didn't we?"

"And I'm glad she's not." Grinning, they shook hands. "One more thing, Lowell. These are not city folk. Please try to contain your natural cynicism. I don't think it will be understood here."

"Freddie, my boy, I know these people better than you ever will. They are my people. They share the same roots as the stalk that sprung me in Iowa. I won't embarrass you."

"Thank you." Freddie took a deep breath and got his jacket.

In the church, Kathy waited in the vestry room behind the pulpit. In the main sanctuary, people were filling the pews as Ariadne Counterpane flailed their ears with her wavering soprano, accompanied by a wheezing organ. Women were gently fanning themselves in the heat.

"It's not Saint Thomas's Episcopal is it?" giggled Honoria. She had changed into a green beaded evening shift and wore dark stockings underneath.

"I wouldn't know," said Kathy numbly. "I've never been inside."

Honoria peeked out at the congregation. "There's your mother, waving. I guess they've got Freddie safely locked up by now. Time for us to go around."

Kathy froze. "I can't."

Honoria put her arm around Kathy's shoulders.

"Darling, it's the only way you'll get to your

wedding night, and I've heard some very encouraging rumors about my brother."

Kathy laughed. "Honoria, how shocking!"

Honoria gathered up flowers and veil. "Let's go."

"Doesn't it bother you to think of your brother in that way?" Kathy asked as they walked around to the front entrance. The night air was still and warm.

"That's when I try to stop thinking of him as my brother, and remember he's just a man. It never quite works out that way, so I guess incest will never be a possibility. All in all, I can't complain. He's too proper for my tastes."

Kathy smiled softly. "That's part of his charm."

"Well, he's not that proper tonight. A regular three-piece suit? He's never gone anywhere after six o'clock without at least a black tie."

"He's taken me a few places without it. But then, they were places where black tie was not appropriate, like here."

Honoria held Kathy at the door, and peeped. "We'll have to wait. The minister isn't out yet."

The minister was chatting with Freddie, who wasn't listening. Reverend Macadam, fully robed and ready, smiled. At least Freddie was acting like a normal groom. Macadam had already talked to Kathy, and found her exceptionally white-faced for a blushing bride.

He checked the wall clock, then nodded at Mrs. Johnson, who signaled Mrs. Carpenter at the organ, who signaled Mrs. Counterpane, who cleared her throat.

"It's time, my boy," said Macadam, clapping Freddie on the back.

Freddie felt his entire chest and abdominal cavity do a giant loop the loop.

"I guess it is," he said.

"Last chance, Freddie," chortled Lowell.

Freddie chuckled and gained courage. "Never, Lowell. I'm going through with it, if only to show you that it can be done."

Macadam laughed. Lowell's divorce had come up in the conversation.

They followed Macadam out, and stumbled into the right places. Freddie was a little surprised to see Honoria preceding Kathy up the aisle, but not much, after noting Teresa in the front row with folded arms and tight lips.

The organ gasped a fanfare and the congregation stood. Kathy appeared at the end of the aisle with her father beside her, and all Freddie could think was that the color of her face matched her dress.

She froze, rooted to where she stood. Jacob whispered in her ear. She wouldn't move. He finally shoved her forward. She nearly lost her balance, but it got her walking.

They made it to the head of the aisle where Freddie and the others waited, well before the anthem ended. So they all waited some more. At last, Mrs. Counterpane shut up, and the organ gasped its final note. Macadam opened the marriage book and began to read.

"Dearly beloved, we are gathered here to unite this man and this..." he paused, trying not to insert the word "poor," "...this woman in the bonds of sacred matrimony. If there be any among those present who knows of a good reason why this marriage should not take place, let him speak now, or forever hold his peace."

Honoria giggled as she debated trying to explain to the minister that if her brother got married, she'd have to leave off getting him married and find something else to occupy herself with. She held her tongue.

Teresa held her tongue, too. Kathy would find in time what kind of an animal she was marrying. Not that it mattered. The girl was desperate for a husband, and at least Freddie had money, or so they said.

Katie-Marie and Jacob both held their breath, and hoped Kathy would hold her tongue. Kathy's lips parted.

"As there are no objections," read Macadam quickly. "Let it be known that Kathleen Mary Briscow and Frederick Gordon Little have come here to be married. Who gives this bride to be married to this man?"

Jacob laughed out loud. Honoria giggled.

"Pa!" groaned Kathy, finally getting some color in her cheeks.

"Reverend, I can't give this girl," explained Jacob. "Especially after all the fuss you made about her doing this on her own free will. Hell, she's her own woman. Ask her if she wants to give herself."

Coughing, Jacob sat down. Macadam sighed, and turned to the next part of the ceremony.

"Will the couple please join hands?"

Freddie had to walk over to get Kathy because the part where Jacob was supposed to have done that had been skipped. He smiled softly at her, and she didn't balk. They centered themselves before Macadam, grasping tightly onto each other's hands.

"Do you, Frederick, take this woman to be your lawfully wedded wife, in good times and in bad, in sickness and in health, for richer, for poorer, to love, honor and cherish, forsaking all others until death do you part?"

Honoria giggled some more.

Freddie swallowed. "I do."

"Do you, Kathleen, take this man to be your lawfully wedded husband, in good times and in bad, in sickness and in health, for richer, for poorer, to love, honor and obey…"

"Wait a minute," interrupted Freddie. "She's not promising to obey me. I won't let her do that."

Honoria giggled even harder.

"But… I… Kathy?" asked the flummoxed minister.

"This is humiliating," Kathy hissed.

"Do you want to obey me?" asked Freddie softly.

Kathy opened her mouth to protest, glanced at Macadam, then shut her mouth.

"He's right," she said. "I'm not promising that."

Honoria held her hand against her mouth to stop the giggles.

"B-but..." Macadam was completely confused.

"Those are the terms I promised her," explained Freddie. "Just read her what you read me."

"Uh, yes. All right. Do you, Kathleen, take this wo—no, man, to be your lawfully wedded wi—husband, in good times and in bad, in sickness and in health, for richer, for poorer, to love, honor and cherish, forsaking all others until death do you part?"

Kathy actually smiled at Freddie. "I do."

Macadam paused and looked at them. "How many rings do we have?"

"Two," said Kathy. "One apiece."

"I've done that before." Macadam looked over the text. "Place the rings on the tray."

Giggling, Honoria put Freddie's ring on the small silver plate. Grinning, Lowell patted his pockets and came up with empty hands.

"Where the hell did you put it, you bleeding sot?" snarled Freddie through his teeth.

Honoria giggled.

"Up my sleeve." Lowell retrieved it and put it on the plate. "Revenge is sweet, my boy."

Honoria continued giggling.

"I'd forgotten about that," sighed Freddie. "Pray continue, Reverend."

"If we ever get through this," sighed Macadam. "The wedding ring is a sign of fidelity. It is a circle, and like the circle, it is unbroken, like the faithfulness of your love for one another. Frederick, please place the ring on the bride's finger and repeat after me." Macadam held his breath as Freddie cooperated. "With this ring, I thee wed. Any problems with that?"

"None," said Freddie. "With this ring, I thee wed."

"Kathleen... You don't have any problems with the recommended text?"

"No," said Kathy slowly.

"Kathleen, place the ring on the groom's finger and repeat after me. With—"

"With this ring, I thee wed," Kathy said quickly.

She fumbled with the ring, and almost lost it but for Freddie's quick save. Honoria was holding her mouth again.

Macadam only waited long enough for Freddie to get the ring past his first knuckle.

"Now, with the blessing of almighty God, and the authority invested in me by the state of Kansas, I now pronounce you man and wife. You may kiss the bride. What God has brought together, let no man tear asunder." Macadam shut the book, and breathed a large sigh of relief.

Kathy and Freddie were already indulging in what was for them the only worthwhile part of the ceremony. Honoria could not stop giggling. Kathy and Freddie continued to indulge themselves until Mrs. Counterpane signaled the organ, and burst forth loudly.

Freddie took Kathy back down the aisle quickly, because Kathy was not only blushing, she was bright red.

"I've never felt so foolish in my life," she gasped as they neared the door.

"The ceremony?" Freddie opened it and let her out before him.

"No, getting out. They were all staring at us." She ran down the steps.

Freddie followed her. "It was rather radical."

"Rather? And is your sister ever going to stop giggling?"

"I hope so for her sake." Freddie grinned. "I'm of the opinion we should go directly to the hotel, and lock ourselves into that suite I have waiting for us."

The church doors burst open.

"Too late, Freddie. We should have done it instead of talked about it."

He smiled softly as the hordes bore down. "Are you

feeling better about this?"

"No."

They received congratulations stiffly as they were herded to the church hall. Undercurrents and murmurs abounded about the radical ceremony, and the strange bridesmaid who laughed through it all.

"Wasn't Teresa supposed to stand up with you?" asked Mrs. James.

"She decided at the last minute not to," said Kathy, looking around for Freddie.

They'd eaten dinner together, but found themselves separated as they mingled with the guests. Bill Javits lurked about, hiding in the shadows, a sullen presence in an otherwise merry feast. Joshua teased Freddie mercilessly.

"You don't want her to obey you," he groaned. "Brother, that is asking for it. Do you have any idea what it's going to be like when you can't even hold that over her head?"

"I'm assuming a mutually rewarding partnership," replied Freddie.

He looked around. Honoria had disappeared. He moved around to Kathy.

"Have you seen Honoria?" he asked.

"No. I was looking for Abraham. Have you seen him?"

They paused and looked at each other.

"You don't think..." Kathy asked.

"She was looking at him."

Together they shook their heads.

"Honoria has better manners than that," said Freddie.

"Abraham doesn't take advantage," said Kathy.

Lowell mopped his forehead, then loaded his plate again.

"Now that's chicken and dumplings," he said between the list of credits he was giving Mrs. Thomassen.

"Well, Life I've heard of," she said. "But those other

magazines, no. Still, I'm confused. I thought writers were starving, and well, you know, different."

Lowell patted his exceptional belly. "I decided a long time ago that starving was against my principles. As for being a long haired, wild-eyed, tieless radical, you have two choices. You can assume that I am indeed the man you see before you, or that I am such in my natural state. I will leave it to your discretion. However, I was born and raised on a farm in Iowa."

"Oh, how interesting. But tell me, Mr. Winters. They're saying that Mr. Little is a writer, too."

"Perhaps not in the sense you're thinking, although he has written a book. But he's not a writer for his living. He's one of the idle rich, living off the fat he's plundered from the masses."

"Oh really?" Mrs. Thomassen turned an amused, speculative eye on Freddie.

Lowell lumbered onto the next dish on the table.

"I wouldn't dream of faulting the man," Teresa was saying to a group of her friends, fanning herself quickly. "I'm sure he thought he was doing the right thing. But my Bill is such a sensitive man. He has to be, to comfort all those mourners. It was just disgraceful what Freddie did to him."

Katie-Marie moved up to Kathy, who had again been separated from Freddie, this time by a small group of her old high school friends.

"Are you happy, darling?" Katie-Marie asked.

Kathy shrugged. "It's not a bad party."

"He's a good man, Kathy. He loves you." Katie-Marie scanned the hall and found that Joshua and some other young men had cornered Freddie and were laughing loudly.

"I love him, Ma," Kathy said. "That was never the issue."

"Then what is?"

"Diapers, for starters. Women's work in general. The tedium of housekeeping. And, Ma, I've worked so hard to get as far as I have. I don't want to lose it."

"There's also love, Kathy. You don't want to lose that, either. You'll be all right, darling." She hugged her daughter.

Freddie finally broke free of the group of young men and started to cross the hall to find Kathy. He never saw the man who whispered the message. But it piqued his curiosity. The sun had finally set, and outside the hall was darkness. Alone, apart from the revelers, Freddie walked towards the back.

The report of the gun spurred him to a run. He rounded the corner and stopped point blank. The body was at his feet, the head lost in the shadows of the alley. Freddie bent, reaching for the wrist. Next to it was a shotgun, the muzzle pointed at the head.

"What do you know?" sniggered a malevolent voice.

Freddie looked up. Sheriff Wimberton came out of the shadows with a rifle trained on Freddie. The sheriff dropped a coat over the body's head, and chuckled.

Other men came running up.

"We heard a gun shot!" yelled one.

"That you did," said the sheriff. "I just watched Mr. Little, here, blow Bill Javits' head off."

Chapter Thirteen

Katie-Marie was beside herself. She had two daughters to comfort, each ready to rip the other's throat out, and both genuinely grieved. She ordered Gideon, Isaac and Gam to take Jacob home, as he was failing. Kathy, at least, shoved her mother off.

"Freddie was set up," she insisted. "He's being framed. What else was Wimberton doing out there? And that little bitch screaming that Freddie killed him. I could just—"

"She's just lost her husband," sighed Katie-Marie, uncomfortably aware that Kathy had just lost hers before she had him.

"I know, Ma." Kathy wiped her nose. "You'd better take care of her. I'll be all right. She's lost more than I have."

"Oh, Kathy, you're so generous." Katie-Marie held her, then went to Teresa.

The Javits children had already been taken by the neighbors. The hall emptied. Kathy looked up to see Honoria. Tears and mascara streaked the young woman's cheeks.

"I can't believe Freddie would have done something like that," sniffed Honoria.

"He didn't," said Kathy. "Wimberton is lying. I'm certain of it."

Honoria dug in her purse. Kathy found the extra handkerchief her mother had tucked under her camisole.

"Here," she said, offering it to Honoria. "It's clean."

"Oh, God. It's Freddie's." Honoria's tears flowed again.

Kathy looked at the monogram on the handkerchief she held. It, too, had been handed to her by Freddie. She struggled with her tears, and gave in. Betty came up and put her arms around both women.

"Josh and Abraham are at the courthouse now," she said softly. "I'll take you down there."

Honoria wiped the make-up off her cheeks and stood tall.

"Come along, Kathy," she said proudly. "We're not going to let them beat us. We're stronger than they are."

"You're right." Kathy sniffed one last time and dried her eyes. "And I'm angry."

At the courthouse chamber next door to the sheriff's office and the jail, Abraham was very angry, but in control. The room was paneled in oak, and the judge's desk was immense. Joshua, a couple officers, and public prosecutor Mervin Meyers watched quietly.

"He has a right to counsel," Abraham told Judge Aherne firmly. "And a right to have bail set promptly."

"And who the hell are you?" demanded Aherne over the top of the official charge that Wimberton had filed. He was a grandfatherly sort in a crisp black suit, with dark gray hair and coal black eyes made larger by his wire-rimmed spectacles.

"I'm Mr. Little's brother-in-law. I'm also a student at Harvard Law."

"Well, if you'll give me a minute, I will set bail. He's pleading not guilty. Don't see why. We'll have the trial tomorrow."

"You can't do that!" snapped Abraham.

Aherne glared. "He also has a right to a fair and speedy trial."

"Aren't you forgetting the part about fair, Your Honor? It'll take his attorneys at least three days to get here from New York, and they need time to prepare a case."

Meyers started to speak, but Aherne waved him to silence.

"They don't have a case to prepare," Aherne said. "The sheriff saw him do it."

"Mr. Little pleaded not guilty. He has a right to counsel, and a fair trial."

"Then you be his counsel." Aherne folded his arms and leaned back in his brown leather chair.

Abraham gaped. "I can't practice law!"

"You're doing fine so far."

"We're talking about basic constitutional rights. You can't even get into law school without knowing those. I've only finished one year. I'm not qualified, and I'm not certified in this or any other state. You try to make me do this, and I'll scream mistrial all the way to the capital."

Aherne glowered. "I'm not letting this roll on forever. We'll set the trial for Friday morning. That will give Mr. Little plenty of time to find a lawyer."

"Assuming he's out on bail," said Abraham, standing firm.

"Bail. Very well. One hundred thousand dollars."

"I believe the constitution says 'reasonable,'" growled Abraham.

"It most certainly does." Aherne smiled. "As I understand it, Mr. Little is worth at least two millions, and he is a pilot, and he has a plane well within reach. Under those circumstances, I think the bail is reasonable."

Abraham glared, then turned for the door. "Come on, Josh."

Joshua gave the people in the room a nervous glance, and followed. In the hall, he caught Abraham.

"Why didn't you tell the judge the sheriff had to have made a mistake?" Joshua asked.

"Because that's what the trial is about," Abraham replied distractedly. "We've got to talk to Freddie and find out who his attorneys are. Maybe they can send somebody out from Topeka."

"Why not someone in town?"

"Because there's no one in town who can stand up to Mervin Meyers in a fair fight, let alone this."

They found Kathy and Honoria in the jail office, arguing with the deputy.

"I don't care," snapped the young man in tan uniform, his hair a dark blond. "No one is going back there. Visiting hours are over."

"That is my husband!" yelled Kathy.

"I don't care if he's Jesus Christ. Visiting hours are over."

Abraham stepped up. "Officer, I'm the closest thing he has to counsel right now. You can't deny me access."

"Don't you people understand?" groaned the deputy. "The jail is closed for tonight."

Kathy was about to start yelling again, but Joshua held her back. They retreated to the far end of the room. The deputy sat down at his desk, and sullenly flipped through a magazine. Behind him was a rifle case and just beyond the desk, the closed door to the cells, and in one of them, Freddie.

"I'm not leaving until I see him," said Kathy stubbornly.

"Kathy, about the only person who's going to get back there is an attorney," said Abraham. "We've got to get him one right away. Judge Aherne set the trial for Friday morning."

"Friday?" squeaked Honoria. "His lawyers will never get out here that fast."

"I've got some friends I can wire in Boston," said Abraham.

"That's not any faster," snapped Kathy.

Abraham glared. "They know people all over the country. They can get someone out here from Topeka. The point is, he'll be good and he'll be able to stand up to Mervin Meyers. Probably get him off on a plea of self-defense."

"Freddie didn't kill Bill," said Kathy angrily.

"Kathy, it is possible," said Abraham. "I'm sure it was an accident, or maybe Bill cracked."

"Freddie didn't kill him," Kathy insisted. "Wimberton is lying. That's why I've got to talk to Freddie. I've got to find out what happened out there."

Abraham sighed. "He was heard threatening to wring Bill's neck."

"I've heard all sorts of things," sniffed Honoria. "Freddie was supposed to put him on a rack, and whip him, too. My god, Freddie has never even lifted his voice."

"There are two witnesses. Etta Levers, and her daughter, Marieanne Peterson," said Abraham. "They came in when Sheriff Wimberton was writing up the charge for Meyers. Freddie admitted they'd overheard him."

"I've got to talk to him." Kathy paced nervously. "Freddie said all he did was catch and pin Bill. And, Honoria, believe or not, he did raise his voice. He was very angry."

"He wasn't happy when that body disappeared," said Joshua.

"Bill knew something about it," said Kathy. "More than he was telling."

"Body?" asked Honoria. "Oh no, are you and Freddie mixed up in another murder?"

"It's a long story, Honoria," sighed Kathy.

"Well, for once, I'd like to hear about it before I read it in the papers." Honoria folded her arms crossly.

"I'll tell you all about it later," said Abraham.

Lowell Winters burst into the office and went straight to the desk.

"I demand to see Freddie Little immediately," he

announced.

The deputy sneered at him over the top of the magazine.

"Mister, the jail is closed. Go talk to your friends, if you don't like it."

"Lowell, where the hell have you been?" snapped Honoria.

Lowell walked over. "Getting Freddie's lawyers. In the midst of the confusion, I alone was thinking clearly, and as the dark forces of the law bore him away, I went straight to the hotel and made a telephone call to New York. On Freddie's tab, of course. His lawyers have called a gentleman in Topeka, who promptly telephoned me, and assured me he would be here first thing in the morning."

"Is he any good?" asked Abraham.

"A crack man, highly recommended by Freddie's firm, and they are no cheap shysters, either. I understand he's even a friend of the governor's. The problem is, I just can't see Freddie doing something like this."

"He didn't," said Kathy. "He's being framed. It's too perfectly arranged, with Wimberton right there."

Frustrated, she walked over to the deputy.

"I understand about the rules," she said gently. "And I'm sorry I yelled earlier. We just got married tonight, and this has all been terribly upsetting." Tears rolled down her cheek. "Please, can you just bend the rules for a few minutes? We haven't even been together. Please?"

The deputy sighed. "I guess. Just you, and it'll have to be outside the cell. And five minutes. That's it."

Kathy smiled through her tears. "Thank you!"

Freddie was pacing when the deputy let her through the door. His jacket, tie and vest had disappeared. He looked up as Kathy entered and went to the bars.

"Five minutes," said the deputy, who remained lounging in the doorway.

Kathy reached around the bars as much as she

could to hold him.

"This is awful," she said.

"Looks like they found a way to stop us tonight," said Freddie ruefully.

"I'll get you out of here," Kathy said softly. "I know you were framed. I just don't know how."

"Wimberton is lying through his teeth." Freddie touched her hair with his lips, and would not let go of her. "I was still on the side of the hall when the gun went off. It was so dark back there, I couldn't tell who the body was. I don't know how Wimberton knew, unless he knew Bill was there. And Wimberton had a coat with him. He covered Bill up immediately, before anyone else got there."

"A coat? In this weather? And if he was covered up, how can we be certain it was Bill?"

"Teresa identified a scar he had on his right hand. I heard you two had a little spat when the news went round."

"It was an out and out cat fight. She accused you of doing it even before Wimberton could. The bitch."

"She must have been in shock."

"It's not going to help you any." Kathy swallowed back her tears. "Lowell got through to your lawyers. There's a very good man coming in first thing in the morning from Topeka. The trial is Friday. I don't know why they're rushing things, but I'm going to find out."

"Kathy, be careful." He squeezed her. "There's a package coming. I had it addressed to your father. It's from my brokers. It should be here any day now."

"Did you wire for it?"

"Yes, Monday. It's information regarding Mr. Tipton. I overheard him asking about a reply to one of his telegrams. It was from brokerage in New York that deals in real estate. All the wire operator saw was his name, and the bank's name. It's a complicated maneuver, but I've had to do it before to beat someone else to a good investment. There's something very strange going on in this town, and that information may just point the way."

"Freddie, what about Bill? They say you threatened to kill him."

He sighed. "I did. I'd lost my temper."

"Over what?"

"Time's up," said the deputy.

They kissed as well as they could through the bars until the deputy snarled again. Sadly, Kathy joined the others.

Lowell took Honoria to the hotel. Joshua drove Abraham and Kathy back to the farm in the truck.

"What did he say happened?" asked Abraham.

"Wimberton lied, and I don't want to talk about it," said Kathy in that tone that meant she wouldn't.

Katie-Marie was waiting in the kitchen when they arrived. Joshua brought in Kathy's trunk from the truck.

"Uh, Ma, does this go in your room?" he asked.

Katie-Marie shook her head. "Teresa's there. Put Kathy in the attic."

Kathy blinked back the tears. She waited while Joshua and Abraham kissed their mother good night, then went to do the same. Katie-Marie stopped her.

"Think you can sit a minute?"

Kathy nodded. Katie-Marie got up and poured a second mug full of coffee.

"Kathy, it was very generous of you to let me go to Teresa tonight," she said, sitting down again.

Kathy shrugged. "She needed you more."

"So did you." Katie-Marie shook her head. "I can't imagine how this all fell out."

"Freddie is being framed, Ma. He told me what happened. Wimberton lied."

"But why?"

"I don't know yet. It has something to do with that disappearing body, and all the trouble we've been having here. Bill knew something. He said he didn't, but I got the feeling he did. He might have told me, but Teresa stepped in."

"Now, Kathy, please. Don't be hard on her. And she does have good reason to believe Freddie killed him."

"You think he did, too."

Katie-Marie looked away. "Right now, I don't know what to believe. Kathy, are you certain?"

"Dead certain. There are too many things that don't make sense. Why was Wimberton there in the first place? And he had a coat, and covered the head before anyone got out there. It's the fifteenth of July, and a warm night. What was Wimberton doing in the back of the church hall with a coat? And that's not even considering what Freddie told me. He didn't do it, Ma."

"You must be right. Now, how am I going to explain to Teresa?"

"I don't know. Maybe I should. She might know something, and not even realize it."

"Kathy, I told you, I don't want you playing detective."

She got up. "I don't have a choice, Ma. The people to go to are the people who are saying Freddie did it."

There was a pause, then Kathy kissed her mother good night.

She stopped at the study door, and went in.

"Kathy?" asked Jacob's voice.

"You're sick again."

He coughed. "Fool doctor said, 'no excitement.'"

"Freddie didn't do it."

"I know that. He's got enough balls, he's not going to waste his time with Bill."

Kathy knelt on the floor next to him. "I can't help being afraid. They're rushing the trial, you know. I don't know if Judge Aherne is involved in whatever is going on in town, or if he's just doing someone a favor."

"What's going on in town?"

"I don't know. Freddie and I think it's where the vandalism is coming from, but we can't find anybody who might be behind it. All we've found is that the banker sends a lot of telegrams and makes loans to farmers, but not townsfolk. And the hotel owner and the mayor don't like you, for some reason."

"Oh, I know all about that. But Standling has no reason not to like me."

"What about Mr. Spivens?"

"I just called him a pompous ass one day when he said I was a damn fool not to get electricity out here. We never liked each other much from the beginning."

"He must have something to control Wimberton with then." She looked at him and sighed. "I shouldn't be bothering you with this."

"That's all right. I ain't that sick."

"Pa, I'm so afraid. After everything that's happened, they could hang him, and I don't even get to be married. Hell, even Honoria got three days with her husband."

"Honoria?"

"She was a war bride, married a doughboy, had three days before he shipped out, then the first thing he did when he landed was get killed." Kathy choked. "Honoria's always joking about how nice it is to be a widow, it's about the only way a woman can get any real freedom. But I didn't want to do that to Freddie."

"Kathy, you didn't do it. Wimberton, or whoever, did. Now, you keep looking. I know you'll find out what's going on."

"Thanks, Pa." Kathy got up. "And thanks for making me do it. We should have run and locked ourselves in that suite."

Pa chuckled and coughed. Kathy kissed his cheek and held him.

"You get better, now. I don't think I could take losing both of you at the same time."

"You're not losing either of us. You just do what you have to do."

What she had to do was think. She spent most of the night pacing the attic room. Neither answers nor sleep seemed within reach, but sleep did overtake her eventually. She awoke shortly after dawn, washed up, and slipped out of house, taking some rolls left over from the night before for her breakfast. Without asking, she cranked up the truck and drove around the countryside for almost an hour, trying to think. She eventually returned to the town and stopped in the park next to the creek, trying to think and waiting for the town to wake up.

The jail was still not open to visitors when she finally gave up and walked there, so she went on to a house in the northwest part of town. The house she was looking for was in a neighborhood that was well known for its fine homes belonging to the most respected, or at least wealthiest, citizens in Hays. At the center of the neighborhood was the only street in town with electric street lamps. Kathy found the house of county prosecutor Mervin Meyers near the end of that street. The house had been built near the end of the previous century when some citizens had finally become respectable.

The housekeeper answered the door. She showed Kathy into the living room.

"I'll get the Missus," said the housekeeper in a soft German accent, and left.

For Hays, the ritual was true gentility. Kathy sighed. Freddie, bred to the real thing, would have found the attempt amusing. The Missus, or Mervin's wife and the daughter of the mayor, came downstairs slowly, wearing an expensive China silk wrapper over a tired underdress.

Jaqueline Standling Meyers was an average sized woman, not gone to fat yet, but would be within a few years. Her eyes were glazed over, and her youthful, snobbish confidence had faded into complete indifference.

"I hope you're not here to ask me to influence my husband in your husband's favor," she asked, flopping onto an overstuffed sofa covered in a bright floral print. An overfed, white long-haired cat wandered over to her and demanded affection.

"I don't believe in wasting my time," said Kathy, who had known such a mission would be.

Jaqueline sniffed sleepily. "I should offer refreshments. I can't remember. Were you Temperance like your ma?"

"When I drink, it's not usually this early in the morning."

"How do you get through a day?" Jaqueline removed a bottle from behind the sofa, and a shot glass from under a cushion. "My morning restorative. After last night, don't you need one?"

"I'm managing."

"I heard he says he didn't do it."

"He didn't. Wimberton is lying."

Jaqueline offered the shot glass to the cat. "Want some, kitty?" The cat snubbed it. "Good. More for mommy." She drank half. "Frankly, I'm not surprised. About Wimberton, I mean."

"Why do you say that?"

"Honestly, Kathy, it's obvious. He's such an ass." She yawned. "Why are you here?"

"Your father. I'd heard some rumors he was angry with my father, and I wanted to know if you knew anything about it."

Jaqueline snorted. "He tells me as much as Mervin does. Thick as flies, those two. I don't think they give a damn about your father. Maybe they do, I don't know."

"Well, somebody in town has something against Pa."

"Kathy, that's so desperately...what's the word? You know, that psychology stuff. Paranoid."

"My husband has been framed for murder. My father's farm has been the target of several acts of vandalism. That does not constitute an unreasonable belief that we are being attacked."

Jaqueline burped. "It does sound like it." She sighed. "Kathy, there is so much going on in this town that nobody talks about. Would you believe my friends have no idea that I drink? I'm serious. I've gone to meetings dead drunk, and no one noticed. As far as everyone's concerned, I'm a pillar of society. I get awards, damn it! The mayor's proud daughter. The beautiful Mrs. Mervin Meyers. No one dreams that I don't give a rat's ass for any of it."

"There are those who say your father likes the prestige of being mayor."

"That's all he's going to get out of life. It's all any of us has." Jaqueline poured herself another drink. "If you say he's angry at your father, then maybe your father wants to be mayor. It's the only reason Pa would hate him, and he would hate him, Kathy. Being mayor is all he has."

"I see."

Jaqueline looked puzzled. "Why don't you want me to try and sway Mervin? It is your husband's neck he's trying to stretch."

"I was going to ask. But I wasn't sure you'd believe me that Freddie is innocent."

"I believe that. You're so cold-blooded, Kathy, and so righteous. You're not going to throw yourself on my mercy for a guilty man. Not that it's going to help. Mervin doesn't listen to me. He's so Victorian. I'm his wife. My job is to look pretty, keep his house in order, his meals cooked and the children quiet and out of his way. In exchange, I get a beautiful house, clothes, a housekeeper, and time to drink. Not as exciting as an accused murderer, I grant you, but I manage."

Kathy nodded and took her leave. She went back to the jail. Deputy Diedrich was on duty. She'd known him since her childhood, and he hadn't been a young man then. If anything, he'd only grown a little grayer at the temples and a lot rounder. He'd always treated her kindly, and looked tolerantly on her petty transgressions, even if he hadn't allowed them.

He let her into the cell with Freddie, but kept the door open between the cells and the office. Freddie nonetheless kissed her passionately.

"Freddie." Kathy started to cry again.

"I'm all right, darling." He pressed her head to his chest. "They're not treating me badly, and we'll get through this mess."

"I just wish I didn't feel so much like David going up against a vague, amorphous sort of Goliath."

Freddie kissed her again. "If it weren't for that open door, I'd suggest having our wedding night right here and now."

"How can you make jokes?"

"How can I not? It's all I can do."

Kathy squeezed him. "This waiting must be terrible for you."

"Have you heard from the attorney at all?"

"Not yet. But the morning train isn't in yet. If he's driving, he's got a long ride from Topeka."

Sighing, Freddie wandered over to the bunk and almost kicked it.

"I wish there was something I could do to make him get here faster," said Kathy.

"You can't." He put on a smile. "They told me Honoria got rather vocal at Western Union this morning. She was trying to wire for my bail, and couldn't understand why they didn't have a hundred thousand dollars in cash at the office."

"I'd doubt they have it at the bank, either." Kathy sighed. "Freddie, what was so important about that missing body that you threatened Bill over it?"

Freddie looked away. "Kathy, that's not something I can talk about."

"You'd better, if you don't want your neck stretched."

"Even if it hurts your family worse than it is already?"

"Freddie, how am I going to find out who is doing this to us if I don't know everything you do?"

Freddie grimaced. "It doesn't have anything to do with the vandalism, or the body, or Bill's death."

"How can you be sure of that?"

Freddie looked at her. She stood with her arms

folded and her face stern. A loving wife, perhaps, but not one who was going to accept anything less than the complete truth, no matter what it cost. He leaned on the bars and stared at the floor.

"Kathy, you must understand that the environment of a prep school is such that it invites and encourages certain cruelties among the students. There was a tendency among some of the older boys to pick out the weaker and more vulnerable of the younger boys and visit upon them the worst kind of perversion."

"Sexual?"

"Yes. I saw it happen several times, even from one or two of the teachers. No one ever talked about it except the boys, in hushed whispers. We never dared. Fortunately, it never happened to me, always having been somewhat tall for my years. But I learned the signs."

Kathy swallowed. "The boy that was killed?"

"I can't say for sure, but given the bruises on his shoulders, I'd say he was. But what I threatened Bill over was another boy who is quite alive, and living with this terrible secret. He wouldn't tell me, but I knew anyway."

"Gammers." Kathy's eyes filled as the pressure in her chest grew.

"It's why he was so afraid of me until I made it clear I did not want him to keep any secrets. It's always kept secret, Kathy. The tormentor usually threatens some dire harm, at least at school they did. I don't know how Bill secured Gammers' silence."

"Bill? He was molesting Gammers?" Shocked, Kathy sat down on the bunk. "How? Bill has no spine."

"Who else was weaker than him? It's probably been going on for years. I have no way of knowing."

"Are you sure?"

"Bill admitted it after I got him pinned. But the way he denied it made me sure. I didn't want him touching Gammers again, and so I threatened to wring his neck if he did. And I had good reason to believe it would be sufficient. I would never have followed through on it anyway, beyond finding a more peaceful means of stopping him."

Kathy put her head in her hand. "Except that Bill's been killed, and someone overheard your threat." She stopped and pressed her lips together. "It's a good thing he's already dead or I'd kill him myself. How dare he do that to Gammers?" She shook her head to clear it. "I'll have to be angry about this later. That boy's body has something to do with the vandalism, but I don't think Bill killed him."

"Nor do I, entirely. But Bill was certainly involved in the vandalism. I found tire tracks near the treehouse that probably belonged to a Chevrolet, and Bill's Chevrolet was parked in the alley when I got there. He must have told the vandals about the treehouse, then thought better of it and retrieved it."

"That's right. It fits, too." Kathy got up and paced. "Remember? We always thought the trouble seemed to be coming from the town, but for the fact that whoever doing had to have known the farm."

Freddie frowned. "Except Bill couldn't have been doing it on his own, could he?"

Kathy shook her head. "No. Even if he had the backbone for it, there had to be more than one person involved. Just look at the barn fire. That car didn't stop, and it would have been impossible to throw a burning bottle that accurately and still keep the car on the road."

"You're right. There are too many potholes there, and a quick underhand toss wouldn't have gone far enough from the first spot where there was a clear shot at the hay pile." Freddie's eyebrows raised. "That does make a conspiracy quite likely."

"Yes, it does. But why? And why kill Bill if he's part of it?"

"If he removed that body, it could mean he was weaseling out, and the other conspirators felt he might be dangerous. And I was framed for it because I must present some danger to them. That information I wired for."

"That would implicate Mr. Tipton. But, Freddie, you could have just been a convenient scapegoat, a sacrificial lamb to cover up the real killer, or the whole thing could have been set up as a diversion from the real conspiracy."

"We won't know until we get that package from New York. Has your mail come yet?"

"It won't be ready until the morning train gets here." Kathy groaned. "I hate this waiting! I'm sorry, Freddie, that was a terrible thing to say when you're stuck here."

"I learned a long time ago that there are times when waiting is all one can do."

He took her hands and kissed them, then pulled her into his arms.

Chapter Fourteen

Mr. Jeffery Eckert, Attorney at Law, was fond of hopeless cases. He truly enjoyed prevailing on the behalf of some wronged individual with little hope of achieving anything. He was somewhat on the small side, but not conspicuously so, with brown hair and short-sighted eyes, for which he wore wire-rimmed glasses. His tastes were conservative, as was his dress. Given his preference for taking the part of the weaker side, it was rumored that he was a Socialist. But his political track record was solidly Republican and impeccable, and it had been suggested that he run for office more than once.

The case of the State of Kansas against Frederick Gordon Little, on the surface, did not appear to be the sort of thing he liked. Little was supposed to be grossly wealthy, and something of a dissipate, according to Eckert's colleagues in New York, with nothing better to do than indulge his whims as he pleased. The victim was a harmless undertaker, a rabbity man, whom Little had ruthlessly threatened with violence, then shot in cold blood right in front of the sheriff, if what Eckert was hearing was correct.

The murder had set the small town buzzing as

nothing else had in years. Eckert marveled that he'd barely had a chance to get his car parked and himself to the hotel desk, and he'd already heard three different versions of the story.

"Checking in?" sniffed the balding man behind the desk.

"Yes, thank you. Just myself. The town's busy today."

"Big trial tomorrow. Murder case. Fellow shot the undertaker in cold blood. That'll be a dollar."

"So I hear." Eckert dropped the coin on the counter.

"If you're doing anything, might want to sit in on the trial."

"I may just." Eckert signed the book and took the key. "I was told to ask for Mr. Lowell Winters. I understand he's staying here."

Spivens' eyes narrowed suspiciously. "What do you want him for?"

"He knows my client, and since it appears my client cannot effect the introductions himself, I must rely on Mr. Winters."

"What are you here for?" Spivens glared at him.

Eckert considered. "I am here as legal counsel for Mr. Frederick Little."

Spivens visibly chilled. "You're not getting him off."

Eckert remained outwardly unchanged. But inside, the familiar, pleasant warnings of a challenge whispered to him.

"We'll have to see. How do I find Mr. Winters?"

Spivens gave him the room number. Eckert took his bag and briefcase to his own room, then went to the other. The door was answered by a well-dressed, slender brunette with arresting hazel eyes.

"Yes?" she asked, a little suspicious.

"I'm Mr. Jeffery Eckert," he said. "I'd like to speak to Mr. Lowell Winters?"

"Regarding?"

"I'm here to defend Mr. Little."

Her demeanor changed completely. "You're the attorney. Thank God! Come in, come in. He's here! Oh, I'm Mrs. Honoria Wentworth. I'm Mr. Little's sister. You mustn't believe a word anyone in this town tells you. Freddie didn't kill that man. He wouldn't hurt a fly. He's been framed."

"Let the man alone, Honoria." Lowell was tieless and without a jacket, his suspenders lining each side of his prodigious belly. "Lowell Winters, Mr. Eckert. And we have Joshua and Abraham Briscow here."

Eckert shook hands. "Are you friends of the defendant?"

"Our sister married him," said Joshua. "The night of the murder."

"I did hear something about that," said Eckert.

"I saw the truck at the jail," said Abraham. "Josh, why don't you see if you can get her to come over?"

Joshua shrugged, leaving. "May as well."

"I suppose you were not able to raise bail." Eckert set his briefcase down on a lamp table and opened it.

"It wasn't unreasonable," said Abraham. "Especially since Freddie's worth so much, and he's got his plane here."

"Try raising the cash in this backwater," snapped Honoria. "The telegraph office I might understand. But the bank was completely uncooperative. It's almost as if they wanted to keep Freddie in jail."

Eckert smiled. "Is that why you think he's been framed?"

Abraham shook his head. "My sister is certain of it. She just can't prove it yet."

"My boy, if she is married to the defendant, she is quite probably biased."

Lowell snorted.

"She is," admitted Abraham. "But she is very clear-headed."

"Quite probably so," said Eckert. "However, at a time like this, things get distorted, and if Mr. Little and your sister were just married, she would not be likely to be thinking clearly."

"You don't know my sister," said Abraham.

"That's the truth," growled Lowell. "That ball-busting wench—"

"Mr. Winters!" groaned Abraham. "There is a lady present."

"I'm used to him, Abraham," Honoria lit a cigarette and turned to Eckert. "Lowell is the personification of rudeness, and there's no cure for him."

"He's also talking about my sister," said Abraham.

"Nonetheless, the fact remains that Briscow is not the sort of woman to let her emotions cloud her reason, even where Freddie is concerned," said Lowell. "She's remarkably man-like."

"Mr. Eckert," said Abraham. "You'll hear her reasoning soon enough, I would imagine. I firmly feel that we should proceed as though Freddie is innocent. The hard part is that a lot of the town is quite happy to string him up. Honoria's observation about the bank is not far from the truth."

"It isn't." Eckert frowned, thinking. The case was beginning to look interesting. Not that the wife's observations would be of any use. But even if Little had killed the man, the thought of a lone stranger against the suspicious townsfolk was inviting.

Kathy arrived just as Abraham finished telling Eckert about the rushed trial, and what had transpired with the judge. Eckert looked her over carefully. She seemed exceptionally alert, though obviously upset. She looked at him skeptically.

"I'm told you believe your husband is being framed," Eckert said finally.

"He is," Kathy replied.

Her calm certainty was a little unnerving.

Eckert cleared his throat. "Mrs. Little, are you aware that the sheriff claims to be an eyewitness to the deed?"

"He's also lying. I knew that before Freddie told me what had actually happened."

"But, Mrs. Little, sheriffs are not prone to lying."

Kathy rolled her eyes. "You have obviously decided that I am just another hysterical female. Mr. Eckert, I am not. Nor am I making up fanciful tales in a vain hope to rescue my husband. I assure you, if Freddie were guilty, I would be discussing a case for self-defense, or even justifiable homicide, which it would have been, had Freddie killed Bill Javits. But he didn't."

"Because he wouldn't do such a thing," said Eckert, attempting to finish her sentence for her.

"He most certainly would to protect himself, or someone else. I told you, Mr. Eckert, I had good reason to suspect the charges were false even before Freddie confirmed it. It was very dark behind the hall where it happened. How could Wimberton have recognized Bill? His profile was exceedingly normal. Furthermore, Wimberton had no reason to be there in the first place, unless skulking about dark byways where no one goes, fully armed in one's off duty hours, is a new form of law enforcement."

"Is this what Freddie told you?"

"It's what I observed. Freddie can tell you the rest, and he will at length, if I know him."

Eckert had to chuckle. "Not the kindest of observations from a blushing bride."

Kathy turned on him. "Just because I love the man does not mean I am blind to his faults, a tendency to digress being among the more serious."

"I see." Eckert had to hold back a smile. Obviously the woman considered ·digression as grave a sin as drunken lechery. "That does remind me, though. Not that I would accuse your husband, but I was informed that he does have a reputation for indulging in alcoholic beverages."

Kathy shrugged. "He's been known to get drunk, and worse yet, go out in public that way. But he only does it when he's bored. There was no liquor at the wedding, by the way. In fact, Freddie was complaining about it. He's done hardly any drinking since we arrived, certainly not to drunkenness."

So digression was a worse sin. Eckert smiled.

"Mrs. Little, I would like to hear your version of last night's events."

"Mr. Eckert, last night is not all that is at issue." Kathy went on to explain all that had happened, starting with the vandalous attacks and ending with Teresa's accusations after Bill's death. "I was naturally very angry, and already being very suspicious of how conveniently Wimberton happened to be on the scene, when God knows, he never is any other time, I told my sister off."

Abraham chuckled. "Reverend Macadam had to hold them apart like dogs."

"I see." Eckert held his tongue. "Well, I imagine the rest is a matter of public record."

"You still don't believe me, do you?" Kathy said coldly.

Eckert paused. "Mrs. Little, I agree you have some grounds for your beliefs, however, I must remain objective. Mr. Winters, I believe I would like to interview my client now."

"Mr. Eckert." Kathy stopped him. "You might want to consider that one of the people who has expressed a dislike for my father is Mayor Standling, whose son-in-law is Mervin Meyers, the man who will be prosecuting this case. Something very strange is going on in this town. I don't know what it is. I'm not even sure who all is involved. But Bill Javits was part of it, and quite probably Sheriff Wimberton, and I wouldn't be surprised if there were some other influential people involved. After all, Judge Aherne did want the trial to take place today, and made damned sure Freddie's lawyers would never get out here in time."

"I will take that into consideration, Mrs. Little," said Eckert, shutting his briefcase. "Mr. Winters?"

Lowell showed Eckert out of the room.

"Quite an intriguing lady," said Eckert as soon as they were alone in the hall. "Your assessment of her,

Mr. Winters, was very accurate."

Lowell laughed. "Freddie's gotten himself quite a handful, he has."

"I personally prefer a more womanly woman, someone quiet to come home to," Eckert said, polishing his glasses. "Your friend must be the harmless type to let her carry him off."

"Except that he carried her off. Her father had to get the shotgun out to get her down the aisle, not him. He wanted to marry her."

"Good lord, what does he see in her?"

Lowell snorted. "A brain, man, and she's not afraid to use it. Fear not, Mr. Eckert. Freddie Little has the balls to handle her, and the grace and polish to do it right. Which, by the way, is all the more reason to believe that he is innocent. After all, he is not going to waste his time shooting a puppy like Bill Javits. Javits' whimpering was annoying, but certainly not worth bothering with."

"Apparently, there was something more behind it."

"Nothing Freddie would blast the man over. You'll see."

Eckert was not convinced. But he was more interested in, and very much looking forward to, meeting Mr. Little. He found Freddie affable, quick-witted, and unfailingly polite, all in spite of being fully aware of the seriousness of his situation.

"Might we have a chair for Mr. Eckert?" he asked the jailer after the introductions were made.

Diederich grumbled, but conceded. Freddie made small talk while it was being fetched. As Diederich shut the cell door, Freddie chuckled.

"This is really rather awkward," he said genially. "I've never studied the protocols of entertaining one's attorney in one's cell. Shall I be the host, or would you like to?"

Eckert cleared his throat as he sat. "Frankly, Mr. Little, I find it remarkable that you are so calm."

"Years of training," Freddie snorted, rapping his fingers against the bars. "And, perhaps it is naive of me, but I firmly feel that justice will prevail, preferably before I get my neck stretched."

"Well, I feel reasonably confident I can assure you of a prison sentence."

"I suppose that is preferable to hanging, but rather galling when you consider I didn't do it." He paused. "Might I trouble you for a cigarette? My good captors insisted on taking mine, and won't give them back. Some rascal has probably smoked them all, and pawned the case."

Eckert offered his. "You say you didn't kill Mr. Javits."

"No, I didn't." Freddie sucked in the smoke greedily. "Ah, relief at last."

"Yet the sheriff says he saw you do it."

"I have no idea what he saw. Bill Javits was behind the hall where we were celebrating my marriage. Someone, I did not see who, told me Bill wished to see me outside. I was walking along the side of the building when the gun went off. I ran around back, nearly stumbled on the legs, and bent to check the pulse to see if the body was alive, and who it might be, since at that time I had no idea."

"Couldn't you see who?"

"It was too dark. I never saw the face. The next thing I knew Sheriff Wimberton was saying hello, very happily, I might add, with a rifle trained on me. He dropped a coat over the head, and then he announced to the other arriving parties that I had blown Bill Javits' head off. I was promptly arrested. Teresa identified his hand. Wimberton did not lift the coat, as he claimed there was no face left." Freddie got up and paced. "I have been framed, plain and simple. I don't know why anyone hasn't thought to ask why I would have stayed around after shooting the poor fool. I had plenty of time to make my escape."

"I assume we are to believe that the sheriff

prevented it."

"That would make sense. Nonetheless, it would appear that the town is getting ready to hang me, and have it done as soon as possible."

"Do you have any ideas who wants you hung and why?"

"Who? There are several suspects among the town's more influential citizens. As to why, you can choose your options. I personally suspect that by attempting to obtain information regarding a Mr. Elias Tipton, I have made myself a danger to someone. My wife prefers one of two theories: that they wanted to kill Bill Javits and needed someone convenient to blame it on, which I am, being a stranger and all, or that the whole mess is actually a diversion to prevent discovery of a still more nefarious plot. Actually, all three theories are quite plausible. There is something very dastardly going on around here. Have you talked to my wife at all?"

"Eh, yes."

Freddie chuckled proudly. "Found her a bit intimidating, eh? I assure you, she would be utterly shocked if she knew you did. I'll leave you to get all the details surrounding these theories from her. She has a remarkable knack for stating a case plainly and clearly." He snubbed out the cigarette butt, and looked at Eckert. "Might I trouble you again?"

"Help yourself." Eckert tossed the case onto the bunk.

"Thank you." Freddie all but grabbed it. "It's revolting, really, allowing myself to be subject to the tyranny of the tobacco leaf." He lit up. "Go ahead and put them on my bill. I won't question it, although the estate might. Damn, I will need to change my will. Perhaps..."

"Let us wait until it becomes necessary, Mr. Little. You're in a damnable position. But it's not entirely without hope. The burden of proof is on the prosecution. All we have to do is prove reasonable doubt. The town's prejudices will be the most difficult part to overcome."

Freddie's eyebrows lifted. "Not the sheriff?"

"He will be difficult. But I think I may be able to discredit his testimony."

"You might want to ask why he was carrying a coat on such a warm night. I suspect he knew he was going to need it to cover any wounds that were not where they should have been."

"That is a possibility. Your wife mentioned that you had a brief fracas with the deceased on Tuesday afternoon."

"Oh, that."

"Did you actually come to blows?"

"No, I merely ran him down and pinned him, and made that blasted threat. It was nothing I needed to back up with action, you know, which is why I chose the threat I did."

"What was it over?"

"Nothing that anyone is likely to believe in this town." Freddie paused, toying with the cigarette. "I had gotten proof that Bill Javits was molesting my wife's youngest brother. If we can keep that out of the proceedings, I would appreciate it a great deal. The boy has been through enough."

"I wouldn't want it out, anyway. It gives you a motive for the killing, and as you say, no one is likely to believe it happened. How many people know about it?"

"Just the boy, myself, and I told my wife. She needed to know to help her investigations."

"Is she taking part in investigating this matter?"

"Of course she is. We work together, side by side."

Eckert shook his head. "The modern generation."

"It is radical," said Freddie with a small grin. "I take it you're the old fashioned sort, with a wife at home peacefully taking care of the house and children."

"Of course. I make my living confronting people. I don't want to come home to it every night."

"I suppose not. But my life was woefully lacking in confrontation until Kathy came along. I have good cause to value her intellect. Her wits have saved my writing, and even my life a couple times."

"I think I'm beginning to understand. You owe her a debt of gratitude."

"Not really. I've saved her life twice. We're even on that account." Freddie laughed softly. "I suppose it is hard to understand, Mr. Eckert, but there is true joy in being with someone with whom you are evenly matched. Kathy may be more stubborn than a forty mule team, but then so am I."

Eckert nodded, and made a few notes. He was certain of Freddie's innocence. The hard part would be to decide how to bring that out in court. Or would it be better to push for a self-defense plea, and accept a prison sentence? If the court was as anxious to see Freddie hung as he said, which Eckert thought likely, trying for prison would be like asking for the death sentence. He shook his head and thought.

A pile of sandwiches sat on the table in the Briscow kitchen for lunch. Teresa sat at the table alone, oblivious to the food, and stared sullenly at the pantry door. She didn't move when Kathy came through the screen door behind her.

Kathy paused. She didn't want to hate Teresa, and her anger could easily do more damage to Freddie's case. And Teresa might know something, something vital that would put the whole case in a clear light. She laid her hand softly on Teresa's shoulder.

"I know you're still angry," Kathy said quietly. "But please hear me out. I know why you think Freddie killed Bill, and you do have reason. But Freddie didn't. The evidence doesn't quite fit, no matter what Sheriff Wimberton says he saw."

Teresa sniffed. "I don't care."

"Teresa, if Freddie is convicted, then the one who really did kill Bill will go free."

"Maybe I want that."

"What?"

"Maybe I want him to go free. To say thank you." Teresa squeezed Kathy's hand. "It's not fair to set Freddie up for it, so I guess I won't."

Shocked, Kathy slid around to the nearest chair. Teresa smiled weakly at her.

"I didn't want Bill to die. Actually, I did. I just wanted it to happen peacefully, like he'd get sick and quietly fade away, no pain. Although, if they blew his head off, I don't know how much he felt. I just wanted him out of my life, Kathy, and I couldn't divorce him because of the kids, and the judge would never believe it if I lied and said he was cheating on me, and I couldn't afford a lawyer anyway." Teresa sniffed. "I sound like such an animal, don't I? That's why I was so angry last night. I wanted so badly to blame somebody because I'd gotten my wish, and I felt like it was my fault. I was already mad at Freddie for telling me off. He was easy."

"He's also innocent."

"I know that. Hell, how did a man who didn't notice a bank robbery going on at the teller window next to him turn up in just the right spot to catch Freddie? And why would Freddie kill Bill anyway? There's no reason for it. I know he threatened to, but whatever they were arguing about, that threat was enough to keep Bill down."

Kathy picked up a sandwich and glared at it. "What do you know about what Bill was involved in?"

"What do you mean? The only thing Bill was involved in was embalming bodies."

"He was involved in the vandalism, Teresa."

Teresa looked at her, puzzled. "He was?"

"He had to have been. The vandals have been too accurate. And when Freddie and I found that body, he was the one who took it back. Who else would have known where it was? Freddie found tire tracks near the scene. Chevrolet tire tracks. We just don't know why, and who was directing it. It has to be someone with a lot of influence, enough to control Bill and Wimberton."

"Where'd the body go, then? It didn't come back.

At least, I don't think it did."

Kathy thought. "Maybe we ought to go out to the funeral home and check."

Teresa shook her head. "Wimberton sealed it off last night. Our house, too. Said he didn't want anybody disturbing evidence. He only let Ma and me inside the house, and that was just long enough for me to get some clothes for myself and the kids. Gideon tried again today, and it's still locked."

"They'll have to open it to present physical evidence."

"Why? There were plenty of people who saw the body. And it was Bill."

"Has Meyers talked to you about testifying?"

"He sent around a Notice to Appear. I'm gonna have to, Kathy."

Kathy smiled. "That's okay. As long as you tell them what you told me, as close as you can manage, it may help. Just let Meyers keep thinking you're going to testify for the state."

Chapter Fifteen

Sitting in court, Kathy pinched herself, hoping and praying that what she was witnessing was just some horrible nightmare, and that she would wake up in the boarding house in New York, or in her mother's room, or in a hotel room somewhere in Freddie's arms. She barely heard the request for a continuance (denied), and the opening arguments.

The courtroom, in all its wood-paneled glory, was packed. Two electric fans swirled slowly above the judge, sitting on his high dark wood bench, and above the attorneys' tables. Windows were opened on the one side of the courtroom, but neither the soft breeze nor the fans did much to ease the stifling air inside. Freddie sat at the defense table between Eckert and Abraham. He looked calm enough, but Kathy noticed that he was wearing the suit he'd worn to the wedding, and she choked.

The prosecution presented first. Prosecutor Mervin Meyers, a tallish man with a foppish air about him, wearing an impeccable black suit and starched white pocket square, oozed confidence to the point of looking bored with his task. He had two men testify that they saw Freddie bending over the body, and that the shotgun barrel was pointed at Javits' head. Eckert cross-examined and got them to admit they did not see Freddie touching the gun, or doing anything that involved killing Javits, in spite of objections from Meyers that Eckert was unfairly pressuring the witnesses, all of which were sustained by the judge.

Then Etta Levers testified about Freddie's threat. Eckert tried to discredit her hearing, but Meyers objected on the basis of relevance and it was sustained. Marieanne Peterson also testified. Freddie whispered in Eckert's ear. Eckert got her to remember that Freddie had implied that he didn't intend to carry out the threat.

Then Wimberton took the stand and was sworn in.

"Sheriff Wimberton, how long has it been since you were elected to your current post?" asked Meyers.

"Fourteen years." Wimberton shifted and wiped his nose.

"And during that time has anybody filed a complaint about your service to this community?"

"A couple here and there. Nothing serious."

"So, since you keep getting elected, is it fair to say that you have been a faithful and competent public servant."

"Hope so."

Meyers smiled. "Sheriff, will you please describe for us the events you witnessed on the night of July fifteenth of this year?"

"Well, I was walking around on patrol, and I started down the alley toward the Presbyterian church hall, and I saw Bill Javits looking for somebody. Then this fellow comes up, raises a shot gun and blasts Javits."

"Is this fellow in this room?"

Wimberton jerked a thumb at Freddie. "Yes, sir, the defendant."

"Are you sure?"

"He's kinda hard to miss."

A murmur of chuckles rippled through the room.

Freddie stretched his long legs and ignored the laughs.

Meyers waited for silence. "What happened then?"

"I did my duty. I stopped him, and covered the body, then put him under arrest for murder, and had the body formally identified."

"And who identified it?"

"His wife, Teresa Javits."

"Sheriff, you said you covered the body. Why so quickly?"

"His face had been blown clean off. It weren't pretty."

"Thank you, Sheriff." Meyers turned. "Mr. Eckert?"

Eckert rose. "Sheriff, I believe two previous witnesses have testified that it was very dark that night. How is it that you managed, while just entering an alley, I believe you said, to not only identify the victim, but the gun the assailant was holding?"

Wimberton stopped. "I got lucky, I guess."

"But, by your own testimony, the victim's face was blown off, beyond recognition."

"I saw him before he got shot."

"But according to the others' testimony, you were facing Mr. Little, and the body's head was at your feet. So unless you took the extra time to circle around to the front of the assailant, who had just shot someone, the deceased's back was to you. I ask you again, how did you identify the deceased quickly enough to accuse Mr. Little of blowing his head off before anyone else knew he was even dead?"

Wimberton fished nervously. "I... Well, hell. I've known Javits since he was a kid. I just knew."

"You just knew. Sheriff, how would you describe the weather that night?"

"It was pretty warm."

"You covered the body. With what did you cover it?"

"My coat. The others saw it."

"Why were you carrying a coat on a night that even you admit was pretty warm?"

Wimberton shifted again. "Uh..."

"Objection, Your Honor," said Meyers. "The witness's personal habits do not need to be defended."

"Sustained," said Aherne.

Eckert took it with grace. "Very well. Did you pull a gun on Mr. Little?"

"He'd just shot someone, of course I did."

Eckert nodded. "What kind of gun?"

"My rifle."

"Is it a hunting rifle?"

"It's standard for police work."

"I see. Sheriff, when are your normal working hours?"

"I'm on call, but I work day shift."

Freddie noticed Meyers frowning.

"I see. Earlier I believe you said you were on patrol. Sheriff, what were you doing on patrol armed with a rifle at a time that is not your normal working hours?"

"Objection, Your Honor," snapped Meyers. "I don't see why the witness needs to defend his presence at the scene that night."

"Your Honor," said Eckert. "If the sheriff's presence was not the result of a fortuitous coincidence, then the fact that it was arranged, with or without the sheriff's knowledge, is very significant."

Aherne paused. "Overruled. The witness may answer."

"Sheriff?" Eckert asked.

Wimberton grinned suddenly. "I sometimes change my shift."

"And do you also patrol with a rifle?"

"It don't pay to take chances."

Eckert was angry, but he held it. "Very well, then. No further questions."

He sat down fuming as Meyers called Teresa Javits to the stand.

"That bastard," whispered Abraham, who was at the table assisting. "Gave Wimberton just enough time to think of an answer."

"This is going to be an uphill battle, gentlemen," sighed Eckert, as Teresa was sworn in. "She is going to hurt."

"Mrs. Javits," asked Meyers, "what is your relationship to the deceased?"

"He was my husband." Teresa's face was stoic, and she remained clear-voiced and dry-eyed.

"When you heard that your husband had been shot, what was your first thought?"

"Relief." Teresa ducked her head in shame.

Meyers looked at her, surprised. "But who did you think had shot him?"

"Well, everyone was saying Freddie had done it, so I believed that."

"Did you not say so quite vehemently?"

"I'm afraid I did."

"And did you not almost come to blows over the issue with your sister?"

"I'm afraid I did."

"Do you have a reason for believing that Mr. Little killed your husband?"

"I did."

Eckert held his breath. Abraham stayed looking straight ahead at the table, almost afraid to hope. Freddie kept the same impassive look he'd kept since the beginning.

"And what was that reason?"

"I told you. Everyone else was saying it, and I wanted to believe he did. I wanted to believe that anybody had done it."

"Stick to the question, please," snapped Meyers. He thought. "Didn't the fact that there had been a previous altercation between your husband and Mr. Little influence your belief?"

"At first, then I thought about it, and realized that Freddie couldn't have done it."

Eckert and Abraham quietly rejoiced while Freddie closed his eyes and put his chin in his hand. Meyers gaped, then recovered.

"But that night, you were certain."

"Not really."

"You were vehement enough to attack your sister."

"I was angry."

Scowling, Meyers noticed Abraham sitting next to Freddie.

"Mrs. Javits, is it not true that the defendant is your brother-in-law?"

"Yes."

"And is it not true that the young man assisting our learned colleague is your brother?"

"Yes."

"Is it not possible that your family has influenced you to change your mind regarding something you were very sure of Wednesday night?"

"No." Teresa smiled a little, her voice perfectly confident.

"Have you had any discussions with your family members since that night regarding the assumed guilt of the defendant?"

"One, yesterday afternoon. I told my sister I didn't think he did it."

"Did your sister try to change your mind?"

"Sort of. I'd al—"

"Yes or no, Mrs. Javits."

"Yes."

"No further questions." Shaking his head, Meyers returned to his seat.

Eckert thought a minute, then slowly rose.

"Mrs. Javits, when you spoke with your sister yesterday, did she succeed in changing your mind regarding the defendant's supposed guilt?"

"Not really," said Teresa with a sheepish smile. "I'd already figured he was innocent."

"And how did you come to that conclusion?"

"I thought about it, and wondered why Wimberton happened to be there when he couldn't even spot a bank robbery happening two feet next to him."

"A bank robbery, Mrs. Javits. Were you present, or

did you just hear about it?"

"I was there, scared to death, too. I know he said he was just waiting 'til they'd gotten out of the bank so people didn't panic, but I saw him, and he just plain didn't notice."

"Objection, Your Honor," said Meyers. "The incident is not relevant to the case at hand."

"It brings into question the sheriff's powers of observation, which are very relevant, as he was the eyewitness," said Eckert quickly.

"Sustained," said Aherne. "The jury will not consider the witness's last statement, and it shall be struck from the record."

Eckert nodded. "In any case, Mrs. Javits, would it be fair to say that your later conclusion was reached after careful thought, whereas your immediate reaction was emotional and based on the prevailing hysteria?"

"That most certainly would be fair to say. That's what happened."

"Did anyone in your family, at any time, apart from the very emotional altercation with your sister shortly after the crime was discovered, try to convince you or in any way pressure you into taking Mr. Little's part?"

Teresa chuckled. "They know better than to try that."

"Thank you, Mrs. Javits. No further questions."

Abraham was jubilant. Eckert squashed it.

"We've still got a long way to go."

Meyers stood. "Your Honor, before the witness is dismissed, I'd like to re-examine."

"Your Honor," protested Eckert. "If my learned colleague re-examines, I will have to call for a mistrial."

"The request is denied," said Aherne. "Does the prosecution have any more witnesses?"

"The prosecution rests."

"The defense will call witnesses."

Honoria squeezed Kathy's hand. "I hope he calls me."

"He won't," Kathy whispered. "You're too biased, and a hysterical woman besides."

Eckert stood. "The defense would like to call Mrs. Frederick Little to the stand."

Kathy was a little startled, but went calmly, and was sworn in.

"Mrs. Little," said Eckert. "On the night of your husband's arrest, did you at any time question his innocence?"

"No."

"Was that because he was your husband?"

"I'd like to think I'm capable of more objective thinking than that."

"I'm sure you are, Mrs. Little. Is it not true that you were somewhat reluctant to marry your husband?"

"Very reluctant. Not about him, you understand. Just marriage."

"So I understand. Then would you say that you do not feel strongly about standing behind your husband at all costs?"

"It depends on what you're talking about. I support what he does, unless he does something stupid."

"Such as murdering his brother-in-law?"

"But he didn't do it."

"At this point, that is not what I'm asking. I want to know if he did do it, would you still stand by him and support him?"

"If it were self-defense, I suppose. But cold blooded murder, I can't imagine him doing it, let alone supporting him in it."

"Mrs. Little, if you had been the only witness to such a murder, committed by your husband, would you help him hide it?"

"Hide it? Good lord, how do you hide a murder? I'd stand with him as far as I could if he turned himself in, I suppose, if it were justifiable. But pure cold blooded murder. I wouldn't want to be near anyone like that."

"Then you would turn him in?"

"Yes. But that's not my husband."

"No, it isn't your husband. And you believe your husband to be innocent. At what point on the night of murder did you first become emotional?"

"When my stupid sister wouldn't stop screaming that he'd done it."

"But prior to that you were calm."

"Yes."

"Will you tell me what your thoughts and feelings were when the news first started to be made known?"

"I was shocked that Bill was dead. When they accused Freddie, I knew that was ridiculous. Then I immediately wondered about Wimberton. Freddie and I, we'd had reason to question his role in another matter, and it seemed very convenient."

"Then Sheriff Wimberton did not necessarily like your husband."

"Not as far as I could tell. If anything, he disliked Freddie."

"Mrs. Little, I understand that some months ago you and your husband were in a situation in which your lives were in immediate peril. To be specific, a madwoman was holding a gun on you."

"Objection," said Meyers. "It's not relevant to the case at hand."

"Your Honor, character evidence is allowed."

"Objection sustained. Counsel will please remain with the matter in question."

Eckert sighed silently. "Mrs. Little, having seen your husband in a number of situations, would you say he is prone to violence?"

"No. The reverse."

"Did you know that he had threatened the deceased?"

"Not right away. But when I questioned him about it, he admitted it readily."

"Did you at any time believe he would follow through with it?"

"Only if lives were in immediate peril, and that would be the only way of saving them."

"Thank you, Mrs. Little." Eckert turned to Meyers. "Your witness."

Meyers stood, pondering. "Mrs. Little, you seem to be an exceptionally rational woman. Yet you persist in saying that your husband is innocent, as any good wife would, in spite of considerable physical evidence to the contrary. Why is that?"

"Because Wimberton's testimony was questionable, as was his presence at the scene, and I have heard my husband's version of what happened."

"So you believed what your husband told you."

"There was also Wimberton."

"But you took your husband's word as to what had happened."

"Not in blind faith, no."

"But ultimately, Mrs. Little, you have only his word that what he says happened, did. Is this not true, Mrs. Little? Yes or no?"

Kathy kept silent.

"Mrs. Little?"

"The witness will answer the question," said Aherne.

"I can't."

"Mrs. Little, if you do not answer, I can and will find you in contempt of court," said Aherne, getting testy.

"Your Honor, I am under oath. I cannot answer that question as Mr. Meyers wants because neither yes nor no is the truth. If that puts me in contempt of the court, then so be it." Kathy gazed out over the gallery to a spot on the back wall.

Aherne sighed. "The witness will answer as she sees fit."

"Thank you." Kathy turned to Meyers. "The fact is my husband's word about the details of what happened has been backed up by the testimony of the witnesses, with the exception of Sheriff Wimberton, and I have already expressed my reasons for doubting him."

"No further questions." Meyers returned to his

seat.

Kathy was dismissed.

"It didn't help him any," she sighed softly to Honoria. "I may even have hurt him."

"You told the truth," said Honoria.

Freddie was called to the stand next. He told his version clearly and confidently, and without putting Wimberton in a bad light, or excess verbiage. But Meyers was smiling as he got up to cross-examine.

"Mr. Little, I'm assuming that you are aware that your description of the events of Wednesday night puts you in direct contradiction with the testimony of our well-respected sheriff."

"I am aware of that," said Freddie.

"Are you, then, accusing Sheriff Wimberton of perjury?"

"I cannot say what he saw."

"Are you accusing Sheriff Wimberton of perjury, yes or no?"

Freddie's lips went tight. "No."

"No further questions."

"Then the witness is dismissed." Aherne paused as Freddie left the stand, then looked at Eckert. "Any more witnesses?"

"No, Your Honor. The defense rests."

"Is the prosecution ready to make its final argument?" asked Aherne.

"I believe I can." Meyers sat confidently on the edge of the table. "Gentlemen of the jury, this case is very simple. It is based on facts. And the facts are that Sheriff Emil Wimberton, on Wednesday night, the fifteenth of July, nineteen hundred and twenty five, saw a man, the defendant, shoot William Javits. Witnesses have confirmed that Mr. Little was bending over the body, and that the gun was pointed at Mr. Javits' head. Witnesses have also confirmed, and Mr. Little has admitted, that on a previous occasion he had threatened Mr. Javits with death. The argument is irrelevant. The defense never even discussed it. But those are the facts, and no one can prove otherwise. Therefore, when you make your decision, no matter what the defense says about those facts, they are facts, and can only lead to one conclusion, that Frederick Little is guilty of murdering William Javits."

Eckert didn't feel like smiling when he got up, but he was not unhappy.

"Gentlemen of the jury, my esteemed colleague says that this case is based on facts, and that those facts can only lead to one conclusion. Well, gentlemen, we all know that the sun rises in the east, and sets in the west. That is a fact. The sun also travels across the sky every day. That too is a fact, and given those facts, one might assume that the sun revolves around us. For over a thousand years, people did. But four hundred years ago, it was proven that we revolve around the sun, and modern science has confirmed this. Mr. Little threatened Mr. Javits with a neck wringing. That is a fact, but it does not lead inescapably to the conclusion that Mr. Little was going to follow through on it. Even the witness admitted that he indicated otherwise, and the people who were immediately involved in the event have said to follow through would have been unnecessary. It is a fact that Mr. Little was seen bending over the body. But the witnesses admitted they did not see him doing anything. In fact, it is quite reasonable to assume that they saw him going to the aid of a stricken person, as Mr. Little said he was doing, a person whose identity was completely unknown to him. But there is the fact of Sheriff Wimberton's testimony. He says he saw Mr. Little fire a shotgun at Mr. Javits. But the fact is it was a very dark night. Even the witnesses could not clearly see, and had only the sheriff's word that the body belonged to William Javits. The fact is Sheriff Wimberton approached from behind William Javits, and could not see his face, so how was he to know? Mr. Little is quite gracious, and does not want to accuse Sheriff Wimberton of perjury. He is very willing to accept that the good sheriff was innocently, but definitely, mistaken. I do not accuse Sheriff Wimberton of perjury. It was dark. Mr. Meyers insists that you rely upon the facts to make your decision. But the fact is facts can be, and in this case most certainly are, misleading. Your job is to determine whether or not there is guilt beyond a reasonable doubt. There is considerable doubt here, and so you must find my client not guilty."

Eckert returned to the defense table slowly while the jury was dismissed. Tension sifted through the courtroom as people stood and stretched. Freddie got hold of a cigarette and lit up, tapping his finger against the edge of the table. Kathy and Honoria made their way to the railing.

"They can't convict you, Freddie," said Honoria, her face white.

"We'll see," Freddie replied shortly.

He looked at Kathy. Her eyes were dry, but it seem as though they would fill at the least provocation. He smiled softly at her and leaned over the railing.

"We'll get our wedding night yet," he whispered in her ear.

She smiled and squeezed his hand. He kissed her cheek.

The minutes passed, then an hour.

"It's a good sign they're deliberating this long," said Eckert. "We've given them something to think about."

"As long as it's the right thing," whispered Kathy.

Fifteen minutes more.

An hour and a half.

At fifteen minutes before the hour, the jury room opened and the jury filed in. The foreman stood.

"Have you reached a decision?" asked Aherne.

"We have," said the foreman.

"What say you?"

"In the matter of the State of Kansas against Frederick Gordon Little, we find the defendant guilty."

Kathy's heart stopped beating.

"The defendant will approach the bench," said Aherne.

Freddie calmly walked forward.

"Frederick Little, you have been convicted of murder in the first degree. You are hereby sentenced to hang by the neck until dead, with the execution to take place tomorrow morning, the eighteenth of July, year of our Lord, nineteen twenty five, at ten o'clock."

Honoria gasped. "They can't do this!"

She got up, but Joshua held her down. Kathy had bent her head, but stayed dry eyed. Deputy Diederich put the handcuffs on Freddie and led him back to the jail.

Chapter Sixteen

Diederich let only Kathy, Eckert and Abraham back into the cell with Freddie. Honoria had to wait outside, sobbing on Lowell's shoulder, surrounded by the rest of Kathy's family.

"Put this under your mattress," said Abraham the moment Diederich's back was turned. He handed Freddie a large, thickly-stuffed envelope.

"What is it?" asked Freddie.

"Your mail. Gideon just gave it to me."

"Now I get it, damn it!" Freddie opened it quickly.

"Freddie, you're not going to hang," said Eckert. "That trial was a farce. I've already telephoned the governor. He's ordered the records, and wants them tonight. Aherne will have to give them up, and he can't stall too long or the governor will be pissed."

"Look at this," said Freddie. "The governor will like it."

"What is it?" asked Kathy.

"Evidence that the judge, and the prosecutor, and the mayor, and the banker, and the hotel owner, and the sheriff are in league with each other." Freddie pulled it out. "These are the articles of incorporation for the bank, and they are all on the board of directors."

"That just means they're connected. It doesn't mean you didn't kill Bill," said Kathy.

"But it is justification for a mistrial," said Eckert, grinning. "To hell with Aherne. I'm taking this straight to the governor. That bastard is going to get himself bounced right off his bench. Keep this quiet. I'm leaving now to hurry his people."

"Wait," said Freddie. "I don't trust him. I want you to make out my will now."

"No, Freddie, they're not going to touch you," said Kathy.

"I want it done now," said Freddie calmly.

He sat down on the bench as Eckert got out a pen and tablet. Kathy curled up next to him, finally letting the tears go.

"Very well then," said Eckert. "Today's date, the last will and testament of Frederick Gordon Little..."

"The third," added Freddie.

Sighing, Abraham leaned against the bars.

"Being of sound mind and body, upon my death, I hereby make the following bequests. To my dear friend and companion, Lowell Winters, all my funds currently deposited in the Megatherian Trust, my cufflinks which he's always envied, and any proceeds from my book, 'The Old Money Story', the which, without his patience, dedication and encouragement, would never have been written. To my beloved sister, Honoria Wentworth, my crystal collection that she has always admired, and my eternal love. To my parents, I only ask that they think fondly of me time and again. To Kathleen Mary Briscow Little, my beloved wife and dearest friend, I leave everything else."

"I don't want everything!" sobbed Kathy. "I want you."

"All the rest of my earthly goods and possessions, including all stocks, shares of the family business, monies deposited in bank accounts, trusts and funds, my apartment, my cars, my airplane, and anything else not specifically mentioned. I ask that should my sister suffer from a drastic reversal of fortune, that my wife see to her care. I hereby assign attorney Michael Callaghan, of New York City, as executor, asking that he watch out for my wife, but not too closely. This will shall supersede any other will of mine dated prior to this date, and render them null and void." He stopped. "Is that in order, then?"

Abraham snorted. "Anyone wants to contest that they'd better have a fortune, 'cause they'll have to spend one to have a prayer of winning."

"It will easily sail through the probate court," said Eckert. He finished writing. "Sign here."

Freddie took the pen and swallowed. "Never did like signing these things."

He took a deep breath and signed, still holding Kathy.

Eckert signed it and had Abraham sign as well.

"We must be getting on," Eckert said, putting his pen away. "We don't have much time. I will leave the will in Mr. Abraham's custody."

"Thank you," said Freddie.

"Don't give up hope," said Eckert. "I'll get you out of this in plenty of time. Good day."

Abraham called for Diederich, and he and Eckert left. Kathy remained behind.

"I'm not going to leave you, Freddie," she sniffed.

"And Diederich's left the door open, so I guess we don't get any privacy." Freddie took her into his arms. "Shall we scandalize him anyway?"

"He'll probably kick me out, and I don't want you disgraced. You're not hung yet, and I'm not going to let them."

"Kathy, you may not be able to stop them. Someone obviously wants me hung very badly." Freddie held up the rest of the papers. "And I suspect these papers are why. Shall we look?"

Kathy looked over the hand-copied sheets and forms with a puzzled frown.

"What are they?"

"Financial statements." Freddie read them carefully as he spoke. "It's all public record, but one does have to know to look for them, which is why I was convicted. The person, or persons, behind this should appear somewhere in these records. And here it is: a prospectus for a new corporation. And look who is on the board of directors."

"The same six as the bank?"

"You are correct, my love. This is interesting. It's for a land development company, selling parcels of land for resorts or vacation homes. That explains why Tipton was telegraphing Levitt and Solomon, the real estate brokers. Or, more accurately, land speculators. Looks like our gang decided if swampland in Florida can sell like crazy, why not farmland in Kansas?"

Kathy took the sheets of paper. "Freddie, this says there's a lake on the edge of town. There's no lake around here for miles and miles."

"But there could be, if the creek was dammed." Freddie sorted out another set of papers. "Tipton has been investing the bank's funds in a lot of stock, I assume raising capital."

"Capital?"

"The cash needed to pull this off. But how is he going to get enough to buy all the land?"

Kathy gasped. "He doesn't have to buy it. The farmers all have mortgages. He can just call in the notes."

"Except one." Freddie looked at her.

"Pa. He won't take a mortgage. The vandals, Freddie. Josh was right. They are trying to drive him off his land."

"Or better, cost him enough money so that he'll have to take out a mortgage." Freddie shuffled through more of the papers. "Oh, my. It looks like Tipton has managed to acquire all of the shares in the new company and almost all of the shares in the bank, and I seriously doubt he's managed to convince his partners to give those shares up."

"Isn't that illegal?"

"Very illegal. But not that hard to do when you're at a distance from New York and even Topeka—or would the exchange be in Kansas City?"

"I have no idea." Kathy sighed. "Unfortunately, none of this proves that you didn't kill Bill, or that Bill was even connected to them."

"I'd just as soon prove it, too. It will save all the hearings and court dates it will take to get me acquitted. The funeral home. Maybe there's some record. And maybe even that boy's body is still there and we can find out who killed him."

Kathy shook her head. "Wimberton locked both the funeral home and Teresa's house Wednesday night, and how much do you want to bet one of those six has already searched both places and removed any incriminating evidence?"

"It's entirely possible they haven't, assuming I was safely tucked away. They didn't view you or Teresa as a threat. You saw how surprised they were at the trial."

"I don't want to think about that." Kathy sniffed and shuddered. "Those jurors probably heard my testimony and thought they'd better convict you than throw you back to me."

"At least you proved your opinion wasn't based on bias."

"Not that it did any good."

"Darling, nothing would have done any good." Freddie shook his head. "Those jurors had to have been hand-picked. Not one was a farmer."

"Oh, Freddie. I hate this waiting."

"We can at least be close." He pulled her into his lap and kissed her hair. "And we can hold each other, and kiss."

Kathy sighed. "We can at least do that much."

Kathy got kicked out at six o'clock. Isaac took her to the hotel, and Honoria's room.

"It's war council time," Honoria explained as Kathy and Isaac slid in.

Besides Honoria, Joshua and Betty were there, as were Lowell and Gideon.

"Ma's gotta take care of Pa," Joshua explained. "And Teresa wants to stay with her kids."

"Is the funeral home open?" asked Kathy.

"No. They're all at the farm. Gam's out spying on Aherne and making sure he doesn't try anything."

"There's only one thing to do," said Honoria. "We're going to break Freddie out of jail."

"No, Honoria!" groaned Kathy. "That's the worst thing we could do. It will only make Freddie look bad."

"So what? He doesn't have to come back to Kansas. He can fly out of here and forget this nightmare."

"And once he's in New York, all they have to do is extradite him. And if he never goes back to New York, all his funds will still be frozen. He won't have any money, and I'm sure he doesn't want to live as a fugitive for the rest of his life."

Honoria glared. "And you're going to let them hang him?"

"He's not going to hang. Mr. Eckert is on his way to the governor now with Abraham, and the governor is expecting him and the records. They'll be back with the reprieve in plenty of time."

Gam slid in the door. "Freddie's in big trouble. Eckert went to get a reprieve from the governor, so Aherne moved the hanging up to seven o'clock in the morning."

"We'd better telephone Eckert and the governor," said Lowell.

"We can't," said Gam. "I heard Aherne on the phone. He told the operator at the exchange not to put any long distance calls through without talking to him first. And he also told the Western Union operators the same thing. He said he didn't want Freddie getting anyone to help him escape."

Silence hung heavy in the room.

Kathy took a deep breath. "Honoria, did you have any specific plan?"

It took some haggling. Kathy insisted that the escape take place just before dawn, so Freddie could take off right away, and that there be plans for getting Honoria and Lowell away safely, or else Freddie wouldn't go. Joshua was worried that his Packard Single Six wouldn't move fast enough to get away, when Kathy remembered the Packard Twin Six engine in the shed. Lowell assured them he could install it in Josh's car. Even Isaac and Gam had a job.

"I guess I'll have to buy Freddie another one," sighed Kathy, as they lifted the Twin Six into Joshua's car. "He was so happy about finding it, too."

Gam and Isaac were busy emptying Mexican firewater into a small milk can.

"What is this?" asked Honoria looking at one of the bottles.

"Try it," said Joshua.

Honoria did and grimaced. "It tastes like gasoline."

"They call it 'to kill ya,'" laughed Joshua. "I've got a friend who was an army ace pilot, and he flies it in from Mexico in his old Sopwith Camel."

Kathy went in and helped Betty finish packing.

"It's been some honeymoon," Betty said, wrapping Little J in extra blankets. She smiled at Kathy. "You'll get yours. I'm sure of it."

At quarter before four in the morning, Honoria slipped into the jail office wearing a black beaded sleeveless dress. A new young deputy was on duty, this one with red hair and blue eyes and freckles that made him look even younger than he was. He stood.

"Hi," said Honoria with a soft voice and a coy smile. "I saw you earlier, but couldn't get away."

"Really?"

"I thought you were just adorable." Honoria lifted her skirt. "Do you mind if I smoke?"

"Uh, no ma'am."

Honoria hiked her foot onto the chair next to the desk, giving the officer the best view of her shapely leg. She slipped her skirt up past her garter, and retrieved the cigarette there and lowered her leg. Then she put her other leg up, and got the holder from her other garter.

In his cell, Freddie had not been sleeping very well and was startled when his flight jacket, cap and boots landed on the floor beneath his window.

"Do you have a light?" Honoria asked the deputy.

"Sure." He scrambled through the desk for matches, and lit one quickly.

Honoria leaned way over, giving the young man a perfect view of the inside of her dress with nothing on underneath. She blew out the match, and caught his eyes. He was melting. She leaned over again and kissed his mouth, and soon had him fully involved in necking, with her hands all over him.

Kathy, dressed in flying gear, slid in the door and around behind the desk. She lifted the deputy's gun from his holster very slowly, and eased the keys off his desk. Outside, on the freshly built gallows, there was the sound of glass breaking and a soft explosion. The deputy suddenly pulled away from Honoria.

"I heard something," he gasped.

Kathy hit him in the back of the neck with the gun. He fell forward, unconscious.

"See? It works," Honoria said, smiling smugly at Kathy.

Kathy ran for the cells. "You get some of those rifles out, and some ammo. I'll get Freddie."

Freddie had his boots on and was waiting.

"Do you have any idea what you're doing?" he demanded as Kathy unlocked the cell. "You could destroy every last chance I've got!"

"Aherne already did," snapped Kathy, pulling him out. "He moved up the hanging time. You'll be dead by the time Eckert gets back with that reprieve."

Freddie slid on the jacket. In the office, Gam and Honoria were loading a kit bag with boxes of shells.

"This is gonna be really heavy," said Gam.

"Hopefully, we won't need it." Freddie swooped up

the bag and grabbed a rifle.

Kathy led the way out of the office. What few people were about were distracted by the gallows going up in flames in front of the courthouse steps. They dashed across the grounds and into the shadows of the public library. Gam slipped off to whatever hiding place he'd found. Kathy sent Honoria off to her meeting place. Then Freddie and Kathy checked the street and dashed across and into the alley.

"They went this way!" someone yelled.

Gunfire erupted, and Kathy and Freddie dove for the pavement.

"Now what?" Freddie gasped, firing back.

Kathy looked at the square panel just above the pavement.

"We're at the funeral home. Through the panel."

"Will I fit?"

"They got Fatman Albright through without a hitch." Kathy wriggled through.

Freddie scrambled after. The room was cool. Freddie could barely make out a high table, and beyond that, shelves holding all kinds of jars and bottles. The sickly sweet stench of a recent death was just starting to ease off. Kathy kept her hand on the panel and held her breath.

"Where'd they go?" someone yelled outside.

"They must have made it out of the alley somehow. Let's go."

Silence once more filled the room.

"Where are we?" Freddie whispered.

"The basement," Kathy whispered back. "We went through the body drop."

Freddie glanced back at the panel. "How creepy."

"We'd better get upstairs and barricade ourselves in," said Kathy. "It won't be long before they look."

They went upstairs and pulled Bill's rolltop desk in front of the back door, and coffins in front of the front door.

"Thank God he kept the windows curtained off,"

Freddie grumbled, going back into the viewing room.

Kathy came in from the back. "Freddie, look what tumbled out of a crack in the desk."

Freddie took the envelope. "It's addressed to Teresa."

"Hm." Kathy pointed to the back of the room. "Well, it looks like Wimberton was pretty lazy."

Freddie looked. "I'll be damned."

He switched on a light. Bill Javits' corpse lay on its back on a body cart in the far corner. The coat had slipped off, revealing a fully intact face, eyes open and staring.

"He's not smelling too good," said Freddie, wrinkling his nose.

"But he's got a face." Feeling a little squeamish, Kathy looked at him more closely. "He hasn't got the back of his head, though." Grimacing, she opened the lips. "And here's the proof you didn't kill him. Powder burns."

"He killed himself. That's why the barrel was pointed at him."

"Wimberton must have seen him do it, then decided he could use it against you."

"He was waiting for me." Freddie looked at the envelope in his hands. "I think we'd better open this anyway."

He ripped open the letter and read.

"It's a suicide note," he said. "'They're going to kill me. I know they are. But it's Freddie they want. That's why it has to be this way. I have to make it obvious, and if they're going to kill me anyway, why should I let them have Freddie? He's the only one who can stop them. He knows about Tipton, and he'll know about the plan they have for the farms. They're going to foreclose on all the surrounding farms, Tipton and Spivens and the whole board. Teresa, don't let your pa take a mortgage or he'll lose his farm.'" Freddie looked up. "Where are those papers, anyway?"

"In the plane," said Kathy. "What's on the second

page?"

"He confesses to molesting Gammers and the other boys."

"Oh, my god. If that ever comes out..."

Freddie folded the sheets and hid them in his flight jacket's inside pocket. "It won't. Sadly, Bill did not say who killed the boy."

"And that body doesn't seem to be here, either."

Downstairs, the panel slammed. Kathy and Freddie grabbed their rifles and slid down the stairway to the basement. Gam was reaching up and shutting the panel. He turned.

"There you are," he said. "We'd better get this bolted."

"What are you doing here?" Kathy asked as Freddie hurried down and helped Gam bolt the panel.

"This is my hiding place, at least since Bill got it." He looked at Freddie. "I was kind of hoping you'd done it, Freddie."

"I'd already made sure he wasn't going to touch you, Gammers," said Freddie softly.

Gam groaned. "Is that what that threat was? Oh, damn."

"It doesn't make any difference now," said Kathy. "Hopefully, that reprieve will get here, and I can get off on mitigating circumstances." She smiled. "We can prove that Freddie didn't kill Bill, and that he was framed, and that Aherne, Meyers and Wimberton all had good reason to want Freddie hanged."

"They'll have a hard time doing it," said Gam, grinning. "Their nice new gallows is all ashes. Those bottles worked great. And Josh and everybody got off."

"Betty, the baby, Honoria and Lowell," Kathy explained to Freddie. "They had the car. We thought splitting up would be better since only two of us can get in the plane."

"It was some chase, too," said Gam. "Josh's car took off like a bat out of hell, with that big engine in it."

"My Twin Six," sighed Freddie.

"I'll find another for you," said Kathy. "At least they're all safe."

"That's somewhat reassuring," said Freddie. "In the meantime, we are trapped here. Let's go upstairs and see what we can do about it."

In the shop, Kathy peeked through a curtain, and nearly took a bullet for it.

"They know we're in here," she said, smiling weakly from the floor.

More bullets followed. Freddie ducked behind the coffin at the door, broke out the glass, and pumped a few rounds into the street.

There was silence for a few minutes, then they heard Wimberton clearing the area.

"All right, Little," Wimberton called. "We know you're in there. Come out peacefully."

"So you can get me hanged before Eckert gets back with the reprieve?" Freddie called back. "Or would you simply prefer shooting me before I let on about the bank's plans for the mortgaged farmers in the area?"

A small rumble wafted in off the street.

Kathy peeked through the bottom of the curtain. "We're getting somewhere, Freddie. There's a few people coming out on the street."

"Wimberton, you might like to know, I've got the prospectus, that's the plan, for the Hays Land Development Corporation, with all that nice talk about the lakefront property around here. And the names of the board of directors, and guess what, Wimberton? Yours is one of them."

"Oh, Freddie, they're really looking at him out there."

"You still killed Javits, Little," Wimberton hollered. "I saw you do it."

"You're lying, Wimberton, and I know it."

Kathy grinned. "Freddie, I've got an idea. Let's get the body."

"We are, as usual, my dear, of one mind. I'll keep Wimberton going." Freddie turned to the door and squeezed off a couple rounds at Wimberton's feet.

"I don't get it," said Gam as he scrambled along behind Kathy.

"The body proves that Freddie didn't kill Bill," explained Kathy. "That's why Wimberton covered it up so fast and wouldn't let anyone see it."

Gam gasped as he saw the corpse. "He's got his face."

Kathy paused. "He killed himself, Gammers. He put the shot gun in his mouth and fired. That's why the rest of his head's gone. Let's get this out where the rest of the town can see."

Freddie taunted Wimberton some more, then blew the lock off the door. Holding the coffin in front, he swung the door open, and Gam and Kathy pushed the cart out onto the street. Women screamed.

"Hey, Javits has got his face!" someone yelled.

"And powder burns in his mouth," Kathy yelled. "And we've got a suicide note. He killed himself! And Wimberton knew it."

"I didn't," yelped Wimberton. "I didn't know, honest!"

The crowd surrounded the sheriff as Deputy Diederich walked up and took the rifle from Wimberton's hands.

Freddie and Kathy remained locked in the funeral home for the next few hours, although Gam slid out through the body drop and returned to the farm. Diederich allowed Katie-Marie to bring Freddie and Kathy some breakfast. Bill's body was taken to the basement of the funeral home, and the basement was locked. When Eckert and Abraham returned, they arrived on the morning train with a lawyer from the state attorney general's office and five U.S. Marshals to help. The marshals promptly went to work rounding up Tipton, Spivens, Aherne, Standling and Meyers. Wimberton was already cooling his heels in the courtroom office.

After consulting Diederich, the lawyer from the attorney general, a man named Smith, let Freddie and Kathy out of the funeral home, but insisted that they remain close by. Reverend Macadam had the two rest in the church office. The remaining Briscow family members stayed close by in the hall. Smith spent another hour going over the financial reports that Gam had retrieved from Freddie's plane, then called everyone involved to the courthouse at noon.

Much of the rest of the town arrived as well, and soon the courtroom was packed even fuller than for Freddie's trial. Tipton and the other conspirators were lined up in the jury box, with Wimberton at the end. Mr. Smith, a medium-sized man with blond hair and glasses covering his watery blue eyes, took the judge's bench.

"This is not a formal proceeding," he announced. "It is merely an investigation. But it looks like this will be the easiest way to get at whatever it is that has been going on here. The first order of business will be to note that Frederick Little was, in fact, falsely convicted of the murder of William Javits, since there is incontrovertible evidence that Javits was not murdered, but killed himself. It would also appear that we have some considerable judicial malfeasance going on, not to mention the harassment of a law-abiding family."

"An investigation? That seems a mite irregular," Jacob muttered.

Abraham leaned over Katie-Marie and whispered. "He wants to exonerate Freddie publicly so Freddie doesn't sue the state over the false conviction."

Freddie, sitting on Abraham's other side, stifled a grin.

"Now, it seems this started over a plan to sell land in the area for vacation homes," Smith went on. "How many people knew about it?"

Several men and women in the audience, including a few farmers, raised their hands. One farmer stood.

"Mayor Standling and Judge Aherne wanted to start it, sir," he said, his gangly hands fidgeting with the side seams of his overalls. "They said Mr. Tipton was going to make us all rich."

"Really," said Mr. Smith.

He caught Freddie's eye. Freddie stood.

"Unfortunately," Freddie said, "the six conspirators apparently had no intention of making anyone rich except themselves. And of those six, Mr. Tipton was about to sell them all out. Among those financial reports is one that shows that Mr. Tipton transferred all shares of the Hays Land Development Corporation to himself, and most of the shares of the bank."

Aherne, Meyers, Standling and Spivens all froze in shock, while Wimberston yelped in anger.

"Furthermore, it doesn't look like there was going to be any real vacation land development," Freddie continued. "Mr. Tipton had arranged to sell all the land through a brokerage to a bunch of speculators. You would have all lost your farms to people who had no interest in them other than re-selling them and quite probably not even succeeding."

"That's not necessarily the case," said Tipton. "You can't prove I transferred the ownership of those shares."

"Well, I sure as hell didn't!" yelped Wimberton. "Unless you're counting all that bribe money you gave me and Aherne and Meyers."

The crowd began to grumble. Smith used the gavel to quiet them.

"We also have the issue of the dead boy that was placed briefly on the Briscow farm," Freddie said. "The corpse is, unfortunately, missing. But Mr. Tipton also has a boy missing from his household. An orphan he claims ran away earlier this week."

"I think you should ask Sheriff Wimberton about that," said Mr. Tipton.

"I didn't kill him!" screamed Winberton. "I didn't kill anyone!"

"Oh, please, Sheriff," Tipton sneered. "It was you. You've done it more than once. And I know how it happens."

Winberton's face colored up as he panicked. "It was an accident! I didn't mean to."

"That's an interesting statement," said Smith. "Especially if you'd said nothing, we couldn't have done anything about it. Want to tell us where the body is?"

"I don't know," gasped Wimberton. "Bill took care of it."

Smith shook his head, then nodded at one of the marshals, who went over and put handcuffs on Wimberton and led him away.

"Mr. Smith," began Aherne. "In my defense, may I point out that Mr. Tipton included me on the board of the bank and on land company board because the speculation idea was mine. Not getting the mortgages, mind you. Merely the idea of an investment. By the time he told me that Mr. Little was going to reveal that he was going to call in the farmers' notes, it was already too late and I would have been ruined. I may have acted rashly in allowing Mr. Little to be convicted, but it was Mr. Tipton who threatened to expose me and the others if we did not see to it that Mr. Little was hung. I was trying to protect my family and their good name."

Spivens stood. "Mr. Smith, Mr. Tipton had a note on my hotel. He threatened to call it in and ruin me if I didn't help with vandalizing the Briscow farm. He needed me to help with the vacation part of the business, he said. But then Briscow wouldn't take a mortgage, and Tipton needed somebody besides Wimberton to push Briscow into doing it."

"Tipton made me steal their cow," said another young man. "Or he wouldn't loan me the money I needed to pay for my mother's hospital stay."

One by one, people came forward, claiming that Mr. Tipton had in one way or another forced them to do something. In fact, so many came forward it was hard to imagine that Tipton had inveigled them all into various and sundry misdeeds around town. Still, it was clear the banker had few friends in the community.

Smith finally insisted that two of the marshals and Mr. Eckert see to taking all the statements from the citizenry while he finished the appropriate paperwork with the court clerk to formally exonerate Freddie.

Freddie and Kathy waited impatiently with the rest of the Briscow family in another office in the courthouse.

"All right, Jacob, go ahead and say it," sighed Katie-Marie finally. "You were right about not taking a mortgage."

Jacob smiled, but wisely chose not to say anything.

"I wonder what Tipton had on Bill to get him to cooperate," Teresa said quietly, looking over the letter Bill had left. "He didn't say in his note. He didn't even sign it. Or tell me he loved me."

Freddie looked at Kathy, who nodded. He took the second sheet from his flight jacket pocket.

"You may not want to know," Freddie said, holding the sheet out. "But I can assure you, he did love you."

Teresa looked at Freddie. "It was the boys, wasn't it?"

Freddie nodded. Gam held his breath. He glanced at Freddie, who shook his head. Gam breathed a silent sigh of relief.

Teresa took a deep breath, then suddenly gasped. "Bill didn't kill them, did he?"

"No," said Kathy, coming up and putting her arm around her sister. "At least, we never thought so, and given Wimberton's display, it seems pretty certain. There's no way of knowing unless we find that one boy's body."

"Bill said he wanted to take extra time with Mrs. Schultz." Teresa gazed into space thoughtfully. "Maybe that's where the body is. Buried with her."

"Wonderful," grumbled Smith, who had just come into the room in time to hear Teresa. "Now I have to swear out an exhumation order. What a rat's nest."

He stashed a small sheaf of papers and a large envelope under his arm, then whipped his handkerchief out and began polishing his glasses.

"Tipton's not saying anything, but everyone else is singing like birds, and I haven't got a judge or a prosecutor because they're the birds singing the loudest." Smith put his glasses back on, sniffed, then handed the papers to Freddie. "Well, Mr. Little, you are officially exonerated. And here are all your possessions that were confiscated at the time of your arrest."

"Thank you, Mr. Smith. I truly appreciate it," said Freddie. He checked his cigarette case. The cigarettes were gone.

"And I, uh, hope this will be the last said on the matter...?" Smith asked.

Freddie glanced at Abraham, who smirked. "It depends. Since the people involved in helping me escape a premature hanging were technically involved in a jail break."

"I think we can consider that matter completely closed," Smith said.

"Excellent. Thank you again."

Smith left, and with big whooping cheers, Kathy's family surrounded Freddie, effectively squeezing Kathy out.

"I knew you'd be all right," Katie-Marie said, giving Freddie a sound hug. She stepped back. "Now, maybe we can get back to celebrating your wedding."

Freddie sent a panicked look at Kathy, who looked like she was about to burst into tears.

"Mother Briscow, I really would much prefer fetching Kathy's trunk and valise from the farm, if that would be possible," Freddie said.

Jacob and Katie-Marie looked at each other and laughed.

"What do you think we were talking about?" said Jacob. "Now, the two of you head on over to the hotel and get busy. We'll take care of Kathy's luggage and see you in the morning."

Freddie took Kathy straight to the hotel suite for which he still had the key. He locked the outer door and put the key in his pocket. He locked the bedroom door and put that key in his pocket.

"Now, at last, short of—"

Kathy clamped her hand over his mouth. "Don't say it. It may just happen!"

Freddie kissed her hand. She removed it and reached up for his lips.

"No rushing," he teased, as her hands wandered.

Some time later, they rested together in bed, sharing lazy, relaxed kisses.

"Freddie, darling," sighed Kathy. "It was wonderful."

"I promised you, Kathy, equal partners." Freddie grinned. "But in the future, we may want to experiment with other positions."

Kathy purred. "The near future?"

"Reasonably near." Freddie purred and kissed her.

Someone knocked loudly on the outside door. Kathy groaned.

"Not again."

"I'm afraid it's my fault, too." Freddie looked at his watch. "I didn't want to rush. I ordered dinner."

"Let's skip it."

Freddie got out of bed. "We'll regret it later. Now, where did my pants go?"

He retrieved the pants from the floor, and the keys, got the tray, sent the hotel boy packing, and relocked the doors to find Kathy in the bathroom.

"What are you doing?" he called. He set the tray down on the foot of the bed, then disposed of his pants.

"Rinsing out."

"What?" He pulled a black tie from the trunk and went to the mirror.

"I'm trying to prevent parenthood."

"Ah, I've heard of the technique."

"It helps." Kathy appeared in the doorway wearing Freddie's dressing gown, and laughed. "What are you doing?"

Freddie grinned as he finished his tie. "I firmly believe in the tradition of dressing for dinner."

She smiled ruefully. "Something was missing, wasn't it?"

Freddie busied himself with setting out the two dinner plates, each containing a steak, roasted potatoes and cold asparagus.

"Nothing that should bother me," he said with offhand ease.

"You were a little put off by it, though."

Freddie shook his head. "I was surprised."

"Surprised?" Kathy wandered over to the bed and sat down. "Good lord, Freddie, I've told you enough times."

"Not in any specific terms."

"I would have thought you'd figure it out."

"I didn't." Freddie took her chin in his hands and kissed her lips. "Largely because, my dear, you are such a terrible seductress. Only an innocent could be so inept."

"Or me."

Freddie laughed and handed her some silverware. "Or you."

Kathy paused. "Are you sure it doesn't bother you?"

"It doesn't. Actually, Kathy, I may be in the minority, but I find deflowering maidens is highly overrated." He grinned at her lecherously. "And you do use your experience well."

Kathy grinned back. "So do you."

Freddie started in on his steak. "I am a little curious, though. How does a hot blooded woman like you manage to get what she wants and still keep her reputation intact?"

"I'm a terrible seductress. I'd lead a boy into seducing me. Well, I thought I was. Anyway, tears and promises later, and of course I had to stick with him for a while, visiting at prolonged intervals and making do with corn cobs in between."

"And how did you manage to feign the obstacle I was expecting?"

"Clamped down hard and cried out at the right moment."

"And the original trespass. A haystack out here, perchance?"

"No. A wonderful experiment in free love my second year at Radcliffe with a Harvard graduate student. Well, it was, until his fiancée showed up. I also had a rather bad scare that month, so I promptly did a lot of reading, and learned to protect myself as well as I could."

"Now, you don't have to worry about it."

Kathy sighed, then swallowed a bit of potato. "Actually, being married is worse. You're expected to make babies."

"Don't you want children?" Freddie shifted, not sure what he wanted himself.

"No. You want them, don't you? Carry on the family name, and all that."

"I suppose I just expected it would happen."

"I'm hoping it doesn't. I've had my share of babies, Freddie. Ma was very good at dropping the baby to pick up the plow, and I got stuck picking up the baby. At least I didn't have to be pregnant first. There's nine months of misery for you. Nausea, exhaustion, blowing up like a balloon, and if the little beast is active, he plays football with your kidneys. And then there's labor, hours of incredible pain and hoping the doctor gets there before the baby does. Then you have baby, overflowing at both ends, both of which smell awful, getting shot at by junior, bitten, wiping off and watching where you sit once junior is out of diapers, because a little boy cannot hit a bleeding ocean."

Freddie mused. "It is a mess, but, darling, that's what nurses are for."

"Nurses? I don't want my children turned over to a complete stranger."

"Not a stranger, a well-trained woman with excellent references."

"I don't know, Freddie. You complain so much about being isolated from your parents."

"Just because we don't change diapers doesn't mean we can't be involved. We won't be strangers to our children. But, Kathy, I really don't want to deal with all the mess of child rearing, and I can't imagine you wanting to either."

"A nurse," Kathy mused, then reached over to Freddie's tie.

He caught her hand. "What are you doing?"

"It's time to undress."

"I'm afraid not, my dear. We've got to pack our trunks and prepare them for shipping, and perhaps prepare a few other things."

"For home? Where are we going to live?"

"If we want to maintain discretion, then Mrs. Lynne's is out, because I do not want to live apart."

"And if you move suddenly it will be fishy. Of course, Honoria said her apartment was available. But are there any stairs between the two? It's too obvious to take the elevator with the operator and all."

"The stairs are in the servants' quarters. I've had to use them when the elevator has broken down. I think we can convince Honoria to take you as a roommate, especially since you'll be downstairs with me."

"At least that's settled. It will be nice to get back to the office."

"But we're not going home, not yet."

"Why not?"

"I thought we might leave a telegram or two with Gideon to be sent out at the proper time, and let your employer think that your father is hovering between this world and the next for, say, another week or so, and take a honeymoon. Niagara Falls seems like it would be rather boring. But we could go to Reno and see if that amuses us, or perhaps fly through the Grand Canyon and see if it's quite the sight that Josh had led us to believe."

"A honeymoon? Oh, how delightful. I'd love it, Freddie." She caught his tie and untied it.

"Wait!"

"Well, Freddie, if Pa is going to linger on for an extra week, he can linger for a few more days beyond that, and we can pack and arrange tomorrow."

"Hmm."

Smiling, he put the dinner dishes on the floor.

THE END

About the Author

Anne Louise Bannon is an author and journalist who wrote her first novel at age 15. Her journalistic work has appeared in Ladies' Home Journal, the Los Angeles Times, Wines and Vines, and in newspapers across the country. She was a TV critic for over 10 years, founded the YourFamilyViewer blog, and created the OddBallGrape.com wine education blog with her husband, Michael Holland. She also writes the romantic fiction serial WhiteHouseRhapsody.com. She is the co-author of Howdunit: Book of Poisons, with Serita Stevens, as well as mysteries Fascinating Rhythm and Tyger, Tyger. She and her husband live in Southern California with an assortment of critters.

Other books by this author

Please visit your favorite retailer to discover other books by Anne Louise Bannon

FASCINATING RHYTHM
The first Freddie and Kathy novel. When Kathy Briscow's boss turns up dead, she's the obvious suspect. Socialite author Freddie Little teams up with her to search the speakeasies and streets of 1920s New York to find an obsessed killer.

TYGER, TYGER
When Brenda Finnegan and her animal trainer boyfriend Bob Zebrinski witness a kidnapping, they end up caring for the little girl the victim left behind. Chased by a cult and just angry enough, Brenda and Bob try to find the kidnappers, helped by Bob's tiger Sweetness.

WHITE HOUSE RHAPSODY
(www.whitehouserhapsody.com)
A light romantic fiction serial
President Mark Jerguessen is single and there's a dark secret why. His aide Sharon Wheatly loves high-achieving, driven guys, but does not want anything to do with their fame. You know there's got to be a way to get them together.

HOWDUNIT: BOOK OF POISONS
(co-authored with Serita Stevens)
The perfect reference work for writers looking for realistic mayhem in their stories. The book not only provides all the facts on toxins, it indexes them by symptoms, reaction times, etc., to make it easy to find the deadly dose your story needs.

Connect with Me!

I'm so glad you read my book. Thank you! I love connecting so here are my social media coordinates:

Friend me on Facebook: http://facebook.com/RobinGoodfellowEnt
Follow me on Twitter: http://twitter.com/ALBannon
Favorite my Smashwords author page: https://www.smashwords.com/profile/view/MsBriscow
Subscribe to the Robin Goodfellow Newsletter: http://eepurl.com/zH0Ab
Connect on LinkedIn: http://www.linkedin.com/in/annelouisebannon
Follow me on Pinterest: http://pinterest.com/msbriscow
Visit my website: http://annelouisebannon.com
Follow me on Google+: http://google.com/+Annelouisebannonfiction

www.ingramcontent.com/pod-product-compliance
Lightning Source LLC
Chambersburg PA
CBHW031232120726
47905CB00002B/561